LADY GYPSY

"A beautiful love story . . . stirring passion, deep-seated prejudice make Pam Crooks's *Lady Gypsy* an unforgettable treasure you will want to take out and read again and again."
—*Rendezvous*

"Pam Crooks's second book proves that she is a writer to watch. *Lady Gypsy* is a unique love story, delving into the practically unknown world of gypsies in the American West. The romance between these two unlikley lovers is filled with all the heat and sensual tensuion a forbidden can evoke."
—*Romantic Readers Connection*

WYOMING WILDFLOWER

"Powerful emotions boil over in this gripping epic. Lyrical prose, complex characters, and clever plot twists combine for a perfect blend of romance and adventure. . . . Ms. Crooks is a writer of immense talent."
—*Rendezvous*

"Pam Crooks is destined to become a powerful voice in historical romance."
—*Romance Readers Connection*

"*Wyoming Wildflower* is a complete Western with all the right ingredients. [Ms. Crooks] is an author to keep an eye on."
—*Romance Reviews Today*

"Pam Crooks writes a much different, but very interesting take from the usual Western fare . . . filled with a lot of emotion . . . a lot of love. [This is] a very satisfying book."
—*Affaire de Coeur*

CHANGING FORTUNE

"What do you see?" Reese asked, his voice low, curious.

For a lengthy moment, she did not answer. Hardly aware of it, she touched her fingertip to his Heart Line, following the groove in a slow, caressing stroke.

"You will have a great love someday, Reese," she said softly. "A woman will wed you, and you will love her as you have loved no other. Your marriage will endure. You will be happy, and the love you have for one another will last forever."

A silence fell between them. Somehow, their fingers became entwined, each coiling around the other's, their grip soon clinging and intimate.

"My turn, Lady Gypsy," he said quietly.

Before she could resist, he pulled her toward him with a subtle strength, twisting their bodies so that she lay beneath him on the tablecloth-covered floor, their entwined hands resting near her head.

Filled with raw emotion, his gaze roamed over her face. "I predict you'll have a great love of your own. A husband who'll hold you in his arms at night and thank God with every fiber of his being that you're his."

Her teeth bit into her lower lip, and she turned away. "Do not tease me, *Gajo*. I cannot bear it."

Gentle fingers took her jaw and turned her back again. "It's the truth. I swear it."

Other *Leisure* books by Pam Crooks:
WYOMING WILDFLOWER

Lady
Gypsy

PAM CROOKS

LEISURE BOOKS NEW YORK CITY

To Gypsies everywhere, for their fascinating customs and beliefs. And for giving me Liza.

A LEISURE BOOK®

September 2001

Published by

Dorchester Publishing Co., Inc.
276 Fifth Avenue
New York, NY 10001

Cover art by John Ennis
www.ennisart.com

ISBN 0-8439-4911-2

Visit us on the web at www.dorchesterpub.com.

Lady Gypsy

Chapter One

Northern Nebraska, 1876

Damned Gypsies.

Reese Carrison reined in his horse and grimly watched the colorful, high-wheeled wagons rolling along the sun-bright horizon. Like a trail of ants, they made their way around the outskirts of Niobrara City and halted near a woodland bordering the river.

There they would camp. One night, maybe two, he guessed. The trees hid them from the townspeople's view; lush rangeland offered unlimited grazing and valuable water for their horses. And then, as quietly as they arrived, they would leave again, their destination as mysterious as the Gypsies themselves.

Reese breathed a silent curse. He didn't need them here. Not today. He didn't need the problems they'd bring, problems that spawned complaints of stolen chickens, unruly children, and women begging in the streets. Niobrara City's

9

saloons would fill with boisterous, dark-skinned men who, in their drunkenness, hurled insults at the non-Gypsy and left a string of frustrated and angry shopkeepers in their wake.

Reese sighed. No, he didn't want them here today. Today was special. He'd waited most of his life for this day. Today his railroad would finally link up with the prestigious Union Pacific line.

The Nebraska-Dakota Railroad grew out of his sweat and blood—and every dime he owned. Niobrara City would've been little more than a row of shanties and false-front businesses if not for him. The N & D provided area farmers and ranchers with a shipping point to Omaha markets. It provided employment for the citizens. It put Niobrara City on the map.

The little railroad was his pride and joy. He lived and breathed the N & D. It was his life. His dream. And he would celebrate its completion today.

All he lacked was a wife to share his satisfaction with and sons to someday hand his hard-won legacy down to. But that would come. Rebecca Ann had traveled all the way from St. Louis for the ceremony. She would make a fine wife. Today, he'd ask for her hand.

His mood lightened. He swept a glance toward the riverbank, and the wagons spread in a wide half-circle. Already, several campfires flickered and danced.

He tugged his hat brim lower over his eyes, then nudged his pure-bred stallion forward. He'd waited too long for this day, and the ceremony that would begin in a few hours time. Nothing was going to ruin it for him.

Not even a band of Gypsies.

"Come with us, Mama." Liza arranged stacks of woven baskets in the battered cart and cast a sidelong glance at her mother. "Our pockets will fill with the *Gaje*'s money quickly. It will be fun."

"Pah!" Mama twisted and spit in the weeds. "I will not breathe the same air as the stupid Gaje! I will stay here in the camp. Far away from them."

"Oh, Mama." Liza shook her head in exasperation, the gold hoops in her ears swaying with the movement. Her mother's vehemence in regard to the non-Gypsy—the Gaje—was deep-rooted and permanent. All Gypsies mocked them, but none despised them more than Mama.

Sometimes, Liza grew tired of the hatred. It had been a part of her life since the day she was born. From the time she had been old enough to comprehend the pain the Gaje inspired in Mama, Liza was forced to live with the consequences. The shame. One *Gajo* had been responsible, and because of him, Mama hated them all. Because of him, Gajo blood flowed in Liza's veins. Because of him, Liza would be forever different from her people.

But the day was glorious, and the afternoon spent in town promised to be a refreshing change from their travels. Rarely did their *kumpania* stop to make camp halfway through the day. Liza was determined to enjoy it.

"Look." Pointing a finger through the trees, she attempted a different approach to convince her mother to accompany them. "There is something special happening in"—she tried to remember what Hanzi, her brother, had called the place—"Niobrara City. See the train? Men and women come from everywhere. Perhaps it is something new."

"Pah! Another of the Gaje's expensive toys. I do not want to see it." With Tekla, Liza's baby sister, toddling right behind, Mama hefted a dented pot full of water toward the newly kindled fire. "Hurry, Liza. The men have already left, and the children are waiting for you."

11

"Mama, do not be so stubborn."

"I am not stubborn." She straightened and faced Liza. A shimmer of tears glazed her ebony eyes. Wounded pride cried out in her sun-weathered features. "I will not embarrass you, my daughter. Go without me."

Embarrass her? Liza's heart plummeted within her breast. The last basket to be loaded into the cart slipped from her grasp, and she threw her arms around her mother's rigid shoulders. "You would never embarrass me. Never!"

"I am no better than an ugly old hag. You love me too much to admit it, but it is true."

Liza drew away and fought the sting of her own tears. Stricken by her mother's words, she could find none of her own to offer comfort.

Involuntarily, her gaze lifted to the faded kerchief wrapped around Mama's head. The colorful cloth helped hide her shame, her humiliation, the judgment handed down by the Gypsy court of law, the dreaded *kris*.

Mama's head was shaved, the punishment for adultery.

As if that were not enough, their wagon would always follow at the end of the line during their travels. For the rest of their lives, they would choke on the dust raised by the wagons ahead of them, and Mama would be deprived of the long braids other Gypsy women wore.

It could have been worse, Liza knew. Mama could have been banished from the tribe, but the kris had given her mercy out of respect for Nanosh, her husband.

Mama had been only fifteen, but already a young bride. A sweet-talking, handsome horse trader with hair the color of newly minted pennies had swayed her impressionable, feminine heart. By the time Nanosh finished his dealings at the horse fair, the Gajo's seed had been planted in Mama's womb. Mama never saw him again.

Nine months later, Liza was born. Nanosh accepted her as his own, but his affections were rare. Through the years, two sisters and two brothers followed, but only Liza was different.

"I made a mistake, my daughter. Now, I must pay for it. I will not go into the Gaje's world and hear them speak of my shame and my ugliness. They will only laugh at a Gypsy woman with no hair."

"You will always be beautiful to me." Liza looked into her mother's face and saw her pride. Her skin was aged too soon from the toils of the weather, and her dark eyes often showed fatigue, but the loveliness from her youth had not been destroyed. Liza tenderly kissed each of her cheeks.

"Enough of this. Go." Mama gently, firmly set Liza aside. "Take Paprika with you. And Putzi is growing impatient."

"Yes, Mama." For the first time, she noticed her five-year-old brother tugging on her skirt. She smiled, tweaked his nose, and hurried back to the two-wheeled cart filled with her baskets.

She picked up the one she had dropped. Of all of them she had made, this one was the smallest. She had experimented with the design, weaving strips of bark in with the dried leaves of a yucca plant she had gathered during the kumpania's travels.

Most likely, the Gaje with their fussy tastes would only turn their noses up. They would not think the little basket fine enough to buy. Nevertheless, Liza tossed it in with the others. She did not care what they thought. The basket was one of her favorites.

"Are you ready, Putzi?" Liza grasped the handles of the cart and turned it toward the road leading into Niobrara City.

"Yeth." He spoke between two missing front teeth. "I been waiting and waiting."

13

"I know, little one. Here. Help me push. You are so strong, do you know that?"

"Yeth." His young shoulders squared, and he leaned into the task with all his weight. Liza pretended not to help.

"Liza, wait."

She turned and found her mother stepping from their wagon, a silk kerchief of vibrant gold-and-crimson stripes in her hand.

"You must not forget this," Mama said and draped the kerchief over Liza's head.

"I do not want to wear—"

"Liza!"

The sharpness in her mother's voice stilled the protest on Liza's tongue. A hint of sadness crept over Mama's features. Her work-roughened hand cupped Liza's cheek, and her tone softened. "You have suffered from my shame, too, my daughter. Wear it so that the Gaje men will not look at you, as . . . they did me."

Liza's mouth curved downward in a pout. She could not yet wear a kerchief tied with the special knot of the Gypsies. Only the married women were allowed that privilege, never appearing in public without their head covered. The unmarried braided their hair, the thick plaits hanging down to their waists, free to the day and the night.

But with the Gaje, Liza could not be so free. The kerchief would hide her hair from their curious, mocking stares, hair that glinted coppery-red in the sunlight, hair that made her different.

It was the one thing she inherited from her natural father. As a child, she hated it, wanting the deep, blue-black color of her sisters and cousins and friends, but eventually, she grew to accept the imperfection while among her own people.

Mama had not. Mama tortured herself with the disgrace.

Mama wanted to protect her from the humiliation she endured.

"Come back hungry," Mama said, tying the kerchief beneath Liza's chin. "Hanzi promised me a fat hen for supper."

"He is craving a stew, I think," Paprika piped up, her bare feet rushing across the tree-shaded ground with a twelve-year-old's enthusiasm. She picked up Tekla, planted a loud kiss on her chubby cheek, then set her down again. "We must hurry, Liza. I want to see the big train in Niobrara City!"

"Me, too!" Putzi grunted with the effort of pushing the cart forward by himself. "Will I get to hear the whithle?"

"Yes, little one," Liza said, laughing. "It will be very loud. *Everyone* will hear the whistle."

With waves and good-byes, Liza left the camp with her brother and sister and joined a group of Gypsy women and children on the road toward town. As they walked, Paprika's excited prattle lifted Liza's spirits, dulled from the somber conversation with Mama.

"I will do some begging today," Paprika decided with adultlike confidence. "So many people will be there! I could easily make a fortune."

"Oh, Paprika." Liza frowned, her tone showing disapproval. Begging was not her favorite thing to do. She had always secretly thought it was hardly more than glorified stealing and certainly did little to improve the Gaje's impression of the Gypsy. "You have plenty of money. Sit with me and help sell baskets. I will split the profits with you."

"And what if you do not sell many?" her sister challenged. "We do not get an occasion like this often. I cannot let it pass without a little fun." She cocked her head, her black eyes alive with mischief. "How about you, Liza? Will you tell fortunes today?"

With one hand helping Putzi push the cart, the other toyed thoughtfully with the strands of gold beads around her neck. "Maybe."

Mama claimed she had a gift. Liza was not always sure. There was a certain skill in hand-reading, of interpreting the moles on one's body, or divining with sticks and stones, but she was wrong as often as she was right. The Gaje were gullible, though. They would believe anything she told them if she told them what they wanted to hear.

Liza smiled to herself. Yes, the Gaje *were* gullible. Paprika spoke the truth. It would be easy to take their money today.

"I want to buy something special in Niobrara City," Liza said.

"Like what?" Paprika asked, skipping slightly ahead.

"A new kerchief for Mama. Silk, of course. In the color of the brightest sunflowers. It will make her feel pretty. And maybe some perfume."

Liza thought of the bottle she had found in an alley once. The crystal stopper had been chipped and broken, but the fragrance inside smelled wonderful, and in her weaker moments, she dabbed a little—just a little—on her wrists and on the tip of her nose.

The Gaje enjoyed such frivolous pleasures, but material possessions were not important to the Gypsy. Her people needed only the basic necessities to be happy in life, yet Liza found a certain fascination with all those things that made her feel . . . like a woman.

Mama never spoke of the frills and lace and lavish dresses of the Gaje world. Paprika was yet too young to dwell on it, but sometimes Liza had a yearning for them so strong—

It was the curse of the Gajo whose seed had given her life that made her feel that way. His lust had ruined Mama.

He was responsible for making Liza different, and she would blame him forever.

"What will you buy *me*, Liza?" Putzi asked, working so hard to push the cart that her heart swelled with love for him.

"She will buy you a big piece of coal. How about that?" Paprika answered impishly. "Or maybe a bag of broken sticks to play with."

Putzi looked so aghast that Liza scolded Paprika for teasing him. "I will buy you anything you want, little one. But you must be good and help me sell many baskets."

"He will not sit still long enough to sell even one," Paprika chided. "And he will always be hungry."

"Will not!" Highly offended, Putzi stopped pushing and took off after his older sister, who suffused into giggles and more teasing. They tousled on the road, alternating between tickling and poking each other, until Liza took up the cart and began pushing it alone.

She left them to their banter and gazed at the countryside, alive and golden with fields of swaying wheat. Wisps of clouds, grayish-white like dirty cotton, dotted a vibrant blue sky. Trees fanned a light, summery wind that tugged at the hems of Liza's skirts and flapped the ends of her kerchief. She took in a slow breath, inhaling the sweetness of freedom. Nebraska was a peaceful place, she decided. No wonder so many Gaje lived there.

An unusual-looking bridge broke into the horizon and snared Liza's attention. She lifted a hand, shading the sun from her eyes, and, in her curiosity, she took a few moments to study it.

A trestle bridge, Hanzi had told her when their wagons rolled past. The Gaje built such a thing so that the big train could cross over the canyon beyond the river. Liza had never seen one before, and she was forced to admit to a

17

grudging fascination at its construction, a complex maze of lumber and steel that rose from the bowels of the canyon and seemed to reach for the sky.

But in the next moment, she chided herself. It was only one more expensive toy the Gaje enjoyed. She would not give it another thought.

The ground shimmied through the thin leather of her shoes, and for a few moments, she did not comprehend the reason for it. A slight frown pulling at her brows, she turned and glanced at the road behind them.

Hoofbeats pounded the packed dirt, thundering louder as a massive horse advanced steadily upon them. Its rider had the wild look of a man possessed, as though the spirits of the dead gave him chase. He charged toward them with no regard to their safety, his mighty arm upraised, his powerful fist clenched.

A scream of alarm bubbled in Liza's throat, and the cart's handles fell from her grasp.

"Putzi! Paprika! Get away!" she cried.

Everything seemed to happen in slow motion. Liza feared she could not move fast enough, would not reach her little brother and sister in time to pull them from the road, and her heart froze within her breast.

The horse and rider loomed ever closer. The roar of hooves bellowed in Liza's ears, shutting out the shrieks and curses from the other Gypsy women. An enormous coat made of buffalo hides magnified the man's size, making him even more formidable, more frightening. A raccoon-skin hat covered his head, the furry tall swinging behind him.

"Out of my way, you fools!" he boomed, irate fury throbbing in the command.

He was nearly upon them, and by the sheer grace of God, Liza found the impetus to move. She threw herself against

Putzi and Paprika and flung them to the side of the road. The horse veered slightly, missing them by mere inches. Clods of earth flew upward, hitting her in the face, the arms, the legs.

In a few horrible seconds, it was over. He was gone, galloping onward toward Niobrara City, out of their sight, oblivious to the danger or the scare he had given them.

Putzi started to cry. Liza hugged him tightly against her, comforting him, soothing his pain from the elbow he had skinned. Paprika trembled and fought tears of her own; Liza found room for her within the circle of her embrace.

The other Gypsy women hastened toward them, concern in their dark faces, but Liza stared past them, past the cart and the baskets strewn about the road, and glared in the direction the wild man had fled.

Only a Gajo would behave so abominably, so carelessly. A Gypsy would never have been as thoughtless toward innocent women and children. A Gypsy would never have provoked such fright. A Gypsy would have shown infinitely more compassion.

The Gaje. It was little wonder the Gypsy despised them.

Her lip curled in renewed disdain. More than ever, she was ashamed to have their blood coursing inside her.

"Does she always take this long?" Reese growled. He snuffed out yet another cigarette, wondering when in hell Rebecca Ann would finally come downstairs.

Amused, Bram Kaldwell, his trusted friend and Rebecca Ann's father, peered over the top of his newspaper. A haze of smoke from the pipe clenched between his teeth curled upward and dissipated throughout the lobby of Niobrara City's Grand River Hotel. He grunted an affirmative reply. "Her mother was always late, too. Better get used to it, Reese."

Reese shifted restlessly. He'd spent the afternoon pleasurably enough with Bram, but after waiting almost an hour, he'd grown increasingly impatient. He had things to do, people to see. It was almost time to meet the governor, and he wanted to view the train—his train—decked out in all its glory before the christening and his dedication speech.

Maybe Bram was right. Maybe waiting was all part of it. Husbands were often left with nothing to do but wait on their wives while they readied themselves for special occasions. And though Rebecca Ann was hardly his wife, he already felt like she was. He had no doubt she would agree to his intended marriage proposal, because she, like himself, needed a spouse.

Her first husband had died unexpectedly, leaving her with a three-year-old daughter to raise. Bram claimed the death had devastated Rebecca Ann, and she had become somewhat of a recluse in St. Louis. She seemed willing enough to travel to Niobrara City, however, and Reese considered that a good sign she wanted to see him.

He leaned forward and rubbed the ache in his right knee, wrenched years ago when he'd slipped on an icy rail pulling a switch. The joint had dealt him trouble ever since, flaring up whenever it damn well felt like it. Bram claimed the ache foreshadowed a change in the weather.

Reese glanced out the hotel's tall, velvet-draped window, and a corner of his mouth lifted. Not today. Only a light breeze stirred the daisies and goldenrods growing wild outside Niobrara City. Few clouds decorated the sky. The temperature was perfect. Not a finer day could be found to celebrate the Nebraska-Dakota Railroad.

He debated lighting another cigarette until a rustle of petticoats drew his attention. Rebecca Ann descended the stairs, slowed by the child clinging to her hand. Reese rose, unmindful of the stiffness in his knee, and watched her approach.

She seemed nervous and fragile. So very fragile. She was petite, with milky skin that glowed in all the right places. It would be easy to love her, he thought with some relief. Someday, he would. But for now, he was content to just look at her. Niobrara City rarely had a woman as beautiful as Rebecca Ann grace its streets, and he was proud to have her on his arm when he dedicated his railroad.

The little girl was a miniature portrait of her mother. A porcelain doll dressed in a confection of pink ruffles and eyelet lace, complete with matching bows in her blond ringlets. Another man's child, but he would learn to love her, too.

"Hello, Reese," Rebecca Ann said softly.

"Rebecca Ann." Reese moved closer, bent, and dropped a kiss to her ruby lips. Her lashes lowered, and she turned away, giving Reese the vague impression he'd been far too bold in his greeting. He fought the feeling, but vowed to be more careful with her. If he were to ask for her hand, he couldn't have her too leery of him.

"We were about ready to come up and get you, Rebecca Ann," Bram said. "Reese was squirming in his seat. He isn't used to sitting still for so long."

"Really?" At her father's subtle admonishment, she glanced at Reese. "I didn't know you were in such a hurry."

Irritation flickered through him before he banked it. Surely she realized how important this day was to him, to his railroad, to the town of Niobrara City, in particular. Yet her expression registered no chagrin, and he knew she didn't realize it at all.

"No harm done. We have plenty of time," he lied and hunkered down to the little girl's level. She stared at him

21

with heavy-lashed blue eyes. "Hey, Margaret. You look almost as pretty as your—"

"Michelle," Rebecca Ann said. "Margaret Michelle. She goes by both names."

"Oh." The child whined and tugged her hand from her mother's. Reese straightened to his full height. "That's a lot of name for a half-pint like her."

"Michelle is the feminine form for Michael. My husband was quite pleased that his daughter bore his name. Even though he is no longer with us"—her voice quavered, but she regained her composure quickly—"I intend to keep his memory alive for her. Margaret means pearl in Greek."

"That so?" he murmured, having no idea what his own name meant. The futility of the conversation frayed his patience.

Bram came to his rescue. "Well, what do you say, Reese? Ready to head on out to that fancy train of yours?"

Reese shot him a grateful glance and opened his mouth to voice agreement, but a gasp from Rebecca Ann stopped him short.

"Where's Margaret Michelle?" She darted a frantic look all around her.

"There she is." Bram pointed toward the hotel doors.

"I'll get her," Reese said and sprinted in that direction. For a three-year-old, she was damned quick, and she had no fear wandering among strangers. He reached her before she left the hotel altogether and scooped her up into his arms.

"No! No!" She howled and squirmed against him. Reese tried as best he could to keep a firm grip on her.

"We're going to have to watch her like a hawk," Bram said grimly.

Rebecca Ann was right behind him. "Oh, put her down, Reese."

"There are a lot of people out there, Rebecca Ann," he said, trying to be heard over the child's tantrum. "More than usual. I'll hold her until we get to the train."

"You'll crush her dress. I spent half the morning ironing it. Please." She pulled her daughter from him and set her down, all the while fussing and fretting, trying to smooth the wrinkles from the fabric. She appeared to be near tears.

"All right. Sure. I'm sorry. Just hold her hand, okay?" He regretted upsetting Rebecca Ann and wished he could start over with her. Pulling the hat from his head, he raked his fingers through his hair on a wave of rising frustration. He took a slow breath, replaced the hat, and vowed the rest of the day would go better.

"Are we ready?" Bram asked.

"Yeah," Reese said. "Let's go."

Outside, Rebecca Ann gazed at the throng of carriages and townspeople crowding the streets.

"Where did everyone come from?" she asked, her features bewildered.

"Everywhere," he said and knew a sense of pride that it was true. To see him *and* the N & D. "The Nebraska-Dakota Railroad is a positive thing for Niobrara City. This celebration has been a long time coming." He gestured in the general direction where his train waited on the edge of town. "It's only a few blocks. We'd best walk. We'll never get a buggy through the crowd."

Bram agreed, and since Margaret Michelle seemed better inclined to behave herself, they joined the throng on the boardwalk. Bram took the child under his supervision, leaving Reese and Rebecca Ann to follow them.

Reese glanced over at Rebecca Ann. He'd yet to really touch her, he thought. If she was going to be his wife, she'd better get used to the idea that he intended to touch her.

Often. He took her hand and curled her fingers in the crook of his elbow.

Her fair features registered surprise at his show of possessiveness. Her initial stiffening eased, and she allowed him the privilege, though she made no effort to move any closer to him.

Reese satisfied himself with the small victory. She would warm up to him soon, and he to her. It would only take a little more time.

As they approached the Empty Saddle Saloon, George Steenson, its jovial owner, stood in the doorway, his arms crossed over his apron-covered chest. Reese knew most of the shopkeepers in Niobrara City, and George was one of the best. He took it upon himself to know his customers, and he knew the comings and goings of nearly everyone in town. The Empty Saddle was the nicest place around for a man to slake his thirst, and Reese had given him a fair share of business over the years.

"Today's the big day, eh, Mr. Carrison?"

"Sure is, George. Going there now. Seen the train yet?"

"Yes, sir. She's a beauty. You oughta be real proud of her."

"I am." Reese couldn't help the spread of a grin. "Been busy today?"

"Yep. Governor was here fer a spell earlier. So was some of them Union Pacific bigwigs. They all went on down to see the N & D. Reckon they're waitin' for you."

"We'll get there." Reese waved and continued walking, but George called him back. Some of the joviality had left his expression.

"Silas McCrae was in, Mr. Carrison. Thought you might want to know that."

Bram halted and turned around.

"And?" Reese narrowed an eye warily.

24

"Lookin' for you, he was. Madder'n a rained-on rooster, too."

"So what else is new?" Bram muttered.

Reese cocked his jaw and fought a stubborn sense of foreboding. The day that should have been perfect had already taken a few troublesome turns. Silas McCrae didn't help matters any.

Instinctively, he scanned the crowd and spied a group of Gypsy women huddled on the street corner. The sunlight bounced off brilliant hues of gold-and-crimson stripes, a kerchief worn by one of the women. A couple of children were with her, laughing and playing, while she arranged stacks of baskets in a two-wheeled cart.

Reese refused to let an ornery three-year-old, Silas Mc-Crae, or a bunch of Gypsy women dampen his spirits. This was his day. Nothing was going to ruin it for him.

The thought had no sooner formed in his mind when lightning flashed through the sunshine. Peals of thunder rumbled, signaling the onslaught of rain sure to fall from the wall of storm clouds hovering over Niobrara City.

Chapter Two

Endless yards of red, white, and blue bunting hung from evergreen boughs looped along the huge train engine. A sculpture of a proud eagle graced the shining smokestack amid ribbons and gold stars. Miniature flags waved from every car, and Liza couldn't help being impressed from the grandness of it all.

"Foolish Gaje!" Paprika snorted, blatantly unaffected by the sight. "They waste their money on stupid pleasures. Do you think the train knows how silly it looks?"

Liza's lips twitched. If the train breathed with life, it would be embarrassed with the extravagant frills, but while Paprika and the other Gypsies were scornful of its splendor, the Gaje were not. It seemed all of Niobrara City crowded onto the depot to see the mighty engine and the long line of cars behind it. Men stood, their hands in their pockets, their hats pushed back on their heads, and stared in wordless wonder. Women oohed and aahed, and children ran about, calling out in excitement.

26

The Nebraska-Dakota Railroad. Liza didn't understand the importance of it, but the occasion had been good for selling baskets. Her skirt's pockets bulged with Gaje dollars. Nanosh and Mama would be pleased, and there would be a great celebration when they returned to camp.

"Liza, I want a flag. Can I have a flag? Pleathe?"

Putzi's plea intruded on her musings, and she glanced down at her brother, sitting quietly and eating ice cream while she tended her baskets.

"Of course, sweetling. You have been such a good boy today." Hundreds of flags adorned the big train. The Gaje would not miss the one that would make Putzi happy. "Paprika, stay with the cart. I will not be gone long."

Liza took Putzi's hand in hers and led him into the crowd. After darting a cautious glance around her, she raised up on tiptoe and plucked a flag from a row above the train's huge wheels and slipped it into her pocket. Certain no one had noticed her theft, she pivoted to make a hasty return to Paprika.

But Putzi held back, his attention snared by a little girl in pink ruffles and lace. Liza had never seen a child so beautiful, so laden in wealth. Her mother was just as lovely, young and fair-skinned, and garbed in what Liza guessed was the newest in Gaje women's fashion. The woman spoke with two men, one older and smoking a pipe, the other taller, his stance erect, his hands clasped loosely behind his back. An air of importance clung to him.

For a moment, Liza stood riveted, watching the woman's husband. He had great pride in the train. Liza could see it in his face, browned from the sun, his features rugged, strong, pleasantly handsome. He seemed to explain something to her, pointing to valves near the bottom of the train, and she listened politely, as a good wife should. He bent

27

and rubbed one of the valves clean with the cuff of his coat sleeve.

Guilt washed over Liza that she watched him so intently. He was another woman's husband, and it wasn't right. Someday, she would have a husband of her own to watch, to stand at his side while he showed her the things important in his life, and she would listen, just as the beautiful Gajo woman did now to hers.

Liza resolutely pulled her gaze away from him, letting it settle briefly on the child. The little girl's mouth formed into a pout, and she pulled free from the older man's grasp. He appeared not to notice, gesturing instead with his pipe and talking animatedly with the woman and her husband.

Again, Liza chastised herself for staring at them, and she urged Putzi forward. He protested, his eyes still on the little girl. Wanting only to return to her baskets and Paprika, Liza dipped into her pocket.

"Play with your flag, Putzi, but do not let the Gaje see you. They will be very angry that we took it without giving them money. See how it waves in the wind?"

"Yeth." His attention diverted, he allowed Liza to lead him back to the cart. Paprika greeted him with due enthusiasm for his new treasure, and he plopped into her lap, happy and content.

Liza counted the baskets she had left and figured a mental total of her profits. Yes, Nanosh would be pleased. Though it was common practice for the Gypsy women to earn the money for the men in the kumpania, today she would keep some of her earnings to buy Mama a pretty kerchief. Nanosh would never know.

She caught a blur of pink in her side vision and glanced up to find the little girl she'd been watching only minutes ago standing at the front of her cart, engrossed with the baskets scattered inside.

She was an exquisite child, even prettier up close than she had been from afar. The sun twinkled over her blond curls, each one perfectly formed and shining, and so very different from the dark, wind-blown locks of the Gypsy children. Liza resisted reaching out to touch them.

"I want a basket," the little girl said.

She spoke clearly for her young age, and from the ring of demand in her tone, Liza guessed she was accustomed to getting what she wanted. At the sound of her voice, Putzi, his black eyes wide with surprise, scrambled to his feet.

"Where is your mama, little one?" Liza asked, sweeping a glance through the crowd. She found no sign of the child's mother or father nearby, or even the man with the pipe. Her brow furrowed with concern. The parents would be very worried when they realized she had wandered away. But the child didn't seem to miss them, absorbed instead with inspecting each and every basket.

Putzi inched closer.

"Look what I got." Proudly, he extended an arm toward her, the flag gripped in his fist.

The little girl rested her long-lashed gaze upon him. Beside her perfection, Putzi looked like a poor peasant, his shirt too small and missing a button, his feet shoeless, his pants a size too large. Ice cream had dripped and dried on his chin; dirt clung to his hands and beneath his nails. In spite of his ragged appearance, or perhaps because of it, Liza's heart filled with renewed love for him.

The little girl's lower lip thrust outward. She snatched the flag from Putzi and flung it to the ground.

"I want a basket," she demanded again.

Appalled, Liza gasped. Putzi's eyes widened, his mouth quivered, and Liza gave him a swift, tight hug of comfort.

Could the Gaje not teach their children better than to

29

hurt another? Gypsies would not tolerate such behavior in
their own kind. Respect toward one another was para-
mount and enforced.

"Give her a basket, Liza," Paprika said tersely. "Then
make her go away."

Liza had always loved children, but this one tested her
tolerance. She searched within the cart and found the
smallest basket, the one made from bark and yucca leaves.

"You may have this. It is just the right size for you." Liza
handed the basket to her and hoped she would not throw
it to the ground, too.

A bright smile erupted on the little girl's perfect face, and
squealing in delight, she took the basket.

"Margaret Michelle!"

At the panic-stricken shriek, Liza jumped. The little girl's
mother rushed through the crowd toward them, her husband and the man with a pipe close on her heels.

"Oh, dear God! Stay away from those people!" the
mother cried and snatched her away, as if fearful Liza
would gobble her up at any moment.

Stay away from those people!

The words stung deeply, and Liza fought the hurt. Her
back stiffened, her chin tilted upward, and her gaze lifted
to clash with the Gajo woman's husband.

Tawny eyes, flecked and ringed with black, locked with
hers. Framed with thick lashes the color of rain-wet earth,
they reminded her of a tiger's, sharp and alert, missing
nothing. Magnetic, intense, he held her suspended for a
fraction of time. Her heart tripped an odd beat, but she
matched his intensity with defiance, silently challenging
him to echo his wife's words, to show the same contempt
and revulsion.

She saw only a guarded wariness. Veiled irritation tautened his jaw, and Liza was unsure if she was the cause of

, but she sensed he kept his impatience tightly under wraps.

His gaze dragged to his wife. "The child's come to no harm, Rebecca Ann. Calm down."

"But they're dirty, Reese. All Gypsies are," she said, embracing her daughter protectively. "They steal children. Everyone knows that."

A small, choking sound escaped from Paprika. Liza's nostrils flared from her own fury; her chin jerked higher. Guilt twinged her subconscious, reminding her of the flag she had stolen for Putzi, but to be accused of stealing a child—a Gaje child, no less—was too much. Once more, those tiger-gold eyes burned into her, singeing her with threads of suspicion.

Paprika's hand lifted to her scalp. Her young features grew impassive, and she began to scratch, first one side of her head and then the other. The movement drew the Gajo's attention. He frowned, and Liza secretly applauded her sister's performance.

It was an old Gypsy trick. Scratching a nonexistent itch, or feigning disease or lice effectively kept the Gaje away. And Liza wanted nothing more than to send the tall Gajo with the disturbing eyes, his whining wife, and spoiled daughter as far away as she could.

"Ooh!" The woman gasped in horror at Paprika. Her nose wrinkled in shocked distaste, and she plucked the basket from the little girl's grasp. As if it were a piece of rancid meat, she held it with her fingertips and tossed it toward the cart. She missed, and the basket fell to the ground.

The child howled in protest. A tantrum was imminent.

"Come on, Reese. Daddy. Let's get away from them." The woman seemed on the verge of tears, but she held her squirming daughter fast.

The incident drew curious stares from the crowd. The man with the pipe studied Paprika, his features kind and sympathetic, yet Liza noticed he carefully kept his distance. He took another step away and tried to console the squalling little girl.

The tall Gajo's glance skimmed over Paprika and Putzi but lingered on Liza before he bent and picked up the basket. Silently, he held it toward her, his eyes seeming to pierce her very soul.

Did he know the game they played? It did not matter. The Gaje would think whatever they wanted of the Gypsy and they would always think the worst. Lowering her gaze, she pulled the gold-and-crimson striped kerchief farther over her forehead and refused to take the basket. She did not want to see his mockery or disdain.

After a long moment, the basket dropped into the cart with a slight thud. He took his wife's elbow in a firm grasp and they all disappeared into the crowd.

Paprika stopped scratching and heaved a relieved sigh.

"Thank goodness they're gone," she said, setting her hands on her narrow hips and shaking her dark head. "That little girl needs a sound thrashing."

"She is only a child, Paprika. I remember you behaving the same way a time or two." Liza refused to turn around to search the throng of people for one last look at the tall Gajo, to feel the heat of his gaze upon her or hear the low smoky tones of his voice.

"I never!"

"Yes, you did. All children do, one time or another."

"Did I, Liza?"

Putzi's sweet face appealed to her, soothing the lingering traces of anger stoked by the Gaje. She managed a smile. "No, little one. You are always very good."

Paprika rolled her eyes. "Why do you favor him so, Liza?

32

He's forever getting into scrapes, and Mama must give him a swat—"

"Paprika, hush." Liza was in no mood to bicker with her sister. She had had enough of Niobrara City. How could she have been so excited to come anyway? She should have stayed at the camp with Mama and the rest of their kumpania.

Her actions brisk and irritable, Liza gathered the last of her baskets and tossed them into the cart.

"Are we leaving, Liza?" Putzi asked.

"Yes."

"Now? Why?" Paprika's tone revealed great disappointment.

"It is time. We have been here long enough."

"But I haven't done a single bit of begging. And Putzi has been looking forward to hearing the train's whistle."

"He will hear the whistle from our camp clear enough."

Liza cared little about a big, noisy train. What use was it to her and her people anyway? Let the Gaje have their extravagant toys and foolish pleasures. She wanted to go home.

"Have you forgotten Mama's kerchief?" Paprika demanded. "And we must bring back candy for Tekla and the others."

Liza nearly groaned. She *had* forgotten her intention to buy the kerchief. Was it not the whole purpose for their trip to Niobrara City, to sell her baskets and do just that?

Remembering a store they had passed earlier, one that had a lovely display of women's clothing in its window, Liza clucked her tongue and grasped the cart's handles. "We must hurry, then. Hanzi has probably already found a hen for Mama to stew. We cannot be late."

"Wait, Liza. Look." Paprika gestured toward the crowd

33

and slanted her a sly glance. "The handsome Gajo must be famous. Everyone knows him."

Liza could not have stopped herself from looking for him to save her soul. She found him almost immediately, a head taller than most of the men surrounding him. He did not take a step without someone thumping his broad back or pumping his hand with exuberant enthusiasm.

His smile shone with pride. He had something to say to everyone, and he made his way with a relaxed ease through the crowd, drawing closer and closer to the mighty train engine.

What was it about this Gajo that made him stand out among his own people? Though she knew she must leave, Liza tarried one minute and then another, watching him with a forbidden fascination, at times forced to stand on tiptoe to keep a clear glimpse of him.

"For that one, you will stay, eh?" Paprika teased knowingly.

"I will not stay for him!" Liza exclaimed. "He is a Gajo!"

"Yet you watch him like he is one of us." Paprika cocked her head, her features considering. "He is better than the other Gaje, I think. Tall and strong. Rich, too."

Liza's gaze inched back toward him. He did indeed appear to have a modest wealth. His tailored black suit clung to his masculine frame with perfection, unlike the threadworn, ill-fitting suits of the men in her kumpania. The fabric laid against his skin and accentuated the flow of muscles whenever he moved. Hair the shade of rich coffee hung beneath his hat and past the collar of his white shirt, gleaming crisp and bright against the tanned column of his throat.

While Liza stared, someone gave him a bottle of champagne. Taking his daughter and handing her to the man smoking a pipe, he gently nudged his wife before him, and together they climbed onto a narrow platform on the train's engine.

The crowd grew quiet. Liza found herself holding her breath with everyone else, an odd fluttering deep within her breast. He began to speak, his words clear and precise, his manner dignified and composed. He welcomed his people, thanked them for coming, and spoke of the importance of the Nebraska-Dakota Railroad for Niobrara City.

Liza hung on his every word as though hearing the English language for the very first time. This man drew her like none other before him, and the knowledge troubled her. He was not of her world. Worse, he was another woman's husband. How could he hold this power over her?

She fought the power, squelched it down, forced it away. She knew a sudden need to return to their camp, to smell the smoke of the scattered campfires, to see Mama and the familiar high-wheeled wagon she called home.

Liza took Putzi's hand and turned, only to find Paprika gone. She darted an anxious glance about the depot and found her with a Gajo, perhaps in his twenties, who appeared nervous and uncomfortable.

Exasperated, Liza shook her head at her sister's stubbornness. With her manner humble yet proud, Paprika would tell him a sad story and persistently beg until he parted with his money. Liza had no choice but to wait until she succeeded with the ploy.

She sought the tall Gajo once more. What else did she have to do while she waited for Paprika but watch him? He carried a champagne bottle in one hand, and his arm lifted and shattered the glass against the train's smokestack. A roar of delight rose among the crowd, and the air filled with cheers of celebration. Men tossed their hats into the sky, women waved lace handkerchiefs, and inexplicably caught up by their enthusiasm, Liza laughed with them.

A gust of wind fluttered the ends of her kerchief about her face. Thunder growled on the horizon, and the air hung heavy with the scent of rain. Ominous-looking clouds rolled and tumbled, restless with the storm soon to come.

Her laughter died. The need to return to camp increased tenfold, and she searched for Paprika again. A mammoth horse blocked her view, his rider swathed in buffalo hides and a raccoon-skin hat. He clenched a rifle in his meaty fists.

He was the Wild One—the Gajo who had nearly run them down on the road outside Niobrara City. Fear welled up inside Liza, and she pulled Putzi closer to her side. The man would bring trouble. She could see it in his bearded face, in the crazed look in his eyes, in the way his mighty chest heaved beneath the huge buffalo coat.

He cocked the rifle and shot into the sky. The crowd did not seem to notice, but Liza flinched and squeezed Putzi's hand tighter. He shot again, and this time, the Gaje listened.

"Carrison!" he boomed. "Reese Carrison!"

Murmurs of alarm rippled through the men and women. The tall Gajo halted. There was no mistake he bore the name Reese Carrison. Even with the distance separating them, Liza recognized the tension in him, in the taut slope of his shoulders and in the rigid, alert way he stood. She imagined his mind racing as he calculated the danger the Wild One presented.

"Now's not the time, McCrae." The terseness in his voice reached over the crowd. "We'll talk later."

"Talkin' won't help. Too late fer it."

"The N & D is here to stay. You have to accept that."

"I told you before, and you didn't lissen. You're ruinin' God's land with your damned railroad, Carrison! I ain't gonna stand fer it."

36

"McCrae, you can't—"

The Wild One leveled the rifle at the train and shot into the smokestack. The bright red, white, and blue bunting jerked from the force of the bullet. Women screamed. Reese ducked, dragging his wife with him and pushing her into the arms of the man with the pipe.

Another shot followed, and then another. Bullets pockmarked the sleek engine. Chaos erupted. Reese jumped from the train into the crowd. Frenzied mothers grabbed for their children and ran for cover. A group of men lunged at the Wild One, trying to pull him from his horse.

Liza had had enough. Hugging Putzi protectively, she pushed the cart at a half-run away from the Gaje's hysteria and frantically searched for Paprika.

"Liza, what's happening?" Paprika emerged from the blur of faces and bodies, her dark eyes wide with fear.

"God's saints! I found you!" Liza had to shout above the cries of the crowd. "We must get away from this!"

"I'll help push the cart. Putzi, give me your other hand and run as fast as you can."

Keeping their brother safe between them, Liza and Paprika dodged panicked townspeople and hastened down the length of the long train stationed beside the depot. Pausing in the shadows of the caboose, Liza glanced behind her. The Wild One kicked free from the men who hoped to restrain him, rode past the train and away from Niobrara City at a full gallop, his empty rifle held high in the air.

Liza was certain he was possessed by the devil. She pressed a hand to her breast and sighed in great relief. He was gone. They were safe.

But why had he threatened Reese Carrison? What was it about the Nebraska-Dakota Railroad that inspired his hate?

With his departure, the chaos ended, and so did the Nebraska-Dakota Railroad's celebration. Joyous smiles were replaced by somber frowns, and Niobrara city's disconcerted citizens began to return to their homes. Buggies and horses filtered into the streets, and Liza hesitated about returning to their camp just yet.

The other Gypsy women with their children had long since left. She glanced at the sky and tried to gauge the storm's arrival. If they hurried, they could find the store that sold the pretty kerchiefs.

"We will take a shorter way." Liza veered into a narrow street. Only a couple of blocks to the store, a few moments inside, and they would be on their way back to the kumpania. They did not have a minute to waste.

"Basket! My basket!"

She halted at the sound of the child's voice. Alone, Reese Carrison's daughter toddled toward them from the depot, her blond ringlets mussed from the wind. Her parents were nowhere to be found, nor was the man who smoked the pipe, and Liza clucked her tongue in concern.

"Not her again," Paprika groaned.

"Maybe she is lost," Liza reasoned. The child obviously had been separated from her family in the fray. Her mother would be frantic.

"I want my basket back." The child peered inside the cart, searching for the basket Liza had given her.

"Where is your mama?" Liza asked for the second time that afternoon.

The child's shoulders lifted carelessly. "I don't know. Do you have my basket?"

Liza could not help remembering Mrs. Carrison's animosity toward Gypsies. What would she think if she found her daughter with three of them now? Given her dramatic, high-strung nature, Liza shuddered. She did not want to find out.

She plucked the bark-and-yucca-leaf basket from the

cart and gave it to the child. "Here it is." Placing her hands on the little girl's shoulders, she turned her around in the direction of the depot and gave her a pat on her pink-ruffled backside. "Now, go. Your mama is worried about you."

The child remained, entranced with the small basket.

"Go," Paprika urged more forcefully, flinging her arms outward. "Shoo, shoo."

Still she made no attempt to leave.

"Stubborn little thing, isn't she?" Paprika muttered.

Liza wallowed in indecision. She did not have time for a lost little girl. Her instincts told her to walk back to the depot, find the child's parents and return her safely, yet the impending storm forbade it. Already, the wind had grown stronger, colder. Besides, she had no desire to risk another confrontation with the child's mother or hear her stinging accusations.

"Let's start walking. Maybe if we ignore her, she'll go away," Paprika suggested.

Liza nibbled on the inside of her lip. Perhaps that would be the best way. The child had no fear among strangers, showed no worry about the loss of her parents. Her independent nature would sustain her well. Most likely, Reese Carrison would turn the corner at any moment and find her safe and content.

Feeling guilty with every step, Liza pivoted and pushed the cart along the wooden boardwalk, despite Putzi's protests to stay. The women's clothing store waited on the next block, but the Gajo child's footsteps sounded plainly behind them. Exasperated, Liza halted again.

"Can you play?" the little girl asked Putzi, taking his hand as if they'd been friends for years.

Putzi turned wide, hopeful eyes toward Liza. "Can I?"

"No, you may not play," she hissed.

Paprika gasped. "Oh, Liza." Horror sounded in her voice. "We have trouble. Look over there."

A horde of Gaje, with Mrs. Carrison in the center, her husband at her side, appeared in the street next to the depot.

"There she is! They're trying to take her away! Stop them!" she cried. Contempt and suspicion was evident on the Gaje's expressions as they increased their pace to a near run. "Oh, Margaret Michelle! Baby!"

In an instant, Liza knew what Mrs. Carrison thought, what they all thought. Gypsies had long been accused of stealing children, and this time would be no different. Having the beautiful child in their midst through no fault of their own would look incriminating enough. The Gaje would ask few questions, show little mercy.

Liza knew of the Gaje jails. More than once, Gypsies had camped out in front of a local police station or sheriff's office when one of their own had been arrested. Too often, she had heard of the treatment Gypsies received, the disdain, the swift convictions. Was it any wonder they had quickly learned to flee arrest?

And Liza did not want to be arrested, did not want Paprika and Putzi to endure the fear of the Gaje jails.

Taking their hands into each of hers, she abandoned the cart and broke into a run, darting between buildings, into an alley and sidestepping boxes of trash overturned in the wind. They found refuge behind an old, weatherbeaten shed.

The child, Margaret Michelle, would be with her people now. Safe, unharmed. Her mother would be happy and relieved. Yet the Gaje would not let the matter rest, would not let a Gypsy go without stern words of warning or worse, and she must spare her brother and sister the humiliation.

The Gaje sounded close, so close. Liza knew they would not be able to outrun them, not with Putzi and his short legs to slow them down. She turned to Paprika.

"You must go without me," she said. "Run with Putzi back to camp. Can you find the way?"

Frightened tears trailed along Paprika's cheeks and mingled with the giant raindrops that had begun to fall. "Yes, but I won't leave you. I won't!"

"You have to. Tell Nanosh the kumpania must leave, or the Gaje will come looking for you and take you away. I will lead them on a wild-goose chase."

A sob escaped Paprika's throat, and she nodded. "But how will you get back? The storm is already here."

Liza shrugged. She was not afraid. "I will follow the *vurma* Mama and the others will leave for me." She scooped Paprika against her in a quick embrace. "Do not worry, sweet sister. Be strong for Putzi."

He was crying, too, and his tears moved Liza, as they never failed to do. She bent and kissed the top of his tousled head. "Run fast for Paprika, little one. I will see you soon."

He hugged her fiercely. With the miniature flag still gripped in his pudgy fist, he and Paprika sprinted away from the old shed, away from the depot, away from the troubles in the Gaje world to the refuge of their own.

Liza swallowed down a sudden surge of emotion at watching them go. Taking a breath, blinking against the pelting raindrops, she lifted her skirts and dashed into the street.

And ran right into Reese Carrison.

It was like hitting a giant oak. His tall, muscular body, solid from head to toe, nearly knocked her over, and she had to step back swiftly to keep from falling.

He looked as surprised as she. His gaze bolted behind

41

her and caught Paprika's and Putzi's tiny receding figures, then slammed into hers. His eyes narrowed, the tawny depths no longer burning and intense as she remembered, but instead, cold and harsh.

With a cry of alarm, Liza scrambled away, evading his grasp with more luck than skill.

"Bram! She's coming your way! Grab her!"

Liza's heart pounded in terror. Shouting, angry Gaje appeared from everywhere, and though she once judged the man with the pipe to be kind and compassionate, she knew he was now as determined to capture her as Reese Carrison.

How could she outwit them all?

She had been a fool to think she could. There were too many against her. Never did it occur to her to surrender, to try to explain that she had no intention of stealing the lovely child they called Margaret Michelle, that the whole thing was all just a horrible misunderstanding.

Because she was a Gypsy. And they were the Gaje.

But she could not outrun them. They were all closing in on her, all of them. Even Reese Carrison.

Horses were tethered in front of the Grand River Hotel. Liza's practiced eye found the finest in the row, a midnight black, pure-blooded stallion, the choicest piece of horse-flesh she had seen in years. She knew instinctively that this animal would be her salvation, strong enough and fast enough to save her from the vengeful Gaje.

And she made her decision.

From almost a block away, Reese slowed his run. On a wave of disbelief, he watched her sprint toward the line of horses, her bright, colorful skirts flying about her ankles, the ends of her striped kerchief flapping in the rain-filled breeze. Of the entire row, she chose the horse in the middle. Without a second's hesitation. As if she knew exactly what she was doing. Her movements deft and sure, she

42

untethered the reins, vaulted into the saddle with more fluid grace than most men he'd known, and maneuvered the stallion into a smooth turn. The giant beast responded to her command, as if she'd trained him from birth, and fairly flew down the street and out of sight.

With the wind and rain swirling about him, Reese tilted his head back and hurled a vehement curse into the stormy heavens.

On top of everything that had gone wrong all damned day, the beautiful Gypsy woman had just stolen his horse.

Chapter Three

"What're you waiting for, Reese?" Bram panted to a stop, his near-fifty years sapping the breath from him. "Go after her!"

"How the hell am I supposed to catch her? She took my horse!" Through the curtain of rain dripping from his hat brim, Reese glared at the empty spot only seconds ago filled by the stallion.

"Yours the only one that can run?" Bram shoved him toward the row of horses tethered at the hotel. "Take mine! Find her! She can't get away with trying to steal my grand-baby!"

Half-hearted grunts of agreement filtered from the men who lagged behind them, their quest for justice fast washing away in the blowing rain. With the Gypsy woman gone and her kidnapping attempt foiled, the need for chase seemed unnecessary. Except for Bram, no one cared whether they caught her.

But Reese cared. A lot. He had a fortune tied up in that

horse. Sired in Kentucky, shipped to Nebraska with the best care money could buy, its bloodline was impeccable. For the past six years, the N & D had taken nearly every dime, nickel, and penny Reese had earned. The stallion was the one extravagance he had allowed himself.

Yes, he cared. And he'd be damned if a troublemaking Gypsy was going to steal it from him.

His stride lengthened into a full-blown run toward Bram's sorrel. Bram shouted something, but his words were lost in the wind. Reese yanked at the reins and leaped into the wet saddle.

From the hotel, he cut between the Empty Saddle Saloon and the barber shop. The sorrel gathered speed as they fled past Gardner's Liquor Store, Masterson's Grocery, and the Niobrara City Bank. One block, another, and then another, until the town faded into a storm-filled blur behind him, and only wide open country lay ahead.

Which direction had she gone?

The possibilities were endless, and frustration welled up inside him. He gritted his teeth and reined the sorrel to a stop. Rain pelted his back, plastering the wool suit against him like a second skin. Grimly, he ran a thorough glance over the sprawling grassland.

He spotted her on the crest of a bluff. She, too, had halted, seeming to search for him as he searched for her. Like lightning, their gazes bolted together, and she started, as if not expecting to find him watching her.

She recovered quickly. The stallion, poised for her command, charged into swift flight, heading northward along the river. Reese vaguely recalled her people were camped to the south. Would she circle the town and return to them in a roundabout way? Or had she grown disoriented in her haste to lose him?

He tossed aside the thought. She knew what she was

doing. She hadn't evaded nearly a dozen men not to.

Determination raged anew to reclaim what was his. With a yell, Reese kicked the sorrel into a run, giving him full rein for the chase. The rain-softened earth gave way beneath the pounding hooves, spewing clumps of mud and grass in their wake. He squeezed his knees against the horse's belly and leaned into the ride, rueing that twist of fate that forced him to pursue his own mount.

Only now did he realize the stallion's speed. It had been important to have the finest horse in Nebraska. A thoroughbred. Strong and lean. Swift-footed. A horse so fast Bram's sorrel didn't have a chance in hell to catch up with him.

Yet the Gypsy rode him well. Had he been of a mind to, Reese would have marveled at her skill. But right now he only wanted to get his horse back and give her a tongue-lashing the likes of which she'd never had before.

Needle-sharp with vengeance, his mind raced to devise a strategy. His only hope to catch her was to head her off, to beat her at her own game. He squinted into the distance and gauged her destination. She seemed to follow the river's meandering course, continuing her flight northward, leaving her people farther and farther behind.

And he knew a shortcut.

Tight-mouthed, he maneuvered the sorrel into an abrupt turn and rode into the wind. The gusts threatened to swipe the clothes from his back, forcing him to ride with one hand on his hat, the other clutching the reins. He laid low over the sorrel's neck, giving his body less resistance against the wind.

Visibility was lousy. Anyone would lose their bearings in the heavy rain, and he understood the Gypsy's reasoning to keep to the river. He glanced over his shoulder, saw her disappear over a bluff, and grunted in satisfaction.

The sorrel galloped through Jack Hadley's cornfield, past the barns and outbuildings, and skirted a windmill. Ever faster he fled over the drenched grassland until, at last, they reached a drop-off leading to the river.

Thick brush lined the bank. Like long, bony fingers, tree roots poked and curled around huge outcroppings of rock wedged among the dirt and sand. Reese gave the horse his lead, letting him pick his way down the embankment. Mud slid and squished beneath the iron-clad hooves, and Reese tensed, fearful the horse would slip and go lame.

But they reached the river's edge without mishap. The current pooled and swirled in angry response to the storm. Here, the Niobrara formed a loop as it twisted and turned through the gently sloping land, and it was here Reese hoped to catch the Gypsy woman by surprise, to end this skin-soaking chase she'd led him on and get his prized horse back.

The ground leveled out along the bank, forming a narrow path. It would be easy to see her when she came around the bend, and Reese turned the sorrel in that direction, the taste of imminent victory sweet on his tongue. He'd be ready for her.

And then she was there. The stallion bore down on them at alarmingly high speed, defying the intensity of the wind-driven storm. Reese couldn't see her face. The rain slanted directly at her; she kept her head angled against the force, trusting the stallion in his run, as if the fierceness of the downpour had become too much for her.

"Hey! *Hey!*"

Too late, Reese realized he didn't know her name, that he couldn't get her attention except through his frantic yell, that, because of the sliver-thin path and the river on one side, the steep bank on the other, the stallion had nowhere to go but to ram them straight on.

At the sound of his voice, her head jerked up; her eyes widened. Immediately, she reacted, yanking the reins tight to halt the stallion's flight. He screamed and reared, his mighty forelegs slashing the air. She nearly lost her seat, her mastery over the horse gone as he pounced and lunged against the muddy riverbank.

She cried out and dropped the reins, clutching the black mane and hanging on with a white-knuckled grip. Fearful she'd fall and be trampled beneath the horse's powerful hooves, Reese swore viciously and spurred the sorrel closer. Again, the stallion reared up on his hind legs. Reese leaned over and tried to grab the bridle, but missed.

"No!" The Gypsy tried to evade his grasp. "Leave me alone!"

"Are you crazy?" Reese shouted and reached for the bridle again. "You'll be killed!"

"Stay back!" She angled away from him even as she clung to the mane for dear life. "Do not touch me!"

She *was* crazy. Reese rose in the stirrups and bent toward her, snaking his arm around her waist, hauling her from the saddle with much determination and little fanfare.

She fought him like a she-cat, refusing to relinquish her hold on the stallion's mane. Bram's sorrel shied from the frenzied animal, and Reese almost lost his grip on her. Each horse dodged the other, their flailing hooves desperate for firm footing on the muddy bank. Through sheer superior strength, Reese overpowered the Gypsy, and she tumbled from her horse onto his.

The sorrel fought for traction. Reese had all he could do to hang on to the squirming woman and stay seated. The stallion stumbled toward them; the sorrel tottered against his weight. Reese instinctively kicked free of the stirrups and pitched sideways from the saddle.

He twisted to take the brunt of the fall. Holding the

Gypsy tightly to him, he hit the bank feet first. Pain shot through his knee, and he buckled to the ground, taking her with him, twisting again, rolling, rolling, to avoid the horses's crushing bulk.

They tumbled to a stop. For a moment, he laid there, caught in the tangled yardage of her skirts, with her body sprawled on top of his, and wondered if he'd broken his leg. Jesus, it hurt. Fire flowed up his thigh and down to his ankle. He drew a breath.

The Gypsy scrambled to her feet and took a cautious step backward. She seemed poised for flight, ready to bolt should he take off after her. Reese groaned aloud and forced himself to sit up. He doubted he'd ever walk again.

She watched him warily. He struggled to get a hold on the pain, relaxing in slow degrees while the fire ebbed to a dull, persistant throb. He gripped his knee and felt the swelling that had already begun.

"Are—are you all right?"

Her uncertain question stirred his temper, and he fixed her with a menacing stare. She flinched from the intensity of it. "What the hell do you think?"

She looked like a half-drowned mutt with her hair smeared across her scalp and cheek. The striped kerchief, its colors once vibrant in the sunlight, laid over her shoulders like a limp rag. Rivulets of rain streamed across her face, dripping steadily from the edge of her chin onto her blouse.

A single drop caught his attention. It snaked a path down her neck, past her collarbone, and settled in the valley of her breasts. The drenched garment clung to the full mounds, highlighting her nipples as if she wore nothing at all.

Something stirred inside Reese, but his foul mood neglected to identify it, refused to let it take root. His gaze slammed back to hers. "This is all your fault."

She gasped, the sound barely audible in the falling rain. "Mine?"

"Yes, yours." In the back of his mind, Reese became aware that the storm had lessened its roar, that the wind had died to a crisp breeze. "Gypsies bring trouble wherever they go. You damn well brought your share of it."

Her chin snapped up, her nostrils flared.

"If you hadn't tried to snatch Margaret Michelle right out from under our noses—"

"I never!"

"—then lead me on a wild-goose chase on my own horse in the middle of a damn storm—"

A strangled sound escaped from her throat.

"—then none of this would have happened."

"You bastard."

"Call me what you want, Lady Gypsy," he snarled. "But this is all your fault."

"Stupid Gajo!"

"You think I'd be sitting here in the mud, my knee wrenched all to hell, if not for you?" Her ire failed to sway his own. His reckless accusations flew free. "Now we're soaking wet, miles from home, and my horse—"

A whimpering nicker stilled the words on his tongue. His glance swung toward the sorrel and found him calmed, his nose at the river's edge.

Reese automatically searched for the stallion at the base of the riverbank. The animal writhed in the mud and tried to get up on all fours. Reese's gut twisted.

"Saints in heaven!"

Her features horrified, the Gypsy woman lifted her voluminous skirts high about her ankles and hastened to the stallion's side. Reese bellowed a blue oath and tried to stand. His throbbing knee protested every movement, sent

50

shards of pain clear to his hip. He gritted his teeth and managed to pull himself upright anyway, giving his uninjured leg all his weight. He hobbled to a cluster of low-lying branches drooping over the bank, gave one a savage yank and tested its sturdiness.

It proved to be a fine enough crutch. He limped over to the stallion and halted. The animal laid unmoving, as if his agony had become too much to bear. His eyes were glazed, wild, filled with panic. Despair washed over Reese.

"He's lame, isn't he?" Reese's voice rasped with the weight of the words, knowing they were true, but wanting her to tell him they weren't.

The Gypsy's hand stilled over the horse's hindleg. Her gaze lifted, meeting his, the dark orbs pools of sympathy. "Yes."

"Damn."

The stallion meant the world to him. A symbol of his success almost more than the N & D. Any man appreciated a good horse, and this one had been one of the best. Grief sagged inside him. He would miss the stallion sorely.

What else could go wrong? The day had been one disaster after another. He'd had a feeling, from the minute he'd first laid eyes on the Gypsy camp outside of Niobrara City . . .

And this woman was a Gypsy. She was part of the trouble, the reason why they were out here in the middle of nowhere, his horse lame and hurting and useless.

The stallion nickered again, low and anguished with pain. Reese identified with that pain. Didn't he feel it as deeply, in his own knee? Didn't he know what the stallion was going through?

A solemn resolve filled him, leaving him empty, dispassionate. He hobbled over to the sorrel, to the saddlebag where Bram always kept a pistol.

"What are you going to do?"

Reese ignored the woman's wary question and checked the chamber. All six bullets were intact.

She straightened, moved to his side, and tugged on his arm.

"I will not let you do this." Her small hands gripped him with the same intensity as her words.

The rain had dwindled to a mere sprinkle. Droplets clung to her lashes, surprisingly long and thick. Reese pulled his glance away and shrugged free of her touch. His lip curled. "Think you're going to stop me?"

She flinched from the nasty drawl in his tone.

"Yes." Her chin lifted. "I can help him."

He snorted in derision. "You've been a big help already, sweetheart. Move."

She remained where she was, steadfastly between him and the stallion. "No. You must trust me."

Trust a Gypsy? He'd never known a more conniving, thieving, underhanded, elusive people in his life. Or one that brought more trouble. "Uh-uh. I don't think so."

He put his hand out to thrust her away, but she swiveled out of reach. Grimly, he lifted the pistol and took aim. Right between the stallion's eyes. His thumb pulled back the hammer—

"*No-o!*" She came at him hard, knocking his arm aside, nearly making him lose his balance. "Foolish Gajo! Do you think you will be a hero, putting the horse out of his misery? Are you going to help him like that?"

"Yes, damn it! Look at him. He can't even stand up! It'll be hours before we can get him to a vet. I won't have him suffer in the meantime."

"I can help him," she said again, a thread of urgency in her voice. "Let me *help.*"

Reese wavered. He thought of the liniments in the tack-room in his barn at home. The poultices and medications and bandages. But they had nothing here to treat the stallion's injuries.

Nothing.

Slowly, he shook his head and raised the pistol again. "That horse means too much to me to put him through the pain. The only humane thing to do is to put him down. Now."

She spun and planted her feet between him and the horse, splaying her arms wide in a protective gesture. "Shoot him, and you will have to shoot me first, Gajo."

Reese cocked his jaw and squelched his frustration. His instincts told him to do what any man would do under these circumstances.

But another part of him wanted to believe in her, to trust that she somehow had the knowledge and skill to ease the horse's misery, to make him walk and run as strong and swift as before.

And, Lord, the woman was determined.

He narrowed an eye. He touched the nose of the pistol to the base of her throat, dragging it slowly upward along the curve of her neck. A slight flick of his wrist, and the pistol tilted her chin a fraction higher. She shivered.

He had her full attention.

"I'm giving you five minutes to prove yourself. Convince me you know what you're doing, and my horse lives."

She nodded, swallowed, and a flash of cautious relief flitted over her features. Satisfied she took his warning seriously, he lowered the pistol and stuffed it in his waistband.

The Gypsy stepped away, knelt beside the stallion, and set to work. Her graceful hands examined every inch of his hindlegs beginning with his hooves and working up to his hips, then repeated the procedure with the forelegs to the shoulder. The horse seemed lulled by the soft, crooning tone of her voice and remained passive beneath her gentle ministrations. An accomplishment in itself given the animal's high-strung nature, Reese thought with grudging admiration. The stallion had never been receptive to strangers.

Her slim fingers returned to the right hindleg and prodded carefully.

"Here," she said. "A sprain in the hock."

"Are you sure?"

"Yes." Defiance shone in her dark eyes, as if she resented him questioning her diagnosis. "He flinches when I touch him there. And I can feel the heat."

Heat. A danger signal. Even so, Reese wanted to feel for himself, to be convinced that she spoke the truth, that she didn't, for reasons of her own, try to con him with a lie.

His knee aching, he bent and ran his hand along the hindleg. The stallion nickered, seemingly impatient with all their poking, and tried to stand. The Gypsy reached out and took Reese's wrist, guiding him to the swollen sprain quickly.

"Do you feel it?"

Her fingers, cold and wet from the rain, looked small and almost delicate against his skin. He had a sudden urge to warm her, to take her body against his and chase away the chill, to keep her dry and safe.

The unexpected need rocked him, and he fought it, forced himself to keep his attention to the matter at hand.

"Yes," he said, his reply curt.

"Help me get him up, then." She released him, straightened and tugged on the bridle. Reese lent his assistance, and they worked the stallion into an upright position. He shied, favoring the injured leg, but allowed the Gypsy to lead him toward the river.

Reese glanced at the swirling current and frowned. "What are you going to do?"

"The cold water will ease the swelling. He must stand in the river for a little while."

"That's not a good idea."

She met his gaze squarely. "It's what he needs."

"The river's running pretty strong. You could be swept away."

She seemed amused by his argument. "Are you worried about me, a poor, simple Gypsy who brings you nothing but trouble? Save your breath, Gajo. I know what I am doing."

Her taunt hit too close to the truth. Reese reached out and snared her chin in a firm grip. Scorn flared in her expression, and she jerked, breaking free of his hold.

The abrupt movement dropped a thick tendril of wet hair over one side of her face. More gently this time, Reese reached toward her again, and tucked the wayward strands behind her ear.

"What is your name?" he asked.

The question appeared to take her by surprise. She glanced toward the river, as if debating whether or not to answer. After a long moment, she turned back to him.

"Liza," she said.

The name fit her. Exotic. Unusual.

And beautiful.

She seemed to dismiss him after imparting that bit of information, channeling her attention solely on the stallion. She stroked his velvety nose and spoke in soothing tones before leading him from the bank into the river. Like a calf to slaughter, Reese mused. Somehow, she had stolen the stallion's heart, winning his trust and confidence like few others.

He propped his foot on a rock and massaged his aching

knee. He wondered at her power, her skill. Each came naturally to her, as if the trait had been inborn. Gypsies were well-known for their way with horses, their opinions highly sought after at horse fairs and the like. Yet he knew, too, that a Gypsy would lie and cheat his way through any deal, cunningly manipulating a trade to get the horse he wanted.

Would Liza be the same? Would she try to steal the stallion again?

He didn't doubt it for a minute.

And Margaret Michelle. Hadn't she tried to steal the child? He couldn't forget that, either.

Despite it all, she fascinated him. From the large hoops dangling from her ears, to the long strands of gold beads hanging jumbled and snarled around her neck, to the layers and layers of skirts she wore, she was different from any other woman he'd known. More important, her concern for his horse seemed genuine; her veterinary talents were authentic. For now, at least, he could trust her.

She stood in hip-deep water that must be as cold as ice, her feet braced against the strong current. Her hands were never still, always stroking the stallion's neck and nose, rubbing the mud off his belly and flanks. The stallion's ears were pricked to the sound of her voice, her words easily carrying over the water to Reese.

Because of the absolute quiet. He hadn't noticed it before, his thoughts only on Liza. But not a leaf moved on the trees. Not a bird chirped. Not a single fly hovered in the air. The rain had long since stopped falling.

His glance darted to the sky. Blue-black clouds rolled and churned. He knew Nebraska weather well enough to recognize that this was the calm before the storm, that the previous gale had only been a prelude to what was to come.

He straightened from the rock. "Liza, get out of the water. It's going to rain again."

She peered at him over the saddle and shook her head. "Not yet. The horse needs more time."

"Get out *now*."

She ignored his sharp command, going about her ministrations as if he'd never spoken. His lips thinned in annoyance. A sudden breeze almost lifted the hat from his head, and he tugged it on tighter.

"Liza," he said, his tone heavy with warning. He limped to Bram's sorrel, took the dragging reins and tied them to a stalwart branch hanging over the riverbank. His uneasy glance slid toward Liza again. She seemed oblivious to the impending storm.

"Woman, if I have to go in there after you . . ." He let his words dangle threateningly.

"A little longer," she called back. The wind kicked up harder, making it more difficult to hear. Her gaze lifted to the sky; she frowned.

Reese's patience evaporated, and leaning heavily on the makeshift cane, he stepped into the water. The wetness seeped into his socks. He grimaced. Damn, but it was cold. How could she stand it? He tried not to think of the damage done to his leather boots, newly purchased for the N & D's dedication and one more casualty on the day's lengthy list of misfortunes.

The current had grown stronger with the wind. He had to walk carefully lest it sweep him sideways. The water reached his knees and raised higher with his every step.

She owed him for this. Owed him big time. He could hardly wait to throttle her for her stubbornness, to exact punishment for all the troubles she'd caused him this whole day. Never mind that she just might save his horse from going lame or that—

Her scream tore into his thoughts. His heart leaped to his throat. The current caught at her full skirts and pulled her down into the greenish-brown water. He hardly recognized the hoarse yell crying out her name as his own.

She went completely under. She seemed miles away, and Reese couldn't get to her soon enough. A raw fear clutched him, stopped the blood from flowing in his veins.

She came up again, choking and sputtering and grabbing wildly for the stallion. Reese reached her then, flung his arm around her waist and lifted her higher out of the water. With the other, he grasped the saddle horn and leaned against his horse.

"You okay?" he panted, out of breath from the scare she'd given him.

She nodded and coughed, clutching his neck in a death-grip.

"We have to get back to the bank, Liza. We don't have much time. Do you understand?"

"Yes." A shiver took her, and she swiped at the hair that had fallen over her face while still keeping a tight hold on his neck.

"I'm going to lower you into the water a little, but I'll keep my arm around you." He had to shout above the roar of the wind. "We have to hurry. Come on."

She responded to the urgency in his tone and released his neck. With his free hand, Reese grasped the stallion's bridle. After a grim glance at the sky, he tugged him forward.

None too soon they reached the bank. Liza trudged from the river and hastened to the stallion's other side, her intent to help Reese tether him next to the sorrel. But her fingers were blue from the cold, and Reese finished the job alone.

They'd run out of time. The wind was a fierce roar; the water lapped angrily at the edge of the bank. They had nowhere to go in the seconds they had left before the storm unleashed its rage, nowhere except to seek shelter against a massive outcropping of stone a short distance away.

Reese pushed Liza toward the largest rock, angled with another to form an open cocoon of sorts. He pressed her back against the rough surface. She gasped against the strength of the wind and shuddered violently.

She was afraid. She was cold. Her vulnerability touched Reese in a way he'd never known before. He dropped the branch he'd been using as a crutch and gripped her upper shoulders. Sweet mother. Her skin and wet clothes felt like ice.

He opened his suit coat.

"Put your arms around me," he yelled into her ear. He expected her to refuse. On a half-sob, she hesitated, then slipped her arms inside his coat and wrapped them around his torso. She buried her face against his chest, and Reese folded her tightly against him.

He wasn't dry, but he wasn't as wet as she was, either. He could offer her little but the warmth from his body and protection from the storm. He hoped it was enough to get them through.

Her head lifted from his chest, and she glanced toward the sky. Her breath sucked inward.

"Reese. God's saints. Reese."

He couldn't allow himself the pleasure that came with hearing her speak his name for the first time, the appealing way it rolled off her tongue, the ease with which she seem to use it. He knew what she saw, what he'd expected to come, what the convulsing black clouds hurled down to earth in all their fury.

With her skirts whipping about his legs, he pushed her deeper into the shelter of the rocks and braced for the tornado headed their way.

Chapter Four

Liza clung to him. Who could have known she would depend on a Gajo for her life, that she would need his strength, his protection, his body over hers to shield her from nature's wrath?

She had never thought it possible. But tonight, she needed Reese Carrison. Without shame, she welcomed his weight against her and ignored the jutting hardness of the rocks at her back.

The tornado shrieked and howled over their heads; the awful wind sucked at their clothes. It seemed her ears would burst from the pressure, the noise, the powerful fear that held her captive in his arms.

She was sure they would be picked up by the whirling torrent and hurtled over the countryside, then dropped like rag dolls and left to die. The roaring seemed to go on for hours, yet she knew it did not, that it must be only minutes. She fervently prayed the wind would stop and return everything to normal again.

But the gusts only eased to a stiff breeze; a chill soon filled the air. Marble-sized hail began to fall, pelting their heads and shoulders like buckshot. Liza sucked in a breath and squeezed her eyes shut. The Gajo shifted, taking her even closer against him, letting his body absorb the battering from the icy pellets.

In time, they softened to slush, then turned to a steady rain. Liza cautiously peered through parted lids and blinked at the downpour. Her cheek was pressed into the Gajo's broad chest, the damp fabric of his white shirt warm against her skin. Beneath her palms, his back was solid and rippled with muscle, and at that moment, she realized how tightly she clung to him under the suitcoat.

Tendrils of humiliation coiled through her, yet it was he who pulled away first, setting her gently from him.

"The tornado has gone over us. The worst is done." His mouth set in a grim line, he squinted toward the heaving sky. "For now, at least."

She nodded numbly and slid her arms out from beneath the coat, crossing them over her breasts. His heat no longer warmed her, and she shivered from the loss.

"Looks like it could rain all night and into the morning," he muttered. The tornado had stolen his hat; he raked a hand through his wet hair. "We have to find some place to get out of this damn rain."

"Yes." Lightning zigzagged across the gray sky; thunder rumbled in the distance. She wondered if Nebraska weather was always so unforgiving.

The Gajo stepped toward the horses, still a little skittish after the hellish winds, yet they appeared to have survived well enough. He rubbed the stallion's neck. "How're you, fella? Doing okay?"

Knowing his concern, she watched him and was moved to reassure him.

"He will do better than you think." Liza tried to keep her teeth from chattering. She rubbed her arms. "But he must lie down somewhere. Keep the w-weight off that leg."

The Gajo glanced at her, his features impassive, and reached toward the saddlebags draped over the stallion's back. Flipping one open, he withdrew a folded bundle and shook it out. "Wear this. It'll help keep you from getting any wetter than you already are."

He tossed her an oilskin drover. Liza caught the coat in reflex but hesitated.

All her life, she had despised the Gaje and anything associated with their world. Why, now, would she wear something that belonged to one of them, especially one who had falsely accused her, chased her like an animal, then blamed her with his scathing temper? Why would she even consider it?

Because she was cold and shaking and miserable. Because the coat would shield her from the rain, like he had said, and would be warm, too. Because she had never been more afraid when separated from her people than she was now, and the oilskin would give her a small measure of comfort, however irrational that might be.

Hating herself for her weakness, she shoved her arms into the mammoth sleeves. The soft, cotton ticking that lined the oilskin soothed her drenched limbs. The coat was heavy on her shoulders, hung down to her ankles, and made her feel small within its folds, secure, and . . . better.

The Gajo untied the horses. He flicked his gaze over her. "Ready?"

Her chin lifted at his curt tone. "Where are we going?"

He held both animals by the reins under their chin straps and regarded her with one eye narrowed. "Does it matter?"

"To me it does."

"We have to find shelter."

"Where?"

His patience wavered under her persistence. "I don't know. Anywhere that has a roof and no mud."

With that statement he left her and led the horses along the riverbank toward higher ground. Liza stood rooted, awash in indecision.

Her people. Were they still camped along the Niobrara? Had Paprika and Putzi reached them in time to escape? Liza knew Nanosh well. He and the other men would waste little time fleeing the vengeful Gaje. How would she find them in the storm? Had they escaped the tornado? Would Mama have had time to leave behind the vurma? The uncertain questions buzzed inside her head like raging bees.

Night had fallen early, the gray-black clouds snuffing what little sunlight might have lingered had the day been clear. She swallowed down a wad of panic stuck in her throat, tried to remain calm, and made up her mind.

She must follow Reese Carrison, at least for now. She had to believe he would find them a place to seek refuge. It would not be forever, only a little while. Then, when the weather cleared, she would leave him and return to the kumpania.

On that fragile thread of resolve, she pulled the oilskin tighter about her and reluctantly fell into step behind him. He walked slowly, his knee clearly hindering him. She hadn't realized he'd been hurt so badly. As an afterthought, she ran back to retrieve his abandoned crutch.

The stallion fared a little better, continuing to show his pain by lowering his head every time his injured hindleg touched the ground. For his sake even more than their own, they must find shelter quickly.

Liza caught up with the Gajo and silently handed him the crutch. "I will lead your horse for you."

He took the tree branch and positioned it under his arm with a grunt of thanks. His glance swung to her. "I can handle him."

"The sorrel, then."

Rain streamed down his temple and followed the strong line of his jaw, set in a taut line, before dripping off his chin. Liza knew he was still angry with her, that he blamed her for the predicament they were in.

"All right." The agreement was clipped and tight. "Can you lead him without getting us into more trouble?"

The barb hit its mark, and she stiffened, yet she knew she had best not test his temper further with a stinging retort of her own. She clasped the sorrel's chin strap and stubbornly held her tongue.

His broad back made a fair beacon in the bleak night. She kept her gaze on him often, more to see that he or his horse did not stumble than to find her way. The terrain gradually leveled out, and the Niobrara River rushed and rippled its course farther and farther behind them.

Dead birds, sticks and debris from the tornado littered the ground. Pockets of water sucked at their feet with an annoying squishing sound, chilling Liza's toes until she lost all feeling in them. She could hardly remember what it was like to have the sun shining on her face or feel the heat from a glowing campfire. It seemed she had been drenched in the torrential rain forever.

The Gajo stopped and waited while she drew closer.

"We can ride from here," he said.

We?

Liza's ears hummed from the tiny word. Riding the stallion was out of the question. Did he intend to share the sorrel's back with her? She almost laughed aloud. What would her people think?

She shook her head. Trickles of water slid down the back

of her neck, and she pulled the oilskin's collar more snugly to her. "I will walk. You can ride."

"You'll ride with me."

His tone brooked no argument, and she glared at him. He considered her a moment, sighed heavily, and rested an elbow on the stallion's saddle. "What's the problem here, Liza? Anyone with a lick of sense would prefer to ride a horse than trudge their way through the mud on foot. Anyone but you. Why is that?"

His condescending attitude worked on her nerves, yet she took care not to raise his hackles. His temper tremored deceptively close to the surface. "We—Gypsy women—are accustomed to walking while our men ride in the wagons. We think nothing of it."

"That a fact?"

"Yes," she defended. "And given your injured knee, I think it is wisest that you ride. I am quite able to walk."

He straightened. "Any man with a sense of decency would never allow a woman to walk when she could share his horse—or his wagon—just as easily." His slur against the Gypsies did not escape her. He gave her no chance to retaliate. "The sorrel's strong enough to carry both of us. Now climb up in the saddle, or by God, I'll throw you into it."

Liza fixed him with her most withering stare, the same one that had always succeeded in keeping leery Gaje at a distance, but it did not seem to faze him. He seemed as immovable as ever.

With a snort of disgust, she gave in. She would ride the Gajo's horse to still his irritable tongue. After all, who would see her? She would tell no one she had given in to him.

Her foot jabbed the stirrup, and she swung onto the sorrel in a huff, settling into the saddle with a piqued flounce and a jerk on the oilskin. He mounted up after her, easing his length behind the cantle.

She heard his breath catch and knew the climb had hurt. In spite of herself, compassion stirred, and she leaned forward to give him as much room as possible. His arms came around her, taking the reins from her unresisting fingers. He bent toward the stallion, took those reins, too, and urged both horses forward.

He surrounded her. Liza could not think of what to do with her hands or feet, for he had taken over the stirrups as well. She could do naught but relax her legs against his, and even through her skirts, could tell his thighs were hard with muscle.

He held the sorrel's reins loosely in one hand, the same hand that rested casually in her lap. She frowned at his boldness. And though the sorrel plodded at a slow pace, her back brushed his chest with every step. Even her head seemed to get in the way of his jaw. Much too often, her temple bumped his chin.

"I have friends who live on the next spread. We'll stay at their place." He spoke somewhere above her ear, his voice muted over the steady rain.

Before she could reply, a low curse fell from the Gajo's lips. The sorrel halted.

Liza peered into the darkness. Planks of wood, sections of pipe, and loose paper were scattered all over the field. The mess seemed to worsen the closer they rode toward the homestead. Among the rubble, a lone dinner plate rested in the grass. The china seemed to be in perfect condition, without a single chip or crack, as if someone had carefully set it there in preparation for a meal.

The twister's peculiar vengeance both awed and frightened Liza. Mama always said storms were unleashed by angry spirits. What had anyone done to provoke such destruction?

Ahead, a cabin lay in near-shambles, its roof half-blown off, the front door gone, every window shattered. Broken pieces of furniture were everywhere.

"Oh, my saints." Liza stared in horror.

A child's shoe hung from a lone fence post. Nearby was a baby's blanket, the soft flannel soiled from mud. Next to that, pillows, towels, toys, a can of beans. The list went on and on.

A family's home. Destroyed.

And what of them?

Liza turned her head. She could easily touch the Gajo's cheek with the tip of her nose. She appealed to him, her heart filled with dread. "Are—Is this your friend's home?"

"Yes." He peered down at her, his breath warm over her forehead. "But they're not here. Went to Omaha to visit relatives."

"Thank God."

"Yes, thank God. But look what they'll come back to." He dismounted awkwardly and grimaced. "Stay here. I'm going to check the place out."

Liza shivered, whether from the cold rain or the depressing sight before her, she could not be sure. The farm had lost its outbuildings, the barn had suffered enough damage that Liza would not dare step inside. Whatever livestock Reese Carrison's friend might have owned had long since run off. Except for the rain, the land had an eerie silence.

The Gajo returned, his dark suit making him difficult to see from afar. "There's a lean-to out back. The horses can bed down there for the night."

She nodded and moved to get down.

He took hold of the chin straps. "Relax. Enjoy the ride," he said dryly and began guiding both horses through the debris. "Unless Gypsy women have an aversion to riding while a man walks?"

"Not any man," Liza retorted loftily. "Just one who is not Gypsy."

To her utter surprise, he chuckled, a low, warm sound that curled around her body like an eiderdown on a frosty night.

They took great care to make the stallion comfortable.

The Gajo found a lantern. Aided by its meager, golden light, he hauled off the saddles and set them aside to dry. Fearing a case of mud fever from the dampness, Liza thoroughly wiped down the animals' backs and legs with their saddle blankets. The lean-to offered enough room for both horses to lie down; its roof promised respite from the wind and rain; fresh hay and a bucket of oats further ensured their comfort.

The Gajo rubbed the stallion's nose. "Have a good night, fella. I'll check on you first thing in the morning."

His glance strayed yet again to the swollen hindleg; his voice betrayed his concern. Liza knew the walk from the river had not helped the sprain. The horse nickered softly, as if to reassure him, and slowly, the Gajo stood.

His attention wandered to the damaged cabin. "I'll see what kind of shape the house is in."

Giving her only a brief glance, he hobbled out from under the lean-to, taking the lantern and saddlebags with him, obviously expecting her to follow.

Yet Liza held back. Her pulse hammered from trepidation. Without the stallion to fill her thoughts, a new worry took over.

She would be spending the night with Reese Carrison.

Alone.

Just the two of them.

Her belly did a nervous flip-flop. She yearned for the security of the kumpania, her family and friends, cousins, aunts and uncles. It was all she had ever known—her kumpania. Her people. Her life.

How would she endure the hours until dawn without them? And with a Gajo, no less?

God's saints, she must.

She would survive the humiliation of it. The dismay and fears. She had no other choice.

She bravely swept aside her apprehensions, pulled the oilskin tighter, and stepped into the rain. Treading gingerly around the debris strewn over the yard, she made her way to the front of the cabin.

The Gajo stood inside what had been the main room and held the lantern high, his head tilted to the ceiling, as if to judge the soundness of the rafters. Shingles ripped from the roof revealed snippets of the black sky and allowed the rain to drip inward at a steady pace. Strips of tar paper fluttered in the breeze; the wooden floor was soaked.

Only the back third of the house had been spared. Save for a scattering of glass and splintered wood, the area seemed intact and reasonably dry.

"It's not the Grand River Hotel," he muttered. "But it'll do."

He paused, as if expecting her to complain. She ran a miserable glance over the ruins and thought of the cozy wagon her family would be staying in tonight, how warm they would be, and *together*. A wave of homesickness washed over her, and she fought a rise of tears.

"Can you cook?" he asked.

Blinking rapidly before she looked at him, she nodded in jerky motions. "Yes."

"Fix us something to eat, then. I'll start a fire in the stove and try to clear the worst of the mess. We need some room to move around."

She grasped at his request. It would keep her mind off her unhappiness and stave off the hunger she had not quenched since midday.

With the lantern in hand, she ventured to the sideboard and eyed the numerous drawers and doors. A shelf was filled with fruit preserves and home-canned goods miraculously untouched by the storm. She hesitated.

She was violating another woman's domain. To help themselves to the food lovingly put up by a Gaje wife who was not there to see them made her uncomfortable.

"Go on, Liza." Reese Carrison's voice reached to her from across the cabin.

Her gaze flew to him. She had not known he watched her nor could she identify the smoky huskiness in his tone. Did he sense the reason for her unease?

"I'll pay them well for what we use," he said.

Her lashes lowered. She turned away with a nod, reassured by his promise. Hardly aware of the trust she had put in his words, she set the lantern aside and went to work discovering the secrets held within the sideboard.

After lighting the stove, the Gajo hurled split logs and boards toward the damaged side of the cabin and swept broken glass, bits of mortar and dust into the growing pile of debris. Locating a length of rope, he strung it along the gaping side of the cabin.

Liza slid chopped tomatoes into a hot skillet and stirred them in with chunks of potatoes, onions, and canned beef, then seasoned it all liberally from the array of spice tins on the stove. The coffee perked and would be ready shortly. All too soon, she had nothing else to do.

"Help me hang these, will you?" The Gajo pulled a pile of quilts from a wooden chest nearly buried under a collapsed wall. "There are only three, but we'll use two of them to help shut out the cold and rain."

The idea was a clever one. After the quilts were hung, Liza was amazed at the difference they made in keeping the stove's warmth closer about them.

And yet it had its disadvantages, too. The quilts made their quarters seem even smaller. Intimate. Definitely more intimate.

She swallowed.

The Gajo hobbled toward the fireplace. Using some broken boards for kindling, he stoked a healthy fire. Its heat would supplement the warmth shed from the stove; its light added to the lantern's.

He turned toward her, one side of his mouth lifted in a wry smirk. He made a grand, sweeping gesture with his long arm. "This is as good as it gets, Lady Gypsy."

"Yes," she murmured and told herself their conditions could be worse.

He peeled his suitcoat from his shoulders and laid it over a mangled table, then yanked off the narrow black tie and began unbuttoning his shirt. "You'd best get out of your wet clothes, too. You'll catch your death."

She sucked in a breath. Take off her clothes?

He caught her reaction and stilled; his eyes narrowed. "You needn't worry about your virtue with me, sweetheart. I'm not in the mood."

She wavered at his dubious reassurance. He was married, was he not? Would that be reason enough to be safe with him?

No, her stubborn mind argued. Her own father had ignored Mama's marriage vows when he bedded her nineteen years ago. The Gaje could not be trusted, married or not.

Troubled, she returned to the stove and stirred the food in the skillet. Water had dripped from the hems of her skirts and puddled on the floor. Her toes were still numb from the soaking her thin leather shoes had received. Soggy tendrils of hair stuck to her scalp, the rain-heavy ends dripping onto the stovetop.

Deep down, she knew he was right. She could not stay in her sopping-wet clothes.

You needn't worry about your virtue with me, sweetheart.

She pivoted. "Do you give me your word?"

His brow quirked. "That I won't touch you?"

"Yes."

He scowled darkly. "I'm not a man who speaks lightly, Liza, nor am I in the habit of deflowering innocent virgins. I won't attack you." He gave her a wicked leer. "That is, unless you want me to."

The bastard. She pitied his wife.

"Very well, then." She turned from him again, giving him her back. Her eyes closed; she willed herself the strength to do such a thing. Then, resolutely, she opened the oilskin a little wider, unbuttoned her skirt and let it fall to the floor. Two more underskirts followed, leaving only her skimpy cotton chemise.

It took a little more doing to wriggle out of her blouse, but she managed, removing the strands of gold beads first. Keeping the oilskin draped over her shoulders, she squirmed the blouse off one sleeve at a time. The chemise was no easier, for the damp, oft-worn fabric clung to her skin, but she pulled it off by way of her head and laid it on the heap.

Her nipples puckered from her nakedness, and she shivered. For not the first time, she was grateful for Reese Carrison's generosity in lending her his coat. She hastily shrugged back into the long sleeves and buttoned the oilskin closed from top to bottom, acutely aware of the strange feeling of wearing it with nothing on beneath.

Lastly, by balancing on one foot, then the other, she removed her shoes.

Her toes curled into the wooden floor. She refused to turn around, to see if the Gajo had watched her undress.

Mama would be mortified. Liza endured a pang of shame, but she could think of no other way to dry her clothes. Surely taking them off would be faster, like the Gajo said!

Their meal was nearly ready. She hung the blouse and skirts over the quilts, keeping only her chemise from view. She discreetly laid the undergarment on the sideboard close to the stove and hoped it would dry soon. With nimble fingers, she wrapped the gold-and-crimson kerchief properly about her head and knotted it at her nape. At least she could keep her hair covered and maintain a shred of decency.

Squaring her shoulders, she turned to face Reese Carrison again.

He sat on the freshly swept floor, his hair combed, his shirt off and tossed to the side. He pulled one boot off, turned it upside down and grimly watched the rainwater trickle out.

His face bore such a pained expression that Liza, in spite of herself, nearly laughed aloud. Only the barest of twitches in the corner of her mouth revealed her amusement, and it was then that Reese Carrison happened to look her way.

"Think this is funny, do you?" he growled, and though his words seemed to bear a touch of temper, his tone did not. He wrung out both socks; the puddle of rainwater grew even larger.

"A little, maybe," she said.

"If it never rains again, I'll be happy."

"A drought grows more appealing by the minute," she concurred.

Across the tiny room, their eyes met again. And held. Liza realized he had been as uncomfortable as she, more so because of his wrenched knee, and she, at least, had had the protection from his oilskin coat.

In that moment, she shared with him—Reese Carrison, a man not of her world—a peculiar, inexplicable bonding that evolved from less-than-perfect circumstances. They were in this together, had survived, and it would get better.

Did they not have a snug roof—of sorts—over their heads? Did they not have a strong fire and plenty of food? Had not Reese Carrison provided her with all that?

Yes. He had. And even Mama could not deny she could show him a bit of courtesy by filling his belly with the hot meal she had prepared.

Liza's lashes lowered, breaking the pull of his gaze, and she hastened back to the sideboard, retrieving a large white tablecloth from one of its drawers.

She spread it on the floor next to him, then returned with a bowl filled with the steaming meat and vegetables.

"I could not find any plates," she said softly, walking behind him, then reaching around his broad back and setting the food in front of him. "I imagine the tornado took them. We will have to eat right out of the bowl." She left him, found two forks, and walked behind him again to give him those in the same manner. "Would you like a cup—"

When she would have stood to bring him coffee, his hand snaked out and grasped her wrist over the long oilskin sleeves, keeping her bent half-behind him.

"What are you doing, Liza?" His low voice sounded suspicious; his tigerlike eyes bore into her.

Her own widened. Had she displeased him in some way? "I am serving you, of course."

"Like this? From behind me?"

"Yes." Puzzled, she stared at him.

74

"Why?"

She shrugged. "It is the Gypsy way."

"This is how the women serve the men? From behind?"

"Yes."

The suspicion faded from his expression. "And they never serve from the front?"

"No." She shook her head. A tardy raindrop fell from a lock of her hair and landed between them. "Except their husbands. And always in private."

"I see." He released her. "Well, serve me from the front, okay?"

She blinked at him, unable to believe he would ask such a thing from her. "But why?"

"Because I prefer it."

"But—"

"We're not in public, are we?"

"You are not my husband!" What would Mama think? And Paprika and all the other women of her kumpania?

"It's just you and me, Liza. Who will know?"

She bit back further argument and helplessly surrendered to his logic, knowing this would be yet another secret she would be forced to keep from her people. She rose and poured two cups of coffee. Almost without thinking, she stepped toward his back, corrected herself, and squatted on her heels before him.

She set the coffee down and clasped her hands around her knees. He nodded his thanks, took a bite of the vegetables and chewed. Again, his gaze rested on her, and she glanced away, uncomfortable from the intensity of it. He took a second bite, swallowed, and set his fork down onto the tablecloth.

"And do the women not eat until after the men have had their fill?" he asked quietly.

"No."

His jaw cocked. She sensed he did not approve of the Gypsy custom. "I'm not kin to eating while a woman who is as hungry as me does without." He leaned slightly toward her. "Eat with me, Liza."

"But I cannot!"

"Because I'm not your husband?"

She pressed her lips together. He had already guessed the answer to his question.

He sighed and crossed his sinewy arms over his bare chest. "I won't have another bite until you do."

She clucked her tongue and rolled her eyes. The man was stubborn as a mule.

"The food will go to waste," he said, goading her.

Stubborn as an entire *herd* of mules.

God forgive her.

She picked up a fork. Slowly, guiltily, she dipped into the bowl and snared a piece of beef, bringing it into her mouth. His tiger-gold eyes never left her, and she realized the privilege he gave her, the privilege she did not deserve.

Wisps of steam curled from the pair of cups between them. Behind her, the fire in the grate warmed her back, crackling and spitting an ageless song, the only sound in the tiny room to compete with the rumbling thunder outside. She took a second bite, and apparently satisfied, his strong mouth bearing the remnants of a smile, Reese Carrison lifted his fork and did the same.

The lantern on the sideboard flickered and flared, then unexpectedly went out. A shadowy dimness filled their quarters, touched only by the fire in the hearth.

"Out of fuel," he grunted. "Damn."

But he did not seem sorry. Or worried. He shifted his long body to lay on his side and propped himself up on an elbow. His new position brought him closer to the bowl of food, to the fire.

And to her.

The soft glow of light danced off the dark hairs on his chest, accented the ridges of muscles padding his shoulder and arms, highlighted the one masculine nipple she could see.

The seasoned beef grew tasteless against her tongue.

Saints in heaven. How would she get through the night?

Chapter Five

She was naked beneath the oilskin.

Reese tried not to dwell on it, but even though she kept her calves and ankles covered, all he had to do was see her clothes hanging over the quilts to know she wore nothing but his coat.

Losing the lantern's light didn't help. It only increased the intimacy in the cabin, made him more aware of her— and her more aware of him.

Was that why she was as skittish as a wild rabbit? Because he made her nervous? Was she afraid of him? The thought filled him with reluctant regret.

He should resent her for all she'd put him through. After leading him on a chase that took him damn near into Dakota Territory, he'd almost lost his horse. His knee hurt so bad he walked like a cripple. He'd gotten soaked to the skin, and he was miles away from the comforts of his own home—that is, if he had a home left after the tornado.

Hell. He had every reason to resent her. But what was

the use? Their situation hadn't been entirely her fault. Who could've known a deadly storm would dip from the sky and wreak havoc on the land? Just his luck he happened to pick today to dedicate his railroad.

He sighed inwardly. He'd pricked her with his sharp temper more than once, unleashing his frustration on her when his control had been stretched to the limits. Why did she bring out the worst in him?

Feeling a need to make amends, he tried to put her at ease.

"Grub's good," he said and meant it.

She hesitated. "Grub?"

"Yes." He spoke around a mouthful of potato and gestured toward the near-empty bowl. "You know, food."

"Oh." The compliment seemed to fluster her. Her thick lashes, dusted with a coppery-red glint, floated downward. "Thank you."

He wondered at their color, finding it unusual they weren't the jet-black hues he associated with Gypsies. "Get tired of my own cooking sometimes. I don't bother with it much." Her lashes flew up again; she frowned. "I'd just as soon grab a bite in town than cook at home."

He reached for the steaming coffee. Was he rambling? Is that why she had that all-too-familiar look of contempt on her face?

He took a sip. The brew was strong, very strong. And sweet. He managed not to grimace and set the cup down again.

"You do not like the coffee," she murmured and drank from her own.

Her astuteness surprised him.

"It's not what I'm used to," he said carefully, not wanting to hurt her feelings.

"The Gaje prefer their coffee weak. Like their women."

She delivered the slur smoothly, drinking her coffee as if they spoke casually of the weather.

He regarded her. "What does that mean—Gaje?"

She met his gaze. "Those who are not Gypsy."

"And because we, the Gaje, like coffee different than this"—he nodded toward his cup—"we are weak?"

She shrugged.

Her logic amused him. "If that were true, what does it have to do with our women?"

Her chin lifted. "A woman who refuses to cook for her husband is weak and selfish. Or, perhaps"—she looked directly at him—"her husband is."

Reese fell silent. He understood now the reason for her disdain.

"Rebecca Ann is not my wife," he said finally.

"No?" Her eyes, black as crow's wings, widened in surprise. "But she was with you at the train."

"She came in from St. Louis for the N & D's dedication. Her father is an old friend."

"And the child?"

"Not mine, either."

"But you want them to be."

Again, her perception struck him. He swirled the coffee in his cup, watched tiny bubbles form on the edges. "Yes. I intended to ask Rebecca Ann to marry me today."

That seemed so long ago. Had it been only this afternoon that he'd waited for her in the lobby of the Grand River Hotel; had chased after Margaret Michelle, held her squirming, three-year-old body in his arms?

His mood grew pensive.

Rebecca Ann. He hadn't thought of her before now, hadn't worried for her safety during the tornado. How had she slipped from his mind so easily?

His conscience gave him no answers. Grimly, he lifted

the cup and sipped. This time, the hot brew slid down his throat a little easier.

"I am sorry, then," Liza said softly, her glance fixed on her cup. "I judged you—and her—wrong."

"Forget it." Reese reached for his saddlebags, flipped one open, and withdrew his tobacco and papers. He rolled a cigarette, lit it, and eased from his side onto his back, using the leather bags for a pillow. He inhaled deeply and crossed his ankles.

His position afforded him a more direct view of her. He exhaled, and through the hazy blue curls of smoke, he contemplated the picture she made.

A picture of contrasts. The striped kerchief kept her wet hair close about her head, outlining its shape and her high, genteel forehead. In the fire's glow, her exotic features were accented, every curve and hollow shaded in shadows. But his oilskin dwarfed her, hiding her arms and legs from view, making her seem somehow vulnerable.

And alone.

In need of protection.

He resisted the feeling, knowing this wasn't the first time she stirred it in him, and knowing, too, she had more strengths than he had yet to realize.

"Do you miss your family?" he asked.

The dark eyes welled with sudden tears; she blinked them away. "Yes."

Her reply was hardly more than a whisper but enough to tug at Reese's heart.

"I have never been away from them before," she admitted.

"Never?"

She shook her head, the gold hoops in her ears swaying with the movement.

"Your husband must be frantic." Reese's jaw tautened. If

81

she were his, he'd have an entire posse out looking for her, tornado be damned.

"Husband! Pah!"

She spoke so vehemently, he stared, amazed at the implication of her words.

"I can't believe you're not married," he said. "You're of age, a great cook, beautiful—"

"The right age? Cook? Beautiful? It does not matter, Gajo. Not to my people."

"Why not?"

She fell silent, her gaze straying to the fire. Reese held his breath, transfixed by this woman before him and all he knew—and didn't know—about her.

"We are very different, you and I. Our worlds are opposite," she said.

"Yes," he murmured and waited.

She bit her lip; then, her spine stiffened, her chin lifted. She seemed fused with a new strength, a raw pride, that allowed her to go on. "And at the same time, I belong to no world of my own."

"You speak in riddles, woman," he said softly.

Her eyes drifted over him, as if needing his trust to go on. She drew a breath, and Reese knew, whatever she was about to say, cost her dearly.

"I bring shame to my people because my mother is Gypsy, but my father was a Gajo. I do not know him, but his blood flows through my veins forever." Once more, her gaze returned to the fire. "His lust made me different. No Gypsy man wants me for his wife. I would only bring more shame to his family and to our children." She turned toward him. "Do you understand?"

He didn't understand at all. The cigarette, virtually untouched, had burned down to a stub. She took it from him and threw it into the flames.

"You really despise us, don't you?" he asked. "The Gaje, I mean."

"Do you not despise the Gypsy as much?"

He sat up, rested an elbow over his drawn-up knee and tried to explain. "There's been trouble with Gypsies in the past."

"And trouble with the Gaje for us as well."

"We're not as awful as you think, Liza."

"Nor are we."

He remembered his experiences over the years with Gypsies, the thievery, the drunkenness and lies. His contempt for them had been no less than anyone else's. Had they all been too harsh? Had they been carried away by the aura, the legend, surrounding Gypsies?

"Tell me the truth." Dead serious, he appealed to her. She met him with a level glance. "Did you try to kidnap Margaret Michelle?"

She snorted loudly. "You would not believe me if I told you."

"Try me."

Her eyes flashed. "Why would a Gypsy want to steal a Gaje child when we have so many of our own? Especially that one?" She sniffed haughtily. "She is a handful."

A slow grin spread across Reese's mouth. "That she is."

It was as if a mountain had been moved between them, clearing the path for what could be, perhaps, a budding friendship. Reese reached out and fingered a soggy curl beneath the kerchief.

"Your hair is still wet, Liza. Take off the kerchief and let the fire's heat dry it."

"Oh, but I cannot! It is not decent."

"Is it decent that you wear no clothes beneath my coat?" Even in the shadows, he could see the blush that sprang

83

to her cheeks. "We've been through one hell of a storm. You'll get a chill if you don't dry your hair."

She made a sound in her throat, as if she warred with his practicality. Reese guessed wearing kerchiefs was another of the Gypsies' stringent customs. In this case, he could see no wisdom in it.

"You're not so different from me," he rationed. "Have you forgotten you're half-Gaje? And Gaje women often wear their hair free at night."

Behind her, the fire spit and crackled. She sat unmoving, saying nothing. Boldly, he bent toward her and plucked the kerchief from her head. She gasped and reached for it, but he dangled it away.

"Let your hair dry, Liza," he said, his tone quiet but determined. "Use my comb if you want."

She made no attempt to take the comb from his outstretched hand. Her nostrils flared. "Are you afraid I have lice?"

"Hardly."

"The Gajo woman was. The one you call Rebecca Ann."

"Ah, yes. Rebecca Ann," he said dryly. "Prone to hysterics, don't you think?"

"Definitely."

She sat so stiffly, she could have been made of wood. Reese wondered what it would take to whittle her down to softness.

"I bathe every day," she said. He sensed she needed to erase whatever apprehensions he might have about her. "I wash my hair, clean my teeth, and launder my clothes as often as I can when we are not traveling."

He listened and tried not to smile.

"I do not have lice," she said firmly.

He couldn't resist curling a hand around her damp neck and pulling her a little closer. She eyed him warily.

"I reckon there are a few Gaje who've had their share of lice over the years, just like the Gypsies. And your people aren't the only ones who've been known to lie and steal. My people do, too. Hell, this country has built an entire judicial system with judges and jails just to deal with them." He paused, letting his words sink in. "Okay?"

She nodded slowly. "Okay."

His thumb stroked her slender nape. "And I reckon, too, that Rebecca Ann hurt you with the things she said and the way she acted with the child and all. On her behalf, I apologize."

"You do not have to apologize for her," she said, a little breathlessly.

"Yes, I do." He released her and tossed the comb into her lap. "Now dry your hair."

For a long moment, she made no effort to obey. Then, as if her trepidation left her bit by bit, she shifted from her haunches and sat cross-legged beside him.

She ran her fingers through the long tresses, lifting their length from her scalp and fluffing them toward the heat. In the firelight, the strands glinted with red, copper, and gold. As the comb dipped in and out, stroke after stroke, they shone like spun silk and tumbled over her shoulders, framing her head like a halo from heaven.

Reese leaned back against the saddlebags and lit another cigarette. His loins warmed at the mere sight of her, a warming that had nothing to do with the flames in the hearth.

Christ. She was beautiful. How could her people reject her for something her mother had done? How could they think her less than perfect? Why would any Gypsy man not want her for his wife?

Fools. Every one of them.

* * *

The Gajo shook out the last remaining quilt and spread it carefully over the tablecloth. A crude preparation, but one that would serve them well enough during the night.

Their bed.

Liza ran a panicky glance over the cabin's shambles, knowing their scant quarters left her little room to lay anywhere but beside him. Dry floor space was limited. Outside the quilt partition, rain pattered through the blown-away roof and soaked the wooden floor. The fireplace provided the much-needed heat the stove failed to give.

She stifled a groan of dismay. The intimacy of sleeping with Reese Carrison threatened to overwhelm her. Never had she dreamed she would share the night with a Gajo, a man who was not her husband, nor ever would be.

How her honor had been tested this night! If Mama were to see her with him in these primitive conditions, her clothes hanging over the quilts, her hair unbound and curling over her shoulders and back, she would be appalled.

And now this.

Sleeping beside Reese Carrison under a quilt barely large enough to cover one body, let alone two, would tear away the last shred of her dignity. How could she face her people? How could she face Mama?

Mortification churned in her stomach.

The Gajo eased down onto the tablecloth and rubbed his swollen knee. "I'll give you one of the saddlebags and the side closest to the fire," he said. "The floor'll be hard as stone, but there's nothing else to lie on."

"I cannot do this," she blurted in a hoarse whisper, her arms folding tautly beneath her breasts. "I cannot."

"What? Sleep with me?" His brow raised, as if the notion had never occurred to him.

Humiliated beyond endurance, her glance fell. "Yes."

"Reckon that's never been a problem until now." Amusement laced his tone. "Most women are willing."

"I do not think that is funny."

Her terse words chased away his mirth. He sighed heavily and studied the burning tip of his cigarette. After taking a final drag, he flicked the stub into the flames and exhaled slowly, deliberately. "The way I see it, you've got two choices, Liza. You can curl up next to a blazing fire with me right beside you. Or you can leave." His gaze, cold and steely, found hers. "But if you're planning on helping yourself to that sorrel out back, you'll damn well regret it. I'll come after you, hard and fast, if I have to use a lame horse to do it."

Her chin lifted. His grim warning left no question he would see it through.

"The rest is up to you. Do what you want." He lifted the quilt and scooted beneath it, pulling the hemmed edges over his broad shoulders. He tucked the saddlebag beneath his head and rolled to his side, his back facing her. "Good night."

She stared at him long after his breathing settled into a deep, even rhythm. He seemed not to give her a second thought. What did he care if she stayed or left? Did it not matter to him that her family had been lost to her this night, that they could be anywhere on the storm-torn Nebraska prairie?

Or that she had no idea where?

The flames hissed and spit in the block, as if to remind her the hour had grown late, that she must sleep, too. She wearily speared a hand through her hair, and, rising, pulling the oilskin closer against the cold, she stepped past the quilt partition and peered outside.

An endless sky shown brazenly where the roof had once been. Thick clouds hid the moon and stars, painting the night as black as pitch tar. Rain fell, as if from a mammoth watering can, and pockmarked the land with countless puddles.

Liza knew she could not leave. Not yet. The drenching she had received earlier still lingered vivid in her mind. She had no desire to go through it all again. But, surely, in a few hours time, the clouds would thin and break up. After a little sleep, she would check the sky again.

When the storm ran its course, she would bid good riddance to Reese Carrison, flee the cabin and somehow find her way back to the kumpania.

The vow strengthened her, gave her something to cling to. She slipped behind the quilts once more, to the relative security of the tiny shelter, and shivered. The damp night air had chilled her bare feet, and the wooden floor offered little warmth. Tiptoeing gingerly toward the sideboard, she retrieved her dry chemise and wriggled back into it, glad to have the undergarment next to her skin again.

With the oilskin draped around her shoulders, she returned to the fire. The Gajo had shifted his position; he lay half on the tablecloth, half off, as if to keep as much space between them as possible. Most of the quilt had slid from his long body, gathering in a heap on her side of the makeshift bed.

In the soft, golden firelight, she studied him. A fine sampling of masculinity, this Reese Carrison. A man of his word. A man with honor. For a Gajo, he seemed a man she could trust. She could have done worse by him. Much worse.

He would not touch her tonight. That she could be sure. If he intended to ravage her, would he not have done so long before now? Instead, he had simply rolled over and gone to sleep.

And he had promised.

Her mouth softened. Perhaps she had worried for nothing. In repose, he appeared incapable of all the distasteful things Mama claimed the Gaje were wont to do. Liza sensed this one would be vastly different.

Her hands lifted to the oilskin and pulled it from her shoulders. Carefully, lest she wake him, she laid the coat over his lean length, giving him the warmth that the quilt had denied.

He did not stir. Relieved, she hastened to her side of the tablecloth and slipped beneath the blanket. She laid down, shifting her position so that she faced the fire.

The flames writhed and snapped in the block. Like melted butter, the brilliant red-orange hues drizzled heat over her body, inviting sleep. But it would not come.

The blaze held her pensive gaze, throwing her back to a time not so long ago when she had hunkered before the fires of the kumpania surrounded by her family, a passel of yapping dogs, and Rollo, her brother Hanzi's scruffy but charmingly talented dancing bear.

But there would be no fires tonight. Not in the rain. Instead, her people would huddle inside the high-wheeled wagons, all of them warm from their stoked stoves and thick eiderdowns.

Loneliness welled within Liza's breast, and she pressed a fist to her mouth to stifle a sudden sob of despair. She could not let Reese Carrison know of her homesickness. How could he understand when he had no family of his own?

She closed her eyes tight and prayed to God her people were all safe, that they had survived the tornado, and they would not worry about her too much.

For she would be back with them again. Soon.

"Mama? Are you awake?" Paprika's whisper skittered through the wagon's darkness, silent but for the endless pelting rain outside.

"Yes, daughter." A quavery sigh followed the hushed reply. Paprika doubted her mother would sleep a minute the entire night.

"Oh, Mama," she said in sympathy and turned on the cot, searching for her mother's prone form next to Nanosh. "Liza is very smart. She will not let herself get into any trouble with the Gaje."

"But how can she not be in trouble with them? She would be here with us if she were not."

"I know, I know," Paprika soothed, hoping not to wake Putzi beside her. "Something has happened. I do not know what, but she will come. She promised me."

"We should not have left without her. What if they keep her in their filthy jails? Or what if she lost her way trying to find us? The storm . . ." Her voice, heavy with despair, trailed off.

"The tornado was a terrible thing," Paprika murmured, shuddering from the memory. "We were lucky to miss it."

When she and Putzi had returned to the camp with the frightening news the Gaje were in pursuit and that Liza had urged them to flee, Nanosh, fearful of arrest, had pulled up stakes in great haste and led the kumpania away from Niobrara City. Then the skies had opened, unleashing their own fury on the land, forbidding Mama to leave behind the vurma Liza needed. The wagons had fled as far as they could, until they could go no longer.

"Lucky?" Mama wailed, heedless of her sleeping family. "What of Liza? How can she have luck when the *mulo,* the evil spirits, are angry and punish us all with a tornado!"

As if her grief had become too much to bear, her cries grew louder. Nanosh awakened, grunted with thin patience, and rubbed a hand over his swarthy face. "Wife, what is this squalling? Go back to sleep!"

"You leave Liza behind because she is not from your

seed!" Mama twisted on her cot and thumped his chest with her fist. Paprika had never seen her so distraught. "But she is mine, Nanosh. And we cannot leave Nebraska without her."

Reluctant to witness this private exchange between her parents, Paprika held her breath. Until now, she'd only sensed that Liza, Mama's bastard daughter, had always been an unspoken rift between them.

"Mama speaks the truth." From his own cot near Paprika's, Hanzi's deep voice pierced Mama's tirade. "We will go back for her."

"The wagon wheels are sunk in the mud to their hubs," Nanosh said. "We cannot go anywhere until the ground dries enough that we can travel again."

"Then I will go by foot."

Paprika's heart surged with pride for her older brother. At seventeen, he was two years younger than Liza, but had the wisdom and bravery of a man. If anyone could find Liza, Hanzi could.

"I will go with you," she said.

"You will stay here. You are only a girl."

Only seconds ago filled with love for him, Paprika sputtered in sisterly outrage. Nanosh hushed their argument with a curt word of command.

"It is settled, then," he said. "Hanzi will return for Liza as soon as he can. We will follow when we are able." He glanced down at Mama. "Is that better, wife?"

"Yes." She sniffed loudly and scrubbed at the tears on her cheeks. "Thank you, Nanosh."

"Did you really think I would not go after her?" he chided and scooped her up against his chest. His smile, not often given, showed the glint of his gold tooth. She snuggled against him with familiarity.

"You left so quickly. Without thought to Liza."

He shrugged. "I was afraid."

"But not afraid for her?" Mama demanded.

A long moment passed. "She is not of my blood like Paprika or Tekla, it is true. But I did think of her. How could I not? I would have returned for her. When the weather cleared."

"Only then?"

He made a sound of impatience. "Enough of your nagging, wife. Hanzi will return to Niobrara City. Until then, we will not speak of this again."

Mama held her tongue and seemed satisfied. Thoughtful, Paprika burrowed deeper into the eiderdown and cuddled Putzi closer.

Her little brother normally slept beside Liza who spoiled him with hugs and kisses until he fell asleep. He'd been devastated when she didn't return and had cried himself into an exhausted sleep.

Paprika kissed the top of his head. Mama and Putzi weren't the only ones who missed Liza with a fierceness deep in their hearts. She did, too.

Her mind turned to Reese Carrison, the handsome Gajo who'd showed great pride in the train at Niobrara City. He'd led the angry Gaje in their chase after Liza, and Paprika sensed he wouldn't be a man Liza could elude easily. Paprika guessed, of all the Gaje, he'd be the one shrewd enough to catch her.

Had Liza fared well with him? Or made her escape? Had she found protection against the storm? Against the Gaje?

Paprika had no answers to the questions spinning inside her head. But she had a feeling, a Gypsy premonition, that wherever Liza was, Reese Carrison was with her.

Chapter Six

A delicious warmth shimmered through the depths of Liza's slumber, and she lingered in the lazy netherworld, reluctant to step over the threshold into full wakefulness. A heaviness draped over her waist, and she knew, without looking, that Putzi had crawled into her bed again, as he often did, and laid sprawled beside her, a jumble of little boy arms and legs.

She would not disturb him. Instead, she burrowed deeper into the warmth, closer to the heaviness against her, and waited for sleep to return.

Rain pattered on the wagon's roof. A damp chill had seeped inside, cooling Liza's nose and cheeks. Nanosh must have let the fire in the stove die out, she mused, finding herself more awake than she wanted to be. Perhaps she should rise and stoke it to save him the trouble. After all, the weather would keep the kumpania sleeping in their wagons much later than usual.

Her ear sought his noisy snores. She heard nothing

through the sprinkling raindrops, nothing but the slow, steady breathing of someone close beside her.

Her eyes flew open. And she remembered.

Her gaze fastened on the rough-hewn planks of the cabin, the fireplace, the wall of quilts. Reality hit hard, sweeping aside thoughts of a past life and pulling her down to one in the present.

She laid very still beside Reese Carrison. Sometime during the night, he had spread the oilskin over them both, sharing the coat's warmth and that of his own body with her. She had slept with the bliss of a newborn babe, and her intent to check the storm's progress had faded with the night.

Now, it was long past dawn. And here she laid, nestled like a wife against her husband, no closer to returning to her family than she had been before.

Oddly, the wave of shame she expected did not come. She had survived sleeping with Reese Carrison. Nothing had changed between them. Nothing had changed *her*. Perhaps it had not been as bad as she thought.

She ventured a peek downward. His long arm rested over her waist and reached past the edge of the oilskin, his fingers curled in a relaxed fist. Thick veins corded his muscular forearm; dark hairs coiled against sun-bronzed skin. The weight of his arm over her was not . . . unpleasing.

Something inside her melted. She dragged her gaze away and attempted to extricate her bare foot, which had mysteriously found its way tucked against his shin.

He stirred. His arm drew back slowly and then halted, fingers splaying over her belly.

"Still raining?" His voice, husky with sleep, was muffled against the top of her head.

"Yes. Can you not hear it?" The words sounded rushed.

She had a sudden urge to comb her hair and wash, to prepare herself for him. She inched away.

"Don't get up," he mumbled, his hand tightening to keep her near. He had yet to open his eyes. "Too cold."

"I must." Like a mouse freed from the trap, she pushed his hand away and skittered from beneath the quilt. Gooseflesh seized her skin, for her thin chemise offered scant covering and even less warmth. She hastened to the woodpile and threw kindling in the block. Soon, the fireplace crackled with flames.

She dressed hurriedly. Fastening the last of her skirts, she remembered the Gaje dollars she had earned selling baskets. Her hand dipped into a pocket and found the wad of bills safe inside. If needed, the money would be invaluable for her return to the kumpania.

Her spirits lightened. The rain would be ending soon; she was a day closer to being back with her family. After breaking her fast, she would check the clouds and hope the sun had broken through so that she could leave.

She combed and braided her hair, splashed her face with cold water, and, with coarse grains of cooking salt, rubbed her teeth clean. The routine complete, she hummed an old Gypsy tune and set about preparing a simple breakfast of biscuits and coffee.

"Are you always so damned cheerful in the mornings?"

Liza stopped stirring the dough and glanced over her shoulder. Reese scowled and flung aside the quilt and oilskin. He sat up slowly.

"Usually." She smiled at his frown. "Are you always so grouchy?"

"Only when I sleep on a floor that's hard as rock." He worked the muscles in his back and arms with a grimace.

"You are used to your own bed with its fluffy mattress and pillow."

95

"I am." He finger-combed his hair and regarded her. "Aren't you?"

She shrugged and resumed stirring. "Sometimes I use a cot. Sometimes I do not. It depends."

"On what?"

"On whether I choose to sleep inside our wagon or outside under the stars. The floor is no different than sleeping on the ground. I did not find it uncomfortable."

He grunted. "You bested me on that count, then."

"The Gaje lead pampered lives." She dropped spoonfuls of dough onto a pan and slid it into the hot oven. "The Gypsy does not need fancy things like a big house or a soft bed to be happy."

"I've spent my share of nights in a bedroll next to a campfire. It's just been a while, that's all."

He looked so defensive Liza almost regretted pointing out their differences. The corners of her mouth twitched. "Would you like a cup of coffee? Perhaps it will take away your stiffness."

"Yes. Thanks."

He made no attempt to get up. She handed him a cup of the black brew, and, for the first time, noticed his fingers massaging his knee, swollen double its normal size.

Compassion stirred within her, and she clucked her tongue in sympathy. No wonder he looked as cross as an old rooster.

"Why did you not tell me you were in pain?" she scolded, gently prodding the swelling with her fingertips.

"What? And have you tell me that Gypsies never complain? Or get hurt? Or—"

"Oh, hush!" Exasperation threaded the words, though his taunt bore the truth. "I do not wish to listen to your whining. Sit still while I see what I can do for you."

Memories of her flight from Niobrara City and the ensuing scuffle at the riverbank when he tried to pull her from his horse reminded her she had been the cause of his wrenched knee. Guilt hurried her movements, and she dipped a length of toweling into a cast-iron pot boiling with rainwater. Thank goodness she had prepared the water for washing their dishes. The heat would be good medicine.

Using a wooden spoon, she carried the dripping towel from the pot over to him. Without fanfare, she dropped it on his knee.

He yelped and nearly spilled the coffee. "Good God, woman! You'll scald me to death!"

"I will not. It is what you need. The towel will cool soon enough, and we will see what a difference I have made." She swathed his knee with the steaming fabric and, nodding in satisfaction, sat back on her heels. "There. Is that better?"

"How do I know? The knee is damn near numb by now." His features pulled into a masculine pout. "I'll probably never walk again."

"Oh, Gajo." She laughed, shaking her head. "You are such a baby. You will walk again, I promise you."

"Go ahead," he growled. "Laugh all you want, but I'd warrant you'd sing a different tune if you were in my place."

"I doubt it. Men can be weaklings at times. In many ways, we women are by far the stronger sex."

"Think so?"

She thought she detected the kindling of a rare twinkle in his eyes. "I know so. Try birthing a baby sometime. Then you will agree with me."

He chuckled outright, all signs of his frown gone, and Liza relished the sound. His amusement spoke of an ease between them, one she never thought she would share with a Gajo, and one that stirred within her an unexpected pleasure.

"Guess I'll never get the chance," he said finally. "I'll leave birthing to you women."

"It is best that you did, Gajo. We are far better at it," she said pertly.

A grin lingered on his lips, but he made no further reply. His tiger-gold eyes drifted over her with an intensity that seemed to bore right through her, leaving her feeling naked beneath his perusal.

She fidgeted and groped for something to say, something to do. She spied his tobacco and papers near the hearth, out of his reach.

"The biscuits are nearly done. By the time you finish a smoke, they should be ready to eat," she said. Without a second's thought, she snatched the tobacco and papers up, expertly rolled a cigarette and tucked it between her lips. Reaching for his metal matchbox, she withdrew a wooden match, struck a flame, and lit the tobacco.

"Where did you learn to do that?" he asked, one brow raised.

She exhaled and handed him the cigarette, the unlit end first. "I do not remember. It was a very long time ago."

"You've been smoking since then?"

She shook her head and wrapped her arms around her knees. "I have never learned a taste for the tobacco, though many women enjoy it. The Gypsy often starts smoking at a very young age. As children."

"You're kidding."

"You do not approve?"

"Can't say as I do."

"Another difference between us, Gajo."

A long moment passed between them. He nodded pensively. "Yes. Another difference."

She wondered what he was thinking, of *whom* he was thinking. Suddenly restless, Liza rose and stepped to the stove. Using a wadded rag, she pulled the hot pan from the oven and set it on top of the stove to cool. She stared at the golden biscuits without really seeing them.

"I suppose your Rebecca Ann does not smoke," she said, her back unusually straight.

He snorted with amused disdain. "God forbid. She would die first."

"I see."

"Ladies don't smoke or swear or drink in my society. It's not proper."

"I see," she said again. She bit the inside of her lip and hated the twinge of hurt his words gave her. How shamed he must feel to be here with her, a Gypsy woman who condoned all the things the women in his world did not.

Women like his betrothed, Rebecca Ann.

"Liza, look at me."

"I cannot. I am busy." She briskly plucked the hot biscuits from the pan into a bowl.

His heavy sigh sounded behind her. "I don't think any less of you or your people for the things you do, smoking or otherwise. You have your customs. We have ours. Okay?"

She lifted her chin and turned, the bowl in her hand. "Of course."

His eyes, sharp and piercing, never left her face. Liza's lids lowered. She could not meet his gaze, could not let him see how torn she felt, straddling her world and his.

She set the biscuits before him, opened a jar of peach preserves, refilled his coffee cup, then hers. He made no move to eat. She busied herself dividing the bread between them.

"Liza."

She ignored him and gathered her share into her skirt, vowing to sit closer to the fire, away from him, away from his shrewd, penetrating gaze. But his long arm reached out and grasped the gold beads around her neck. He gently tugged, bringing her closer, persistently closer. Fearful the strands would break, Liza did not resist and eyed him warily.

"I'm starting to like all this, you know."

His change of topic flustered her. His voice, sultry, seductive, hardly more than a whisper, wrapped around her like the finest goose down. Her heart pattered a little faster within her breast.

"Like what?"

"This. Being taken care of by a woman. By you."

Her pulse hammered a steady beat; she was certain he could hear the blood pounding through her veins.

"It is best that you do not, Reese Carrison," she said, her tone quavery. "I will not be with you much longer."

Something flickered over his features, something she could not define. His nearness disconcerted her, left her feeling out of sorts. Did all Gajo men have that power?

"You're different from other women I've known," he murmured. "Stronger. You roll with the punches and come out standing on both feet."

The scent of him, dusted with tobacco, surrounded her. Morning stubble darkened his cheeks, giving him a primitive air, a wildness that incited shards of awareness within her. His chest, bare to the waist, rippled and bulged with muscle, and invited her palms to explore the manly contours.

"Roll with the punches?" She could hardly think straight. Her fingers tightened into a fist. She must not touch him, must not give in to the weakness that these strange longings brewed deep inside her belly. She eased away, but he only tightened his grip on the beads.

The firm line of his lower lip softened. "Let's just say

Rebecca Ann would never have lasted through what we went through. Not the way you did." His voice deepened, stroked her with its smoky timber. "You're quite a woman, Lady Gypsy. Y'know that?"

Her gaze dropped to his mouth. A man's mouth. Meant to pleasure a woman. Liza held her breath, knowing that if he wanted, he could easily, so very easily, rest that mouth against hers, and she would let him.

Slowly, he loosened his grasp on the gold beads. Her lashes lowered, hiding the yearnings that surely showed in her eyes. She would not think of the feel of his arms around her, of the strength he possessed, or his warmth and tenderness. She would not think of laying beside him, of feeling the weight of his body against hers. She would not think of Reese Carrison in that way.

He was a Gajo.

And he belonged to another.

The stallion nuzzled Liza, his black nose poking her braid beneath the striped kerchief. She laughed, crooning in some Gypsy lingo Reese didn't understand, and lifted her arms to circle the horse's sleek neck.

Reese marveled at the sight. She'd bewitched the animal. She'd bewitched him. All with a few soft words and gentle touches and a wealth of loving care.

He could hardly tear his gaze from her. Her vitality shone amid the gray clouds and puddles of mud; her spirit, unfettered from convention, flew free. She had a quiet, unassuming allure that touched him in places he'd never been touched before.

Deep inside. In his heart. In his soul. She forced him to realize, for not the first time, she was like no other woman he'd ever met, a difference that went far beyond gold hoop earrings, ebony eyes, and hair like gleaming copper.

And she wielded that same power over his horse. Normally high-strung and skittish, the stallion allowed few near him, but like an eager puppy, he'd scampered to his feet to greet her this morning and had endured her inspection of his lame leg with amazing patience. She'd rewarded him with a treat of succulent corn husks, and Reese knew his prized mount had been lost to him for good.

Behind the cabin, the lean-to protected them from the heavy mist coating the dreary day. Bullfrogs croaked in the distance, their calls blending with the caw-caw cries of crows flying overhead. Reese tossed Bram's sorrel the last of the oats in his bucket, and leaning heavily on his crutch, limped over and patted the stallion's neck.

"His leg is better today," Liza said and pulled the last husk from the oilskin's deep pockets.

Reese's glance fell to the right hock. The swelling had gone down; the sprain was healing. Obviously, last night's dip in the cold Niobrara had paid off. He nodded his approval. "You're as good as any vet. Maybe better."

Her kerchief-clad head cocked to one side. "Vet? I do not know that word."

"Veterinarian." He gestured vaguely and tried to think of a way to make her understand. "Animal doctor."

A tentative smile scooted across her lips. "Ah. That pleases me, then. The Gaje put great trust in their doctors."

"We do." The stallion gobbled the husk and rooted against her pocket for another. "How do you know so much about horses?"

"From Nanosh. Since I have been old enough to ride, he has taught me their ways. Gypsies are not so different from the horse, you know. Like the wild mustangs, we love the freedom of roaming the land, of feeling the sun against our backs, the wind in our faces."

"Who is Nanosh?" Her past intrigued him. Reese wanted

to know everything about her, her family, friends, the life she led in that elusive world so opposite from his.

"My mother's husband." A veil of sadness drifted over her features and pulled at Reese's heart. "He has given me little since I have been born, but at least he has shared with me his gift with horses."

"He's taught you well," Reese said softly, knowing instinctively that this man whose love Liza craved had been the one to hurt her the most. Not wanting to see her pain, he steered his questions onto a different course. "Do you have brothers? Sisters?"

Her expression softened. "Two of each. Paprika and Putzi, who were with me at the train depot, and Tekla and Hanzi."

He tested the strange names on his tongue. "What are their ages? Are you the oldest?"

She laughed and reached toward him, touching her fingers to his lips to silence his curiosity.

"So many questions, Gajo. There is time for answers later, but now, I must see to your horse."

The movement was a simple one, that of laying her fingers against his mouth, yet it urged within Reese a need for more. Much more. Without thinking, he curled his hand around her wrist, keeping her near. Her words from earlier that morning—the statement that she'd be leaving soon—returned to haunt him.

"Will there be a 'later,' Liza?" he murmured.

Her gaze wavered against his. She pulled from his grasp and ran a troubled eye over the rainy horizon. "I cannot leave yet. Not in this weather." Her chin lifted; she faced him again, her stance defiant. "But soon I will."

In spite of the stubbornness in her tone, he realized the words bought him more time with her. And he relished the thought.

As if jealous for attention, the stallion nudged her. She crooned softly and rubbed his velvety nose.

"Do you have a name for him?" she asked.

Reese shook his head. "Most days, fella works just fine."

"I shall call him Zor, then."

"Zor?"

"It means 'strength.'" She smiled. "Because he will be strong again very soon." Her admiring glance drifted over the black, gleaming flanks. "He is such a fine horse. Nanosh would pay you well for him."

Reese grunted. "He's not for sale."

She smiled. "I thought not."

He remembered his attempt to spare the horse pain and misery, and Liza throwing herself between them. She'd saved the stallion's life, and for that Reese owed her.

Now, he longed to get the horse back into prime condition, to see him as swift-footed and graceful as before. Reese could hardly wait to mount him, to ride him hard and fast, to feel the power in the muscular limbs. Under Liza's care, it wouldn't be long.

He stepped closer to examine the sprain and gauge the heat that concerned her so. The horse snorted and shied.

"Whoa, boy," Reese murmured and stroked the broad back. He bent, running a hand along the hock. The stallion twisted toward him, his lips parted and giant teeth bared.

Reese narrowly missed the bite and swore. Liza gasped and tugged at the bridle.

"Did he hurt you?" she asked, dark eyes wide with concern.

Reese straightened and glared at the horse. "I'm fine. But he nearly took a piece of my hide." He tossed her a petulant glance. "Something he's never tried with you, I'd warrant."

"He is *te'sorthene,* my friend, bonded by heart and spirit." An impish light danced across her face. "Besides, he knows you tried to shoot him last night. No wonder he wants to bite you today."

"Well, hell," Reese said, defensive and frowning.

"Watch your language, Gajo," she said, not looking the least bit offended. "Is it not improper in your world to swear in front of a lady?"

"It is." He inclined his head. His defenses fell away, and he hid his smile. "I apologize, Miss Liza, for you are, in fact, a true lady."

His off-hand compliment seemed to fluster her. A faint blush crept across her cheeks; her lashes lowered, and he knew his words pleased her.

With a swift flare of skirt hems, she pivoted. One hand on the stallion's bridle, she stepped out from under the lean-to into the misty rain.

"What're you doing, Liza?" Reese hobbled after her, stopping just beneath the end of the slanted roof. He had no desire to get a good soaking all over again or to dodge the muddy puddles and storm-tossed debris scattered everywhere.

"Zor must have more cold water for his leg," she called back.

The soggy ground failed to deter her. Barefoot, she picked her way toward an overflowing horse trough. Reese leaned against the structure's edge, hitched his shirt collar closer to ward off the damp chill, and watched her.

She was amazing. How she managed to coax the strong-willed horse to stand placidly while his hind leg soaked in the trough, he'd never know.

Unbidden, thoughts of Rebecca Ann seeped into his mind, distracting him from the sight before him. Though he tried, he failed to form a vivid image of her, as if they'd been a lifetime apart, as if he'd almost forgotten her.

Maybe he had, a little. Too soon, he'd return to Niobrara

City and ask for her hand in marriage. Too soon, Liza would return to her people, and he'd never see her again. Their lives would go on as planned.

He squinted an eye toward the sky and found no break in the clouds. Until the sun broke through, Liza would stay. As long as it rained, he would, too.

He found himself wishing it would rain a very long time.

Darkness had long since fallen. Pensive, Liza squatted on her heels near the fire and listened to the steady rain outside. Reese had allowed her a few moments of privacy, then had stepped outside for some time of his own. Though she had been bitterly disappointed at being forced to spend the day away from her family, the hours with him had not been unpleasant.

Best of all, he had called her a lady.

She basked in the memory. It had long been a secret dream of hers. To be liked and admired and respected. To shed the scorn the Gaje showed whenever they looked at Gypsies. To be above their contempt.

A lady.

If only it were true. She could enter any room, walk down any street, mingle with the Gaje and be above their ridicule.

Would it ever be possible?

Liza closed her eyes and let the dream take flight. She would wear dresses that cost more Gaje dollars than she had ever seen in her lifetime. She would smell of the finest perfume, one that came in a tiny crystal bottle from a far-away place called France. Fine jewels would grace her ears and fingers and neck, jewels that glittered and shined, nothing like the cheap tin—

Shame burned her cheeks. What was she thinking?

Where was her pride? How could she let herself be so weak, pretending to be one of *them*?

There was great honor in being Gypsy. She must never forget that. Honor in being free, of needing nothing more than what nature offered. She had gifts, strengths, that went far beyond other Gaje women.

Had Reese not told her so?

She stared into the brilliant orange and yellow flames. What did it matter that her clothes were mismatched and often torn? Or that she wore necklaces made of old coins and worthless beads? Or that her hair glinted with shots of copper and gold instead of the blue-black hues of her people?

She was Gypsy. Why was that not enough?

A wave of despair crashed through her, for she knew the truth. She would never be the lady in her dreams. She would never be like the perfect Rebecca Ann, all soft and fragile and beautiful. She would never have the respect she longed for, not from her own kind and certainly not from the Gaje.

Because of Mama's sin.

Her lip curled. She cursed her Gajo father and his lust. She cursed the Gajo blood swimming in her veins.

And she cursed Reese Carrison for making her want to be part of his world.

Chapter Seven

Liza hardly noticed when he returned. Her troubled thoughts held her in their grip; she struggled with their power to draw her back into the dream she had long harbored even as a child. The allure of what could never be was far more difficult to shed than she ever imagined, and for that she blamed *him,* the Gajo with whom she shared this storm-ravaged cabin, the man who ignited forbidden feelings within her like a match to dry tinder.

She thought of Mama instead. Her scorn and mistrust were easy to recall. In her mind, Liza heard the stories her mother often told with bitter relish. Liza nurtured the familiar hate, clung to the loathing, relived the disgust every Gypsy felt for the dishonorable Gaje.

And soon, like unwanted dirt under a rug, she was able to thrust aside the dream, a dream that was silly and foolish and totally impossible to achieve. She allowed the old cloak of revulsion to wrap around her, and she held herself tight within its folds.

"That's a mighty fiercesome frown you're wearing," Reese said, his low voice vaguely bemused.

Liza finally turned from the fire. He was sprawled behind her, his hurting leg stretched out before him, his good knee raised in a casual masculine stance.

Her heart tripped an odd beat. It seemed he cared little for wearing a shirt, even in the cabin's chill, and the firelight's play on his taut-muscled chest threatened to melt her resolve.

"What do you care of my frown?" she demanded, shifting from her haunches to face him.

His brow arched at her shrewish tone. "I prefer a smile. It becomes you."

She had not expected the compliment and steeled herself against its impact. "I have little to smile about."

The flames sizzled in the block, the crackling sounds muted against the pelting raindrops outside. He regarded her intently. "Missing your family again?"

"Again?" Haughtiness veiled the query. "I have not *stopped* missing them."

"Of course not." His piercing gaze remained steady. "I'm sorry they're not here with us, Liza. If I could bring them back to you, I would."

Liza fought the sudden sting of tears. His kindness would be her undoing.

"It does not matter," she said and glanced away.

"Like hell it doesn't."

She bit her lip. She could not tell him of Mama's hate, or of her dream and the sheer futility of it, or how out of place she felt in his world. He was only a Gajo. How could he possibly understand?

"I had a schoolmarm once who always wore a frown. We called her Pickle Puss because her face was all pinched and wrinkled like a pickle."

Liza's eyes widened. "I do not look like a pickle!"

The corners of his mouth crinkled. "If you keep frowning, that's exactly what you'll look like."

Of its own accord, her mind conjured the image of a green-faced, sour-looking Gajo woman. Liza dipped her head. She did not want to smile.

"So tell me about Gypsies." Reese settled more comfortably on the floor, rolling to his side and propping his head up with one hand. He waited expectantly.

She peered at him from beneath her lashes. "What do you want to know? You have already asked many questions today."

He grinned and charmed her fickle heart. "Can they really tell fortunes?"

"What do you think?" she hedged.

"I think it's all trickery."

She shrugged. "Telling fortunes takes great skill. Gypsy women practice many years to learn how. It is a very honorable thing to make money telling fortunes to the Gaje."

"And my people actually believe that stuff?"

"Of course. Those who are unhappy need a good *dukkerer* to give them hope."

"So you tell them what they want to hear."

"And what is wrong with that?" she challenged, her pride stung.

"If someone is fool enough to believe Gypsies can look into the future and are willing to pay good money to hear about it, then I reckon nothing."

"You are a cynical man, Reese Carrison," she said, sniffing.

"Not cynical, sweetheart. Just practical."

And shrewd, she thought. *Very shrewd.*

"Can you do it?" he asked, his tone curious. "Tell fortunes, I mean."

She sat a little straighter. "Some say I am very good."

If he disapproved, he kept it to himself. "What else can you do?"

"I can cook and weave baskets and sew whenever I find a piece of cloth—"

"No, no." He waved aside her deliberate evasion. "What other *Gypsy* things can you do?"

"You will only mock me if I tell you."

"I won't. Promise."

He flashed her a disarming smile. Liza weakened and knew she would tell him anything he wanted to know. He had that effect on her.

She sighed and tossed her long braid over her shoulder. "I can interpret moles and divine with sticks and stones. I can read tea leaves, a fire's flames, and a Gajo's hand. I can—"

"You're a palmist, then."

"Yes."

"Read mine." He thrust his hand, palm up, toward her.

She eyed him warily. "Why? I do not think you will believe a word I tell you."

"I'll try anything once." His tiger-gold eyes rested on her. "Besides," he said softly, "I want to know just how good at this you really are."

Perhaps he sought only to salve her testy mood, or perhaps he really wanted his palm read. Either way, she could think of no logical reason to refuse him. Yet she hesitated. To touch him so freely . . .

God's saints. What was the matter with her? He was only a Gajo, and she had read many Gajo palms before now. His would be no different.

She knelt in front of him and took his hand, turning it palm downward. Tiny obsidian hairs dusted his skin, deeply bronzed from hours in the sun and roughened from physical labor. His nails were well-trimmed and clean, but it was his warmth she noticed first. How could he feel so warm when it was such a cold night, and he did not even wear a shirt?

She swallowed and forced herself to concentrate.

"The outline of your hand is square, your fingers are supple and long," she murmured. "It shows you have energy to work hard, to persevere."

"One wouldn't build a railroad if he didn't have energy to work, would he?" he commented. "That's easy enough to figure out."

Her chin lifted; she released his hand and moved away. "I told you you would mock me."

He grasped her forearm in a firm grip, pulling her back toward him. "Don't stop, Liza. I won't say another word."

He had the look of the devil about him, teasing and mischievous and more than a little skeptical.

"You will listen, then?" she demanded, exasperated.

"I will."

She clucked her tongue in annoyance. This whole thing was silly and pointless.

But she turned his hand over and studied his palm anyway.

"See this line?" she asked, tracing the groove near the center and extending around the base of his thumb. "The Line of Life. It is narrow and deep and circles the Mount of Venus." She tapped his thumb knuckle. "That is favorable. You will have health and a good life. It shows character."

He nodded politely and appeared to hold back a smile.

She ignored him. "And this one. The Line of Head. It is not connected to the Line of Life so you have much confidence in yourself and a clear mind. You are very determined and show good judgment."

Pausing, she glanced at him. His brow was slightly furrowed. He listened intently.

"Go on," he urged. "What's next?"

"The Line of Heart." Her fingertip trailed along the groove extending from his first and fourth fingers. "It runs from the Mount of Jupiter to the Mount of Mercury. That means you have a big heart, full of affection and love."

She halted, silently studying the Heart Line closer. It was unusually long, longer than she could ever recall seeing in another Gajo. The woman who held Reese's heart would possess a powerfully noble love, one few men were capable of giving.

Thoughtful, she bypassed the lesser lines and examined the horizontal indentations at the base of his littlest finger. Again, a single line was predominant, nearly joining with the Heart Line.

"What do you see?" Reese asked, his voice low, curious.

For a lengthy moment, she did not answer. Hardly aware of it, she touched her fingertip to his Heart Line, following the groove in a slow, caressing stroke.

"You will have a great love someday, Reese," she said softly. "A woman will wed you, and you will love her as you have loved no other. Your marriage will endure. You will be happy, and the love you have for each other will last forever."

A silence fell between them. Neither spoke of the delicate, milky-skinned beauty whose image was conjured by Liza's words, and yet her name hung between them as if she had said it aloud.

"Liza."

She pulled herself from her reverie and blinked up at him. The flames' glow cast his features into sharply shaded planes and shadowed his unshaven cheeks. Dark and windblown, his hair was carelessly swept back past his temples. Liza had the unnatural urge to smooth every strand.

She must not. She tensed and drew back, yet his hand upon hers tightened. Somehow, their fingers became entwined, each coiling around the others, their grip soon clinging and intimate.

But again, she tried to pull away. He refused.

"My turn, Lady Gypsy," he said quietly.

Before she could resist, he pulled her toward him with a subtle strength, twisting their bodies so that she laid beneath him on the tablecloth-covered floor, their entwined hands resting near her head. She gasped with surprise. He towered over her, and with his free hand, began unbraiding her hair.

"What of you, Liza? What fortune can you predict for yourself?"

Like hazy blue smoke, his voice curled around her and held her motionless. She uttered no protest that he took liberties with her hair for he held her under his spell as if he had uttered the most powerful of chants.

"I have no fortune to tell, Reese," she whispered and grew dismayed that she had used his name twice with such familiarity.

"None? No great loves in your future?"

She pressed her lips together and shook her head. He seemed absorbed with spreading the coppery-red tresses in a thick halo before him, stroking their length as if they were spun gold. He touched them with reverence, and in all her days on earth, she could not remember anyone treating her hair like he did, without a hint of shame.

"Ah, but you're wrong this time, my sweet." Filled with raw emotion, his gaze roamed over her face. "I predict you'll have a great love of your own. A husband who'll hold you in his arms at night and thank God with every fiber of his being that you're his."

Her teeth bit into her lower lip, and she turned away. "Do not tease me, Gajo. I cannot bear it."

Gentle fingers took her jaw and turned her back again. "It's the truth. It'll happen. I swear it."

Her eyes pooled with tears. "It is what I want more than anything, but it can never be."

"Trust me. It will. And he'll be a man to be envied."

She stared up into his handsome face and longed to believe all he said. It would be easy to trust him, to let herself be swept away by all he promised and allow herself to hope, for it seemed, with this man, anything was possible.

He lifted a hank of her hair and held the strands up to the firelight. He appeared enraptured with the sheen bouncing off the flames' glow, and with an unhurried twist of his wrist, let the strands drift through his fingers.

"Keep your hair loose," he murmured. "Don't hide it away in that godforsaken braid you insist on wearing."

He was far too bold in his bidding. A woman allowed only her husband to touch her hair so freely, to see it unbound, but what would he know of the old Gypsy custom?

And she would not tell him. In the short time they had left, she could not deny him what he wanted.

Slowly, she nodded. "I will do as you say."

A corner of his mouth lifted. He seemed satisfied she had given him no argument.

"You're a hell of a fortune-teller, y'know that?"

She gave him a tentative smile, keenly aware he still held her hand and showed no inclination to let go.

"Am I?"

"Yes." His thumb moved over her pulse in lazy little strokes that sent her heart into an uneven rhythm. "But there's one thing you didn't tell me."

Her brows quirked in silent question.

"There's a kiss in our future," he said. "Between you and me. Sometime, before we part ways, we're going to bring our worlds together in a kiss neither of us will forget."

Her breath left her, stealing her will to reply. Anticipation gripped her, a deep wanting of this remembrance he spoke of, a tender keepsake she could store in her heart forever.

But it seemed he spoke only of a casual kiss between strangers. His hand slid from hers, and he eased away.

"It's late," he said. "We'd best turn in for the night."

She tried not to show her disappointment, the vast emptiness she suddenly felt at being denied the pleasure of his kiss, the gift of his passion.

He took the quilt and spread it over them both. He reached for her, then, slipping his arm about her and bringing her close to his side. As if it were her right, Liza went willingly, without reservation. Resting her head upon his broad shoulder, her hair spilling over his arm in rare freedom and, with no further words between them, she closed her eyes to sleep.

Beneath her hand, his heart beat steady and sure, as strong and solid as the man himself. She thought of Rebecca Ann and knew, in time, he would be hers alone. He would touch Rebecca Ann in all the places a wife would want to be touched; his kisses would be hers to take at will, their lives and bodies would be as one.

Part of Liza's soul knew the truth of reality, the other clung to the elusive dream, and no matter what the future held, she would cherish this moment.

For now, Reese Carrison was hers.

He awoke to sunlight peeping through cracks in the cabin's walls. Outside, birds chirped noisily, their cheerful songs slipping in with the sunlight to announce the dawning of a new day.

The rain had finally stopped. It seemed strange not to hear the steady pelting on the roof, but Reese had no regrets. He'd had his fill of the storm, and he had a mountain of work to do back in Niobrara City.

He awakened fully and eased the kinks in his muscles from sleeping on the floor. Pain shot through his knee, and he grimaced, deciding he'd need another of Liza's heat treatments to loosen the joint before he left.

Liza.

He glanced down to find her nestled against him, one leg thrown over his thigh. She slept deeply, her breathing sending little tufts of air skipping across his chest.

A piece of him warmed and melted. He'd gotten used to being with her. He knew her honor and smile and the captivating way she tilted her chin every time he tweaked her pride. She'd been fascinating company, and there wouldn't be another woman like her in his life.

Even so, he'd do well to forget her after today. He was anchored in Niobrara City and the N & D; she was destined to roam the land with her people. Neither had room for the other in their lives.

But where his logical mind made the decision, his heart rejected it. Knowing a sudden need to observe her more fully, to press the vision of her into his memory, he raised up on an elbow and studied her.

She made a pleasing sight. Long, dark lashes rested on her cheekbones, daintily tinted with pink and carved in delicate curves. The gold hoop earrings glinted in the sunlight and lay against her smooth neck.

He reached out and brushed a finger against her bottom lip. He found it soft and warm, and his manhood stirred to life.

Her mouth puckered from his touch. Her eyes opened slowly.

"Mornin'," he said, his voice low, gentle.

"Good morning." She blinked away the last of her slumber and dragged her leg off his. "Why are you looking at me like that?"

"It's not often I wake up next to a beautiful woman. I was just enjoying the view."

"Oh." Her lashes lowered, a shyness took her. "Did you sleep well?"

"You kept me warm and cozy. I slept quite well."

A faint blush crept up her cheeks. "I have never laid next to a man before you."

The quiet admission sent a wave of possessiveness coursing through him. How he'd managed to keep from touching her more intimately, from bedding her completely, he'd never know. His manhood throbbed anew.

"The rain has stopped. The sun is shining," he said abruptly.

Her gaze darted to a small window, the glass panes a spider web of cracks. "We will be leaving today, then."

Did he detect a hint of regret in those black eyes? If not, they must have reflected his own. "Yes."

She stared up at the ceiling and swallowed. "I will miss you, Gajo."

Her honesty both surprised and moved him. Gone were the fortresses of stubborn pride and unbreachable honor she'd built around herself. Somehow, those walls had tumbled down, leaving open a raw and gaping glimpse into her soul.

"It hasn't been so terrible being here with me, has it, Liza?"

"No, not like I thought it would." Turning to him, she cupped her hand against the side of his face. "You could

118

have forced yourself on me, the way a man lusts after a woman and cannot control himself. But you have treated me with respect. For that, I will always be grateful."

She looked delectable with her coppery-red mane tousled from the night, her features a beguiling mix of trust and innocence. Deep in his loins, sparks of arousal burst into flame.

"Grateful? I've got to be the craziest man on earth," he muttered. "Having you here with me like this and not doing a damn thing about it."

She appeared perplexed and drew her hand away. "Why do you say that? Have you forgotten your Rebecca Ann?"

Rebecca Ann.

He thrust aside the quilt and sat up. Frustration lanced him. He had to admit it. Thoughts of her were virtually nonexistent when he was with Liza.

A curse on his tongue, he rolled to his feet with as much grace as he could manage, given the bum knee. He needed a cigarette and a thorough dousing of crisp morning air to cool the heat brewing in his body. He grabbed his shirt and boots and tossed her a terse glance.

"You'd best get up and fix us some grub, Liza. I'll see to the horses."

With that curt command, he left her.

He took his time rolling the cigarette and smoking it. By then, he'd managed to bank his desire for Liza with a fair degree of success.

He was glad to have the stallion and Bram's sorrel to care for. They took his mind off her, gave his hands something to do when they'd rather be doing something else.

Like holding her. Or kissing her. Or discovering the secrets hidden in every dip and curve of her body.

He wondered if she truly understood the effect she had

on him and decided she probably didn't. It'd been a gradual thing, this wanting, and until now, he'd been adept at keeping it under control.

She'd taken good care of him and his horse the past couple of days. Maybe that was it. Gratitude. And with the minutes ticking away one by one, his time with her would be gone. He'd never see her again, and that knowledge raised an odd panic within him.

"You're going to miss her, too, aren't you, fella?" he asked, rubbing the stallion's long neck. "She spoils you. Gives you too many treats." The horse seemed not to listen, but kept his big, brown eyes riveted toward the cabin, as if expecting her to come out any moment. "Well, it's going to be just you and me again. Like it's always been."

Smoke curled from the chimney. The aroma of baking biscuits and strong coffee wafted to his nostrils. Their breakfast would be ready soon, but he had enough time to give the stallion's hindleg a soak in the water trough before he went in to eat.

Reese grasped the chin strap and tugged. The stallion nickered and jerked back, breaking Reese's grip. Swearing in exasperation, Reese reached for it again.

He guessed the stallion's intent a split second before the huge teeth connected with his shoulder. He swiveled out of the way and speared the animal with a venomous glare.

"Why, you damned fool horse. I—"

A scream from the cabin stopped him short.

Liza. His heart leaped in his chest, and he broke into a limping run, his mind filled with torturous visions of a half-crazed bear ready to attack. Or hostile Indian braves. Or a band of lusting outlaws. . . .

Another scream rent the air. Swearing at his lack of weaponry, he reached the cabin and yanked aside the hanging quilts.

He saw nothing. No one except Liza standing near the stove, frozen in fear, a wooden spoon clutched in her fist.

"Liza? What is it?"

"Oh, Reese!" She flew to him and shuddered in his arms. "Over there!"

The wooden spoon gestured wildly. He bundled her tight against him, then stabbed a glance around their tiny quarters.

"Where?" he demanded. "I don't see anything!"

"There. In the corner."

"Liza. There's nothing here." His eye searched for a rat or a mouse or even a skunk, anything that would frighten her. He saw only a bullfrog squatting near the fireplace. "You mean the frog?"

She shrieked and buried her face against his chest.

"The frog? You're afraid of the frog?"

Her head bobbed. She refused to look at it.

For a moment, he stood stock-still.

The frog.

He couldn't help himself. Full-blown laughter tumbled from his throat, and he locked his arms about her trembling form, rocking her from side to side while his shoulders shook in unabashed merriment.

Her head came up again.

"What is so funny?" she demanded, thumping his chest with the spoon. "They are the devil's image! Filthy! Repulsive and disgusting! How can you not be sickened by the very sight of one?"

"Is this a—a Gypsy thing?" he managed to ask.

"Do the Gaje not feel the same way?" She stared up at him, wide-eyed.

"No, we don't. Not at all." His mirth filled the cabin to the rafters. "Probably came in from the river with all the rain. He's harmless. I'll show you."

121

"Do not touch it!" she gasped in horror.

The bullfrog croaked and leaped toward them. Liza jumped and squealed and clutched at Reese, covering her eyes with one hand. "Do not let it get near us. It is the devil! Do you not understand?"

"Oh, Liza. Sweetheart." His laughter erupted all over again.

She ventured a peek around him, her dark eyes riveted to the poor creature, who, amid all the commotion, hop, hop, hopped around them and finally disappeared outside.

"Thank the saints," she breathed and hastily crossed herself.

"I'd warrant he was more afraid of you than you were of him."

"You mock me with your laughter, but I tell you, Gajo, I can think of nothing more revolting," she said, her tone offended. "It is the truth."

"Okay, okay. I believe you."

He drew back.

Their gazes meshed.

His chuckles died away in his throat.

In that moment, something changed between them. Something powerful and indefinable that stole the breath from his lungs and threatened to knock him to his knees.

A slow heat flickered deep within him. Their surroundings faded into oblivion. He was aware of only Liza and the softness of her breasts crushed against his chest. He could drown in her eyes, deep obsidian pools that bewitched him like a sorceress's curse. His hand slid beneath the weight of her hair and curled around her nape.

She stared up at him. With a certainty that rocked him to the core, he knew his prediction from the night before would come true, that their kiss was imminent and unquestioned, and that he wanted it more than he'd ever wanted a kiss from a woman before.

Slowly, his head lowered. The wooden spoon slipped unnoticed from her fingers, and she moved closer, lips parted, her head tilting back to meet him.

At last, his mouth covered hers, gently at first, giving her time to refuse. But she did not. She responded with a boldness that surprised him, her mouth moving and hungry under his. Her slender arms wound around his neck and clung, as if she couldn't get close enough, as if she wanted him as much as he wanted her.

The fires of desire raged unchecked inside him. To hell with respect and gratitude. He'd been a fool to stay away from her until now. The need to crawl between her thighs, fill her with his seed, to brand her as forever his, was almost more than he could bear.

He groaned, deep, fierce, and hardened the kiss. So little time left. Their worlds, too different, too far apart, would never be conquered, but for now, he had her, he had this kiss, and it would have to be enough.

But it wasn't. Not even close. He wanted too much from this Gypsy woman, wanted more than he should, but her passion toppled his, and he could deny himself no longer.

"Liza, Liza."

The aching rasp begged to be answered. She trembled in his arms and whispered his name in kind, giving him what he asked with no more than that. Moist and inviting, her mouth sought his again, and Reese thought he'd die from the pleasure of it.

His hand moved across her ribcage and found the fullness of her breast. She made a primitive sound, as if eager for all he had to give. Impatient with the barrier, he pushed the loose-fitting blouse off her shoulder, to the chemise he did the same, baring a rounded globe of feminine flesh and filling his palm with its delectable weight.

From somewhere, a horse nickered. Absorbed with Liza, with her heat and softness and all she made him feel, he fought the intrusion.

"Reese?" The man's voice cut into his comprehension like an icy gust of wind. "What the hell's going on in here?"

Chapter Eight

Liza tore away from Reese and clutched her blouse and chemise to her bosom, a moan of mortification spilling from her swollen lips. It was all Reese could do to keep from pulling her into his arms again. He didn't want it to end like this.

Bram's timing couldn't have been worse. Muttering an oath, Reese straightened and faced him, keeping his back to Liza that his body might offer her a measure of privacy.

"You should've knocked, Bram," he said, the words husky, heavy with irritation.

"Given the circumstances, maybe I should have."

But Bram's tone offered no apology. His thick, silvery brows were furrowed in disapproval. He stood in the cabin's opening, the hanging quilts thrust to one side. Sunshine and crisp morning air billowed inward, and Reese glimpsed a carriage parked in the yard.

"You found the Gypsy girl, I see." Bram's sharp glance darted to Liza.

"I did."

"The stallion, too?"

"He's with your sorrel out back."

"Both doing well enough, I hope."

"Fine, fine," Reese snapped, impatient with the small talk.

"Rebecca Ann's waiting outside. She's been worried about you. We all have."

Reese made no reply and dragged his gaze to Liza. She stood angled away from him, her back stiff, her fingers still clutching the blouse in a white-knuckled grip. He willed her to look at him, that he might offer silent reassurance, but she did not.

He limped toward Bram, and placing a hand to the older man's back, firmly nudged him outside. Liza needed the time alone.

From the driver's seat, Rebecca Ann peered around the edge of the buggy and lifted a gloved hand, her delicate features bearing a tentative smile. She looked as beautiful as ever in a deep-blue velvet gown that must've cost a fortune. The feathers in her hat fluttered in the breeze. Margaret Michelle slept peacefully on her lap.

Reese waved back, but he didn't go to her; instead, he dipped into his jacket pocket for a rolled cigarette. He needed a shave, a hot bath, and a change of clothes. He doubted Rebecca Ann, in all her perfection, would find the sight of him appealing.

Bram hooked his thumbs into the waistband of his tweed wool suit pants and sighed heavily. "What's going on between you and the Gypsy?"

Reese cupped the match's flame, surprised to find his hand wasn't quite steady, that the blood Liza had stirred to fire had not yet cooled.

"The kiss should never have happened. It just did," he growled.

"Damn right it shouldn't have happened. Thank God Rebecca Ann wasn't there to see you two."

"What happened with Liza is my business. I invite you to stay out it."

Bram looked so offended Reese immediately regretted his outburst. They'd been friends for as long as he could remember. They rarely argued, and certainly never over a woman.

"I can recall a time or two when you were glad I was involved . . . in your business," Bram grated.

Reese took the blow. If not for Bram and his shrewd financial mind, the Nebraska-Dakota Railroad would not have been a dream come true.

He exhaled in frustration, knowing he should apologize but unable to find the words. An uneasy silence reigned between them while the cigarette smoldered, forgotten, between his fingers. Down the road, a wagon and a pair of workhorses plodded through the mud.

Bram took in a heavy breath, then blew it out again, letting the argument dissipate between them. He studied the cabin. Disbelief formed in his expression. "You been holed up here all this time?"

Reese nodded. The structure looked far worse in broad daylight. With the lightest breeze, the heavy logs seemed ready to tumble to the ground like a pile of matchsticks. No wonder Bram looked appalled.

"We had provisions and part of a roof over our heads," Reese said. "We were warm and dry. It could've been worse."

Shaking his head, Bram swept a glance across the debris strewn about the yard. "That was some twister that hit."

"I know. We were lucky to make it through." He paused. "How did Niobrara City fare?"

"Pretty good, considering the strength of the storm."

"And the train?"

"Untouched. The bridge is fine, too. We didn't lose a splinter."

Thank God, Reese thought silently. It was a favorable sign, his train and its trestle bridge making it through. He couldn't help feeling the N & D would survive most anything.

"A search party was out yesterday looking for you and the girl. When we couldn't find a trace of either of you, we expected the worse. Never dreamed you were here all along. Thought for sure we lost you to the Niobrara."

"I appreciate the concern." Funny how he'd worried far less about them. Taking refuge with Liza had thrust him into a world vastly removed from civilization. She'd been one hell of a diversion.

"This is Jack Hadley's place, isn't it?" Bram asked, his tone thoughtful.

"Yes. They went visiting relatives. Omaha, I think."

"Damned awful thing to come back to. Feel sorry for Maudeen. Going to be real hard on her to see this."

Reese fell silent. Jack and Maudeen Hadley's cabin had been a godsend, despite its ravaged condition. Without the shelter it gave, he and Liza might never have survived the storm.

A snippet of color drew his attention. Liza emerged from behind the quilts, her chin taut, her spine straight, the gold beads around her neck jangling lightly with her every step.

From the carriage, Rebecca Ann gasped softly, her fingers flew to her mouth in surprise. The women's gazes locked, as if each sized the other up, judging for themselves the threat either presented.

Reese's eyes narrowed. Liza wore the kerchief again. The striped fabric hugged her head like a second skin, hiding the copper-gold tresses. She wore the damn thing like a shield, holding herself apart from them.

From him.

He sensed the change in her instantly. No impish light danced in her eyes, no soft, gentle smile warmed her mouth. The haughtiness he'd always associated with her people had returned in full force, stealing away the Liza he knew and bringing in its place a woman filled with scorn and contempt.

A stranger.

He'd have no part in her game. He stepped forward to make proper introductions, to destroy once and for all the misconceptions she had about his people, the Gaje. And it was time Bram and Rebecca Ann learned, too, that Liza was as human as they, no different, but in fact a beautiful, caring person who'd touched a part of his heart like few had before her.

But another woman's anguished cry stopped him cold.

They all turned in unison. Jack Hadley guided his team into the yard and commanded them to a halt. Beside him sat Maudeen, her arms clutching their two young sons. They stared at their damaged home, shock draining their faces of all color. The reins fell from Jack's fingers and dropped to the ground.

His glance traveled over his land with a misery-laden thoroughness, as if searching for the outbuildings that once stood, touching upon the barn that leaned precariously to one side, the stalks of corn lying broken and mangled in their fields. Without a word, he slipped his arm around Maudeen. She sagged against him with a sob, and Reese's gut twisted.

He felt their loss keenly. If there was a way he could make this easier for them, he'd do it.

"Mr. Carrison?" Jack's raspy voice cut through him, pleading for a plausible explanation.

"I'm sorry, Jack." Reese's reply sounded meaningless and trite. What good would sorrow do for a man who'd nearly lost everything he'd worked for? "A twister came through," he went on solemnly. "We'll help you and Maudeen get back on your feet. You know that."

"Why us?" The tiny words cracked with despair. "We've done nothin' but scratch out a livin' on this place day and night. And now it's gone."

"You'll build it back up again. You've got no choice, not with Maudeen and the boys to think of."

"We'll put you up in town, too," Bram offered. "Won't take long until the cabin's livable, just like before. You'll see."

"No." Maudeen pulled away from Jack and sat up. She swiped at the tears on her cheeks. "I'm not leaving."

Reese attempted to reason with her. "Only for a little while, Maudeen. We'll get the neighbors to help. Bram's right. It won't take long to make repairs, not with everyone pitching in. Don't you agree, Jack?"

But Jack didn't seem to hear. He'd grown very still. By subtle degrees, his expression changed from despair, to puzzlement, to outright suspicion.

"Why are you all here?" he demanded.

Uneasy with the shift of his mood, Reese chose his explanation with care. "We got caught in the storm and stayed here a couple of days, that's all. Bram and Rebecca Ann just now found us."

"We?" Jack asked, spearing a glance at each of them.

Toby, the Hadley's four-year-old son, scrambled from his mother's arms and jumped to the ground, landing feet first in a water puddle. Jack paid him no mind. Instead, his gaze found Liza standing at the front of the cabin.

It appeared he hadn't noticed her before. The suspicion etched in his young face deepened.

"A Gypsy?" he snarled, his eyes slashing over her. "What's *she* doin' here? Tryin' to take what ain't hers?"

Disgust from Jack's accusation rolled through Reese. Liza's lip curled with disdain, her nostrils flared.

"Speak of her with more respect, Jack," Reese warned. "She's done nothing wrong."

Oblivious to the turmoil brewing about him, Toby ran toward Liza with eager curiosity.

"Hello," he said. "Who're you?"

His innocent greeting bore no trace of his father's animosity. Liza hesitated, then, her hand moved, as if she intended to reach out and touch him.

"Toby! Git away from her!" Jack snapped. "She might have somethin' catchin'!"

"Jack!" Maudeen appeared horrified.

Liza recoiled. The Gajo's words ripped through her like a whip, stinging to the quick, laying her open to bleed in front of all of them. No one spoke. No one did anything but stare at her. Even Reese.

Especially Reese.

She hated them. She hated *him*.

She had to make them go away, frighten them, make them run like fat jackrabbits from a hungry wolf. She had to stop their awful accusations.

Her fingers curled into claws. She hissed and spread her arms wide. Her eyes narrowed. A monotone chant spilled from her lips, and in a voice snapping and cutting, she cursed them with a vehemence dredged up from deep in her soul.

In unified alarm, they drew back. Only Reese remained unmoved.

"Liza, what the hell are you *doing*?"

He seemed stunned by her actions. She repeated the curse, the chant louder, more forceful, and moved her arms in slow, sweeping gestures.

"Liza, stop it. *Now.*"

She wavered beneath his ominous warning. Grim-faced, he stepped closer, looking as if he wanted to strangle her. She knew he saw through her ploy, that with him the old Gypsy trick had failed. She broke into a run, but too swiftly he caught her, holding her in a grip of iron.

"Let me go!" she spat.

"You crazy fool!" His eyes brewed with golden thunder in a tempestuous storm that rivaled the one two days past. His fingers dug into her upper arms; she sensed only supreme effort held his temper in check. "I don't know what you're trying to prove, woman," he said in a growl, his voice so low that only she could hear. "But you're doing damned little to improve your precious Gypsy image to my friends."

She wilted under his attack. His broad shoulders hid the others from view. The feel of his hard body pressed against hers brought crashing back memories of the searing kiss they had shared inside the cabin.

"Get away from me!" she said, the demand sounding appallingly like a whimper.

She pushed against him to no avail. Her hands clenched into fists. She fought his power, clung to the hate that had given her strength only moments ago.

"Something's burning!" Maudeen shrieked.

The biscuits.

Saints in heaven. Liza had forgotten them. But so what? She did not care if they caught fire and burned the stupid Gaje's cabin to the ground!

132

Her gaze involuntarily darted to Maudeen who frantically thrust her baby son into her husband's arms and hurried from the wagon.

Liza swallowed and submitted to the truth. Yes, she did care. In spite of everything, it was not right that this woman should lose what was left of her home to a fire.

She twisted from Reese's grip. With her skirt hems flying at her heels, Liza sprinted back into the cabin, scant steps behind Maudeen, already disappearing behind the quilts.

Smoke curled from around the oven door. Maudeen coughed and waved away the haze before reaching for the oven's handle. Too late, Liza saw the danger as the young woman's fingers gripped the hot metal bar.

Maudeen cried out and snatched her hand away. Liza swiftly pushed her aside and plucked from the floor the tablecloth she and Reese had slept on. Wadding the fabric to save her own palms, she yanked the door open and pulled out the blackened biscuits, tossing the pan onto the stove top with a harried clatter.

The door slammed shut again. Maudeen stared at Liza with wide, uncertain eyes.

Liza stared back.

The woman was close to her own age. Looking frazzled and defeated, she appeared near tears and clutched her burned hand to her breast. Liza waited for her scorn, a match to her husband's, but Maudeen's tongue remained silent.

A wary moment passed. Then, Liza moved, taking Maudeen's hand. Dipping into a tin of lard near the sideboard, she salved the blisters already forming on Maudeen's work-roughened skin.

Maudeen's breath caught in surprise. Again, their gazes met. A flicker of gratitude shone through the shimmery tears, but Liza turned away. She did not want this Gajo woman's thanks. She had no need of it.

Reese and the others entered the cabin in a rush, Maudeen and her injury taking their full attention. None of them paid Liza any notice.

She saw her chance. Without another thought, she stepped around the quilts and made her escape.

"Where's Liza?" Reese asked sharply.

Bram frowned, his puzzlement clearly matching Reese's. "Gone, obviously."

"Jest like them Gypsies to sneak away like that," Jack muttered. Reassured that Maudeen's burn had proved minor, he seemed more concerned with the damage done to the cabin's roof than Liza's disappearance. "Can't trust 'em for nothin'."

"Why do you speak of her so unkindly, Jack?" Maudeen asked, taking their pink-cheeked baby son into her own arms again. "What has she ever done to you?"

Reese didn't wait to hear Jack's reply. He hobbled outside and searched the yard, then the road leading back into Niobrara City. He finally saw her, the gold-and-crimson kerchief drawing his eye as her form grew steadily smaller in the distance. He headed for the lean-to.

Bram followed. "What're you going to do, Reese?"

"Go after her."

"Why? What's the use—damnation! What'd you do to your leg?"

"Twisted it." Reese hefted the saddle onto the sorrel and tightened the cinch.

Bram dodged a pile of broken boards. "Why aren't you taking the stallion?"

"He's lame."

"Lame? What happened?"

"I'll explain when I have more time." Reese mounted the sorrel and shot a glance down the road. Liza had all but disappeared from sight. "I'll get my horse later. Tell Jack and Maudeen I'll be in touch."

Bram swore and snatched the sorrel's chin strap. His eyes met Reese's.

"You're wasting your time on the Gypsy girl," he said in a snarl. "I don't know what all went on the past couple of days between you two, but I strongly suggest you forget her. You've got Rebecca Ann to think of."

"Liza and I have unfinished business." Reese fought irritation at Bram's interference. "Leave me alone, Bram. I know what I'm doing."

"I hope to hell you do."

Bram released the strap and stepped back. The sorrel cantered out from under the lean-to toward the front of the cabin, taking Reese past the buggy as they headed toward the road.

Rebecca Ann still waited on the driver's seat. Odd she hadn't left the rig, if for nothing more than to see to Maudeen's welfare—or his own, for that matter. Maybe she hadn't wanted to sully her kid leather shoes in a mud puddle.

The notion annoyed him. She glanced his way, a pout on her ruby lips. With his mind focused on Liza, he struggled to re-track his attention to managing a few civil words with Rebecca Ann.

He lifted a finger to his hat brim but remembered too late that it'd been plucked from his head by the tornado. His hand came down again and gripped the reins.

"Hello, Reese," she said.

He detected little warmth in her tone and surmised she was miffed with him. Aware of the seconds ticking away, he shifted restlessly in the saddle. "Good morning. You survived the storm well enough, I see."

"Yes. And you?"

He resisted the urge to scan the road again and hoped Liza hadn't vanished completely. "Good. Made it through just fine."

"With *her*?"

Reese stiffened at the hurt in her query.

"Her name is Liza," he said. "And yes, I made it through the storm with her."

"Oh, Reese, how could you? After what she tried to do to Margaret Michelle!"

"It was all a misunderstanding, Rebecca Ann. She had no intention—"

"I saw it with my own eyes. She tried to kidnap my child. You saw her, too. Everyone did."

Reese had no inclination to deal with another of Rebecca Ann's hysterical fits. A frustrated breath hissed through his teeth. "I'll tell you all about it later. Maybe we can have dinner or something."

"You're going after her, aren't you?"

"Yes," he said, his tone curt. "I am."

With a refined pout, she turned on the seat and stared straight ahead. On her lap, Margaret Michelle stirred in sleep, her cheeks flushed pink, a frown puckering her porcelain features. Reese well knew the tantrum she'd make should she awaken.

"I'll call on you soon. Would that be all right?" he asked.

"I don't know. I'll think about it," she sniffed, refusing to look at him.

Hell. What did she expect him to do? Get down on his knees and beg?

His mouth tightened. He kicked the horse into a gallop

and put her from his mind, channeling his searching gaze on Liza's pinpoint form instead.

She had walked with amazing speed, her hips swaying with each long stride, as if she couldn't put distance between them fast enough. The sorrel easily outpaced her, and soon Reese caught up with her.

She glanced at him over her shoulder. Her eyes widened at his close proximity, and she increased her stride to a run. Reese maneuvered the horse to a stop directly in front of her.

His position blocked the road. And Liza. She veered to one side, then the other, but ditches overflowing with rainwater forbade an escape. She glared up at him.

"Out of my way, Gajo!" she snapped.

"We're back to that again, are we?" He leaned forward and rested an elbow on the saddle horn. "Stupid Gajo. Foolish Gajo," he mimicked. "What happened to plain ol' Reese?"

He detected the faintest tremble in her lower lip. She yanked her gaze away and stubbornly held her tongue.

Reese studied her profile, arrogant with hurt pride.

"Jack Hadley behaved like an ass," he said quietly. "The shock of finding his place in shambles brought out the worst in him. I've known him for years. He's a good man."

She sniffed haughtily. "I do not believe it. He behaves no differently than any other of your people."

"Liza, be reasonable."

"I cannot!" Her eyes sparked with ebony fire. "You are all the same! Selfish and despicable, and you treat the Gypsy like pigs!"

"Some, maybe. But not all of us. Not me."

"Ha! You are Gaje. No better."

"You didn't think that earlier," he retorted. "Not when I held you in my arms."

Her hand flew to her mouth; a sound of dismay slipped from her throat. She swung around toward the roadside ditch, as if she thought she could leap over the wide cavern of water to get away from him. Her fists clenched from the futility of it, and she spun back to face him.

"Get out of my way, Reese," she demanded.

"You're not going anywhere." He straightened in the saddle. "You owe me, Lady Gypsy."

She gasped. "For what?"

"My horse. Don't you remember? You promised to help him, to cure his lameness."

"But I have! He is getting better. Soon he will be as strong as before."

"Only with you." Reese shook his head. "He adores you. He won't let me get close to him. Damn near bites my head off every time I try."

Panic flickered across her features. "You cannot make me do this. I must find my people!"

He steeled himself against the anguish in her tone. A force beyond his control governed his actions; of its own accord, the command to keep her with him, to work her magic on his horse, had formed. Little did he understand it, but a tiny, powerful part of him refused to let her go.

"I'll cut you a deal." Her attention sharpened, and he continued. "Take care of my horse, like you promised, and I'll help you find your people."

"How?" She narrowed her black eyes in suspicion.

"I have contacts. Friends. All along the N & D line. They'll let me know if they see a band of Gypsies driving by."

She grunted, seeming to digest his explanation.

"How?" she asked again.

Her refusal to trust him amused him. Few women were as stubborn. His mouth curved. "We have amazing machines called telegraphs. Ever hear of them?"

She shook her head, her long, thick braid swiveling across her shoulder. "I do not know what that is."

"I'll show you sometime." He studied her intently. "What do you say, Liza? Do we have a deal?"

She nibbled on the inside of her lip. "If I make your horse strong again, you say you will help me find my people. What if I refuse?"

"I won't let you," he said softly.

She tossed him a harsh glance. "Then I will make a bargain of my own."

"Such as?"

"Before I agree to your deal, first you must take me to the river. To make sure my people are not still camped there."

He considered that. If for some reason, the Gypsies had ridden out the storm, waiting for her to return, then he'd simply share her with them. He'd show them the Gaje weren't as terrible as they believed, that their worlds could mesh and much of their animosity could be eliminated.

"Fair enough," he said and extended his hand. "I'll take you."

She hesitated, then reached up and placed hers within his grasp. He pulled, and with surprising agility, she leaped up onto the sorrel without benefit of a stirrup and settled behind the cantle.

Her arms wound around his waist. He took the reins and kicked the sorrel into a run, the iron hooves pelting over the muddied road.

Another time, Reese would have enjoyed the ride with her pressed to his back, her warmth soaking into him. Her body flowed with the horse's gait, her skirts flapped in the breeze and offered forbidden glimpses of a well-turned ankle.

But not today. Not now. His thoughts were filled with what they'd find at the Niobrara's edge. If nothing? Liza would be devastated, her hopes dashed. And if her people were there? He braced himself for the confrontation. He wouldn't be welcome.

Along the way, the tornado's ruin was evident. Trees—some snapped in half, others overturned, their roots clawing the air—were abundant, yet as they drew closer to the Niobrara, the destruction thinned. Only a scattering of branches broken from the wind were visible, and relief flooded Reese that the area had escaped the storm's vengeance.

He reined the sorrel to a stop. In his mind's eye, he recalled the band of wagons creeping along the horizon as they skirted Niobrara City the day his railroad was dedicated. They'd filled the woodland with their horses and rigs and people.

Now they were gone. The woodland was stark and empty. Only the gentle rush of the river's current reached his ear.

Without a word Liza slid to the ground. Her tread light and quick, she hastened to a cluster of low-growing shrubs. She bent toward them, searching their foliage, then straightened, tilted her head back and stared into the trees. She hurried from one to the other, as if she looked for something hidden within their branches.

Reese pondered her actions. What did she hope to find?

Finally, she turned toward him and crossed her arms tightly over her breasts.

"The vurma. It is not here," she said in a voice hardly above a whisper.

He'd heard of the signs Gypsies left for one another, a strange code they alone knew. Why had her family forsaken her? Had she somehow missed their message?

"I'll help. Tell me what to look for," he said and moved to dismount.

"No." She waved a hand, dismissing his offer. "It is too late. There is nothing here for me."

"Are you sure?"

"Yes."

Her dejection pulled at him. "I'm sorry."

She looked away. Her gaze settled on a dented pot sitting near an abandoned campfire, its blackened coals long since cold, and she grew still.

Rainwater lapped at the enamel brim. Leaves and twigs covered the murky contents inside—someone's dinner perhaps—and Reese surmised it'd been left behind in great haste.

Liza stepped closer and ran a finger over the chipped handle.

"Mama's," she said softly. He strained to hear. "She was to make a stew that day. Hanzi promised her a juicy hen—" Her voice broke off, and she appeared to fight tears.

Within moments, she won back her composure. She straightened from the old pot and faced him squarely.

"My family is gone. I do not know where to find them." Pride rang out in her matter-of-fact tone. "And I have nowhere to go."

He considered a boardinghouse. The Grand River Hotel. Friends. In the end, he rejected them all.

"You'll stay with me," he said.

She drew a long breath.

"Yes," she said simply.

He gestured toward the campsite. "Do you want to bring your mother's pot?"

"No." She shook her head firmly and sent the hoop earrings swinging. "Soon, another kumpania will camp here. I will leave it to share with them. It is the Gypsy way."

Understanding, he nodded.

She walked toward him. Without speaking, she clasped his outstretched hand and swung up into the saddle. Her arms slipped around him.

With a gentle slap of the reins, Reese turned the horse and headed for home.

Chapter Nine

To Liza, his house was magnificent. Far more magnificent than she could have imagined. A house perfect for Reese Carrison.

She stared in awe. The structure towered over them and touched the sky. Painted a sparkling white and trimmed in deep green along the roof and around each window, his home stood proudly over his land, a symbol of his wealth and success.

Saints in heaven. She had seen few finer than this.

But, then, she reminded herself as he dismounted and looped the reins at a hitching post, her experience with Gaje houses was limited. She had never even been inside one before. Who was she to know?

"What're you looking at so hard?" His features bemused, Reese peered up at her, both hands on his lean hips.

"Your home. It is so big." She could not understand why one man needed this much room when her own family, seven of them, lived comfortably enough in their old wagon.

"Big?" His brow raised. "Compared to what you're used to, maybe. But you should see Bram's. Makes mine look like a cracker box."

Liza frowned. "You should not be ashamed just because your friend has something a little fancier."

"I'm not. Far from it." He ran his gaze over the house and the barn situated nearby. A faraway look crept into his tawny eyes. "I've lived in some real dives in my day. Whatever I could find to get out of the cold. Haven't had a true home since I was a kid." He turned back to her. "Hell, no. I'm not ashamed. I've got plans for this place. I'll raise a family here. Die here. I'm going to see my railroad thrive right along with Niobrara City. Fifty years from now, I'll be right on that porch, gray-haired and senile, watching the world go by."

His declaration riveted her. Fifty years? How strange he would know his life fifty years from now when she and her people hardly knew theirs from one day to the next.

He was far different from the Gypsy, a man with roots who worked hard for what he wanted and hung on tight to all that was his. A grudging admiration flowered inside her.

"Are you going to sit there all day?" His tone half-teasing, he reached toward her, offering assistance to dismount.

Liza hesitated, her foot already in the stirrup. She could not recall the last time anyone helped her down from a horse. Not her uncles or cousins, nor Hanzi, the older of her brothers. And certainly not Nanosh, who had plopped her on top of a horse at the age of two and sent her trotting off by herself.

She gave in to the luxury. Reese clasped her waist and pulled her from the sorrel, easing her to the ground in front of him. Her hands found his shoulders for support and discovered the hard, sinewy muscles hidden beneath his suit jacket.

Her gaze lifted and met his. The sun shaded the chiseled planes of his face and bounced off his unshaven jaw. Her pulse quickened. He was like a wild animal, this Gajo. Primitive and rugged. With the power to hold her captive with nothing more than the touch of his skin against hers.

Her mind reeled back to the memory of his devastating kiss. He had wanted her with the fierceness of a man who needed a woman. She had been weak in his arms, for his kiss had made her want him just as much.

The tawny depths darkened. Like hot whiskey, they drizzled her with a captivating heat. His gaze shifted and drifted downward, settling upon her mouth, and she knew, then, that he remembered, too. The kiss between them, no matter how right or wrong, or how opposite their worlds, would not be forgotten.

Liza's lashes fluttered; she glanced away. She did not know how much longer she could resist him when he looked at her like this. His fingers tightened about her waist, as if he was not yet ready to let her go, but she resolutely stepped back, and he released her.

"Let's go inside." His voice carried a rough, unsteady edge. "I'll show you around."

He limped up the stairs to the porch and opened the door, but Liza followed at a slower pace. She needed a few moments to shake aside the effect he had on her and adjust to the realization that she had agreed to stay with him in his house.

A worried part of her insisted she made a mistake.

A Gypsy staying in a Gajo's home. Mama would be aghast and would cross herself in prayer to God, asking forgiveness for Liza's stupidity.

But Liza climbed one step, then another. The wooden planks were thick and strong and did not creak like the one outside her family's wagon. The porch floor shone with fresh paint, and she surmised he had not lived here very long, that he'd only recently built his house.

Sunlight bounced off a green-trimmed window. Unable to help herself, she gently rapped her fingers on the pane. Real glass. She hastily snatched her hand back lest the fragile thing would somehow break. She caught Reese watching her.

He seemed amused. "Coming?"

She swallowed down her trepidations. She would be safe with him. She had nowhere else to go, and she reassured herself it would not be too terrible to stay with him in his house.

He held the door open. Mustering her courage, she swept past him and went inside. The latch clicked shut behind them.

A few feet into the main room, she halted. Her curious gaze left nothing untouched as she stared at all that belonged to him. A huge stone fireplace occupied one wall, its mantel laced with a model train stretching from end to end. A couch and pair of chairs, covered in a tapestry of blues and golds, sat positioned so their occupants might enjoy the warmth of the fire. Leather-bound books lined rows of shelves on an adjoining wall. Small tables holding fringe-shaded lamps, miniature replicas of steam engines, and one very neglected fern lay scattered throughout.

The hominess of the room called out to her and offered a glimpse into his life and loves. Even the furniture, as strong and solid as the man himself, reflected a stability so much a part of him.

"What do you think?" he asked, plucking a shirt from

the back of the sofa and tossing it into a woven basket overflowing with laundry near the door.

"It is beautiful," she breathed.

He grinned, his pleasure obvious. "I built this myself, when I could spare the time away from the N & D. Took me forever." His glance blanketed the room. "But it's mine," he said softly. "Every sliver and nail."

"You should be very proud to own such a fine home."

"I am." He grimaced and scooped up a stack of newspapers from the floor. "I'm not much of a housekeeper, though. Don't have the time for it." He dropped the papers next to the laundry basket, then seemed to forget them. "Are you hungry? I'll find us something to eat. The kitchen is back here."

On his way, he peeled his suit jacket off and flung it over the back of the sofa, on the same spot where he'd retrieved the shirt in his attempt to tidy up for her. Liza doubted he even noticed, and a small smile found her lips.

He disappeared into the kitchen. Careful not to touch anything, Liza trailed after him and paused in the archway dividing the two rooms.

A sigh of delight escaped her. What a pleasure this kitchen must be to work in, she thought longingly, charmed with the yellow checkered curtains and whitewashed walls. She eyed the big cast-iron stove with reverence. A far cry from cooking over an open fire. And while Gypsy women had prepared meals that way for generations, Liza knew the stove would make the chore much easier.

Reese pulled out a pitcher of lemonade from the icebox. She stared in wonder. An icebox. She had seen them in the Gaje stores before when the kumpania had ventured into the big cities, and this one was as nice as any of them with its polished hardwood door, carved panels, and shiny brass

147

hinges. She could not imagine owning such a luxury.

"Ham sandwiches okay?" Reese asked, pulling a plate of the smoked meat from the icebox's compact shelf. "It's nearly lunchtime."

Liza's stomach gurgled, reminding her they had had no breakfast. "Yes. A sandwich will be delicious."

He set a bowl of fruit on the wooden table with one hand and balanced a cutting board and loaf of wrapped bread in the other. Opening a drawer, he retrieved a knife and pushed the drawer shut with his hip.

"Grab some glasses from that cupboard over there, will you?"

She did as he requested, picking two that looked as if they had never been used before, and set them on the table next to the pitcher. He began slicing the bread, wielding the knife in sure, even strokes.

Not knowing what else to do, Liza stood to one side, her hands clasped tightly in front of her. It did not feel right, a Gajo preparing her meal, even one as simple as a ham sandwich. And it did not feel proper to accept his hospitality so quickly. She reached over and covered his hand with hers. The slicing motions stopped.

"I will pay you for the food I eat," she said firmly.

He set the knife down and regarded her. "I don't want your money, Liza."

"I cannot take advantage of your generosity. You wait on me as if I were a helpless child."

"Helpless? Hell." His piercing gaze seemed to bore through to her soul. "Has a man never showed you kindness before?"

Reluctant to admit the truth, even to herself, she sniffed with disdain. "That is none of your concern."

A tiny muscle moved in his jaw. "Maybe it isn't. Sorry." But his features showed no remorse. "Let's get one thing straight right now. We have a business arrangement here. You take care of my horse and make him well again. In the meantime, I give you a place to stay and food to fill your belly until I can find your family. Got it?"

She wavered. His horse was strong. His leg would heal soon enough with only a little skill on her part. Reese's end of the bargain required far more effort. Finding her family would not be easy.

"I will cook for you, then." She pushed his tall frame aside and picked up the knife. "It is the least I can do. And maybe wash the laundry, too. I do not mind."

"I have a laundress in town, Liza. I don't expect you to clean my clothes."

"Hush. I will not take no for an answer this time." She heaped portions of ham on the bread with an efficiency borne of many years at Mama's side at mealtime. "Do you want one sandwich or two?"

"Make it three. I'm starved. You're a stubborn lady, y'know that?"

A pleasant sensation wrapped around her. She would never tire of him calling her a lady, even if she were a stubborn one.

They ate in a companionable silence. Afterward, Reese departed to return to the Hadleys' and bring the stallion back. Before he left, he surprised her by dragging a copper-lined tub into the kitchen so she might bathe.

She warmed at his thoughtfulness. A bath. In a real tub. What a treat that would be, and she hastened to heat plenty of water. With the table cleared of their lunch and the dishes cleaned, Liza shed her clothes and kerchief, leaving them in a pile on the floor.

She tested the water with her big toe before gingerly slipping into the lusciously hot depths. Water lapped about her and cocooned her in luxury. She sank deeper, bringing

149

her knees up at one end and resting her head on the back of the other.

Saints in heaven. A bath in the middle of the day. How lucky she was. And how wickedly lazy.

She sighed and closed her eyes. If only Mama and Paprika were here. They would enjoy it just as much, taking turns washing and splashing in the splendid tub and feeling rich and spoiled.

Liza basked in the quiet and privacy, a rare thing when traveling with the kumpania. Of their own volition, her thoughts turned to Reese and the bargain they had made.

If anyone could find her family, he could. She trusted him in that. She had learned many things about him in the time they had spent together. His honor bound him to see the promise through. He would use every means within his power to ensure that soon, very soon, she would be reunited with the kumpania.

Ah, a fine man, Reese Carrison. Smart and generous and thoughtful. Even Mama would have to agree.

Liza did not feel so lonely now, in his house, in his tub. He wanted her to stay here with him. He would not mock her or show contempt, not like his hateful friend, Jack Hadley.

The water lapping about her shoulders and neck eventually cooled, taunting her skin with a chill. Abruptly, she sat up and soaped a thick washcloth. She had been lazy long enough. There was work to be done. She had a promise of her own to keep.

And Reese would be home soon.

George Steenson dried the last of the whiskey glasses and set it on the shelf beneath the mahogany bar. Out of habit, he swiped his towel across the glistening top, then folded the damp fabric into a neat rectangle and draped it over a brass knob. He sighed heavily.

At a far table, several cowboys, the only patrons in the saloon, gambled their wages on a quiet game of poker. George had little inclination to join them, as was his custom when business was slow at the Empty Saddle. He just wasn't in the mood for it.

He'd had no word on the whereabouts of Mr. Carrison. No one had. If he'd been found, or even that dadblamed Gypsy girl he went chasing after a couple of days back, George would've heard by now.

He expected the worst. Reckon everyone did.

And a damned shame it was, too. Mr. Carrison and his railroad were the best thing that had happened to Niobrara City. He'd taken the little town under his wing and made it grow. He gave Niobrara City respect, a sense of purpose, a place of prominence on the Nebraska prairie. Just wouldn't be the same without him.

Splaying his arms wide, George gripped the edge of the bar with both hands and gazed unseeing out a saloon window. He shook his head grimly.

Bram Kaldwell sure was taking it hard. Yesterday, after spending long hours in the rain with other concerned citizens looking for Mr. Carrison, he'd come back, defeated and worried. Didn't seem fair to lose a good friend like that, George mused. Not with Bram hoping to marry his widowed daughter off to him and all.

Shrugging aside his troubled thoughts, George turned and made a half-hearted attempt to take inventory of his liquor supply. If he intended to get an order sent to Omaha, he'd best quit feeling so danged morose and get back to work. He had a saloon to run.

Dutifully, his pencil scratched across a sheet of paper. Though intent on his task, his practiced ear detected the soft scrape of a boot sole on the wooden floor behind him. George lifted his head and glanced into the large mirror hanging behind the bar.

A Gypsy stared back. Stiffening, George set the pencil down and faced him.

"What'll it be, son?"

He asked the same question of every customer who patronized the Empty Saddle, but his gaze darted suspiciously about the room. He half-expected to see a whole group of the dark-skinned people, none of whom could seem to go anywhere without their father, brother, uncle, or cousins tagging along.

Yet the young man was alone. George relaxed. One Gypsy wouldn't be too much trouble.

"A beer." Brown fingers slid a gold coin across the bar.

"Comin' right up." He tilted a glass beneath the barrel-shaped keg's tap and covertly watched the Gypsy in the mirror.

George guessed him to be about seventeen. A dusty wool cap covered most of his shaggy, jet-black hair. Several days' growth of youthful stubble shadowed his chin and upper lip, and a weariness dulled the piercing, black eyes. The kid looked like he could use a good night's rest.

"What brings you to these parts?" George asked, setting the glass in front of him. Beer sloshed over the edge and slithered down the side; he dropped the coin into the till.

"I am looking for someone." The Gypsy lifted the glass and gulped heartily, his throat bobbing with every long swallow.

"Reckon I know most everybody around here. This someone got a name?"

He eyed George with obvious distrust. "You would not know her."

"I might."

Contempt flashed across his features. He dragged his threadbare shirtsleeve across his mouth. "She would not come in here. How would you know her?"

George fingered his graying, handlebar mustache thoughtfully. "Not much happens in a town this size that everyone doesn't hear about sooner or later. Maybe I can help you, son. You lookin' for kin?"

The fight seemed to go out of him. He nodded. "My sister."

George had heard enough about Gypsies to know they would never voluntarily leave their womenfolk behind. Especially one alone. Sympathy welled inside his chest.

"The only Gypsy I know about got in a bit of trouble here a couple of days back. Something about trying to steal a little girl. Might she be the one?"

Outrage sparked from the ebony eyes. "She would never steal a Gajo's child! Only the Gaje would accuse her of something so foolish!"

George held up a hand. "Simmer down now, son. That's not the point, is it? Point is, might she be the one?"

Pride stiffened the young man's spine. "Your people are too quick to blame the Gypsy. Yes, she is the one."

"I see."

George wrestled with the notion of telling him Bram and the others had found no sign of her and Mr. Carrison, that the Niobrara had been a raging monster, and the storm had been heartless, that they all feared the worst.

Furrowed lines at the ends of the young Gypsy's mouth and between his dark brows revealed the responsibility he carried on his shoulders. The desperation to find her. The panic and fear that he would fail.

George decided he had a right to know.

"There was a chase," he began quietly. "Mr. Carrison, a respected townsman here in Niobrara City, took after her.

153

Seems she stole his horse. Naturally, he wanted him back."

"Liza was riding a horse?"

He nodded. "A fine horse. Mighty fine. Mr. Carrison had a hell of a run on his hands. That horse can't be beat."

The Gypsy appeared to take hope from the news. "Do you know where she—they—went?"

"That there's the problem, son." George grimaced. "They haven't been found yet. Far as I know, nobody's seen hide nor tail of 'em in all this time."

"None?" Stricken, the young man stared. A low, moaning sound slipped from his throat, and his chin dropped to his chest, his head rolling back and forth in obvious despair.

"Now that don't mean they aren't doing just fine somewheres," George hastened to reassure him. "We just haven't found them yet." He hesitated. "Have you checked the jail?"

"I have checked everywhere. And I will not give up until I find her." Proud determination seemed to inject a new energy into him. He lifted the glass to his lips and finished off the remaining beer in one gulp. He stepped away from the bar.

"They headed north, if that's any help to you," George said softly.

Gratitude flittered across his features before the Gypsy banked it with a veil of haughtiness. "My sister is very strong. With a horse beneath her, Liza will save herself. I know I will find her."

"Good luck to you, son."

With a curt nod, he headed toward the saloon door, then disappeared into the street.

His visit did little to salve George's troubled mood. With another heavy sigh, he dropped the beer glass into a pan of soapy water and wiped the beer spill until the bar reflected its usual shine. That done, he picked up his pencil and forced his attention back to the liquor supply list.

"What's a man gotta do to get a drink around here?"

George jumped at Bram Kaldwell's gruff greeting. He set the pencil down again.

"Sorry, Bram. Didn't hear you come in. Reckon I got too much on my mind." Dismayed at his carelessness, he scrambled to serve his old friend. "What'll it be? The usual?"

Bram nodded, and George reached for a bottle of Old Town gin and splashed an exact amount in a small glass.

"Found Reese and the Gypsy girl today," Bram grunted with a frown.

Gin jerked over the edge of the glass and onto George's hand. "What?"

"Just this morning. They've been staying at Jack Hadley's place all this time. Both of them fit as a fiddle."

"Lord Almighty." George set the glass down with a sloppy thud and scuttled around the end of the bar. With as much speed as his arthritic knees would allow, he hurried to the saloon's door and thrust it open wide.

He found no sign of the young Gypsy. Stepping onto the boardwalk, he scrutinized both sides of the street, his gaze darting right and left and all around the townspeople, horses, and rigs for a glimpse of him.

But the dark-skinned youth had already disappeared. George cursed himself for not taking better note of the direction he'd gone. If only Bram would have arrived five minutes sooner . . .

Saddened by the poor timing, he returned to the bar.

"What was that all about?" Bram asked and propped one boot heel over the brass rail.

George refilled the glass with the proper amount of gin and reached for the tonic water. "That Gypsy girl you found with Mr. Carrison. Her name Liza?"

"I believe that's what he called her. Why?"

"Her brother was just in looking for her. The kid was pretty worried."

Bram scowled and downed the drink. "Rotten luck he couldn't have found her sooner and taken her back with him. The girl is going to be nothing but trouble."

"That so?"

"Yes." His features sullen, Bram handed him the empty glass in mute invitation for another. George obliged him. "Worst of it is, I think Reese has taken a fancy to her. And where the hell does that leave my Rebecca Ann?" He tipped his hat onto the back of his head and wearily rubbed a hand over his face. "The Gypsy is no good for him. Why can't he see that?"

"Maybe he will, Bram. In time. Going through a twister together like they did is bound to make friends out of 'em. Reckon it's harmless." Tending bar at the Empty Saddle Saloon had taught him a skill for lending an ear to a man's troubles and offering advice. Words of comfort came easily. "Rebecca Ann's a mighty pretty woman. They'll be married one day. She'll make him a fine wife. You'll see."

His features doubtful, Bram fell silent. George wiped his hands on his apron and left him to his drink. He picked up the pencil.

Mr. Carrison was safe. George delighted in the news and admitted to a burning curiosity about this Gypsy girl named Liza. If she'd managed to catch Mr. Carrison's eye, she must be one hell of a woman.

Chapter Ten

Reese slid the wooden bar across the barn doors, straightened, and rubbed a hand along the back of his neck. God, he was tired. It'd been a hard day.

Dusk had long since settled over the prairie. He should've been home hours ago. But there'd been endless chores to do at Jack and Maudeen's, and he'd lent a hand organizing neighbors to help clear their place of the storm's wreckage. Afterward, it'd been slow going hauling the stallion home in his wagon. He'd been careful not to jar the lame leg while driving over the muddled roads.

Now, with the horse bedded down for the night, Reese looked forward to calling it a day. He headed for the house and halted in mid-stride.

A light shone in his kitchen. The golden glow reached out to him with welcoming arms and touched a corner of his soul.

His fatigue fell away like an unwanted cloak. It was a strange thing, having someone waiting for him when he came home. He couldn't recall having the pleasure before. He'd lived alone far too long.

Liza waited for him inside. The knowledge warmed him. He'd been half-afraid she'd be gone when he returned. She'd been on his mind all day.

His step quickened as much as his throbbing knee allowed, and he took the back stairs in a couple of awkward leaps. He pushed the door open wide.

The delightful scent of cinnamon and raisins assailed him. The kitchen blazed with brightly lit kerosene lamps and a homey warmth from the cast-iron stove. A pair of delicately browned loaves of bread sat cooling and next to them, a cake.

Liza stood at the table, her arm curled around a mixing bowl as she briskly stirred the contents. Barefoot, she wore only his white cotton shirt, the hem hanging down past her thighs and nearly reaching her knees, the sleeves rolled well past her wrists. She had slim, finely muscled legs, legs she would never reveal in public, but which were now his alone to see. Her hair tumbled and bounced about her back and shoulders in a red-gold profusion, and a heat that had nothing to do with her baking curled deep in his loins.

She glanced up at him in surprise. He shut the door without a word and moved toward her, drawn like a bee to honey.

She cried out in dismay. He froze.

"Do not walk on my clean floor with those muddy boots, Reese Carrison," she said, shaking her spoon at him in dire warning. "Or I shall have you scrub it all over again."

His mouth softened. "Yes, ma'am."

He retreated. Leaning against the door for support, he wriggled one boot off, then the other.

"Put them on the back step. I left a rug there for you to use."

"Okay, okay." Recalling the many hours he'd spent varnishing the wooden slats, he did as she bade without complaint.

Apparently satisfied, she resumed her stirring. Holding back a smile, he padded to her in his stocking feet, and leaning toward her, gripping the table's edge with both hands, he held her pinned between him and the table.

"You nag me like a wife, y'know that?" he taunted softly, his breath stirring the wisps of baby-fine hair along her temple.

She stood very still within the circle of his arms and glanced at him uncertainly. "I did not mean to offend you."

"You didn't." She smelled clean, fresh, like a field of rain-washed wildflowers. Unable to help himself, he dipped his head lower and nuzzled the shining tresses with the tip of his nose. Her scent filled him. "Enjoy your bath?"

"Very much." Her voice was hardly above a whisper.

"You make a fetching sight in my shirt."

Her cheeks pinkened; she clutched the bowl tighter. "I had nothing else to wear."

"It's okay." Over the top of her head, he noticed the laundered skirts, her blouse and chemise hanging on a rope near the stove's heat. He vowed to string her a line outside tomorrow.

"I hope you did not mind me going through your things."

"Not at all."

She bit her lip and glanced away. "You will not think I will steal something, then?"

Rebecca Ann's rash accusations tumbled back into his memory. And Jack Hadley's. No wonder she worried. "Help yourself to anything I have, Liza. I trust you."

Her dark eyes widened. "Do you?"

"Of course."

Relief floated over her features. And raw pride. It pleased Reese she believed him.

"You are late," she said, relaxing a bit and tilting her face closer to his. "I expected you home sooner."

"You're nagging me again." Her eyelashes were black as coal, thick and lustrous. From his close proximity, he could almost count every one.

She drew back. "I am not!"

She seemed so appalled he regretted teasing her. He grinned. "I got delayed at the Hadleys'. I hadn't intended on staying so long. Sorry."

"You must not be sorry. Your friends needed your help." Her full mouth pursed. "And Zor? He is doing well?"

"Very well. Made the trip back without a problem."

"That is good." She nodded her approval and resumed stirring in slow, thoughtful strokes. "I waited supper for you."

He could stand here like this all day long, keeping her close with his arms bracketed on either side of her, her sweet scent and innocent femininity surrounding him, warming him, filling him.

"What're you making?" he asked, angling his head and moving his jaw in a lazy sweep against her hair. He closed his eyes and savored the satin texture against his three-day-old beard.

"Icing. Do you like raisin cake? It is a Gypsy favorite."

"Smells delicious." Slowly, his eyes opened. He struggled to stay with the conversation.

"It is." She dipped a finger into the white frosting and opened her mouth to sample the confection, but Reese snared her wrist, bringing her finger into his mouth instead.

Her breath caught. His hand covered hers. With a slight sucking motion, he drew her finger deeper into his mouth and swirled his tongue along the tip. The icing melted quickly, but still he tasted, laving his tongue around her fingernail, one knuckle and then another, and back around again.

She breathed his name on a sigh and swayed subtly toward him, as if her knees could not quite hold her upright. Gently, he slipped her finger from his mouth, but kept her hand held to him, his lips forming a kiss across a moist knuckle.

He thought of taking the bowl from her and sliding it onto the table. He thought of undoing the shirt she wore, button by button, parting it wide and dragging the white cotton off her smooth shoulders. He thought of her standing before him, a masterpiece of womanhood, with breasts rounded and high and perfectly fitted to his palms.

He had only to lower his head mere inches and touch his lips to hers. He could do it so easily. Already, he knew their softness, their warmth, the way they felt eager and rolling beneath his. He could thrust his tongue inside her and know hers would be ready to meet him, to lead him in a timeless mating, to share with him the hot pleasure.

He thought of all those things. Lusted and craved. He thought of taking her right now, right here in the middle of the kitchen floor.

But he did not.

He clung tight to his dwindling rationality and realized he played a dangerous game with a beautiful woman who could never be his, who lived in a different world, but who wore next to nothing and whose lush curves and feminine softness invited his passion and weakened his control. How long could he resist her?

How long would he want to?

"I'll wash up," he said roughly and let her go.

She drew a breath, then resumed stirring with a vengeance. "I have water heated on the stove."

He needed some time to cool his blood. Hefting the heavy pot of water, he left the kitchen.

In the main room, a brisk fire snapped in the block and lighted his way toward the loft, which contained his bedroom. A tidiness not often seen from his own housekeeping graced the quarters. The usual stack of newspapers near the stairs had disappeared. There was no laundry basket of dirty clothes. Even the sorry-looking fern with its brown, shriveling leaves was nowhere to be seen.

Liza. Just thinking her name stirred his manhood anew.

She'd invaded his home and made it sparkle. She gave the house he'd labored to build a new life and meaning.

Had she done the same with his heart?

By the time Reese returned to the kitchen, Liza had iced the cake and prepared heaping portions of spicy rice and beef. Knowing he had worked up an appetite at the Hadleys' she filled his plate to near overflowing, then served herself a smaller amount. After pouring two cups of black coffee, she sat across from him at the table and tugged his shirt as far over her bare knees as she could.

"You spoil me, woman." His tawny eyes lifted from the steaming fare and smoldered in appreciation.

"A man needs to be spoiled once in a while," she said and treasured his words. An unexpected contentment wrapped around her just hearing them.

He picked up his fork and scooped up a mouthful of rice. Liza's glance lingered on him, watching him eat, captivated with the way the little muscles in his jaw worked every time he chewed.

He had shaved. His smooth cheeks lent an air of sophistication about him, a worldliness, that only added to his sensuality. She had thought him ruggedly handsome with his shadowy beard these past days, but this look reminded her of his success with his people, his town, his railroad. He inspired her awe.

A trill of arousal wound through her belly. His powerful presence filled the kitchen. The table. Her. She had learned of his preference for going shirtless in the time they had spent at the Hadley cabin, and he wore none now, having doffed his rumpled suit for a clean pair of denim jeans and nothing more.

She swallowed and picked up her fork. He might as well be naked. Deeply tanned and thewed with muscle, his chest filled her range of vision, dominated her thoughts. She imagined him at his train, laboring beneath the hot sun, sweat glistening over the bands of sinew, rendering his body hard and lean and a perfect match for her womanly softness.

Her fist curled against her belly as she tried to still the wild fluttering raging within. How could she eat when he excited her so?

"We managed to repair the Hadleys' cabin enough to make it livable," he commented, reaching for the cup of coffee. "Maudeen refused to spend the night anywhere but in her own home."

Lamplight gleamed off the onyx glints in his hair, casually swept back from his temples and forehead, as if he had run a comb through it quickly. Liza dragged her gaze away.

"Thank goodness the rain has stopped," she said and toyed with a mound of rice at the edge of her plate.

Nodding his agreement, he sipped the hot brew and set the cup back down. "Their place is a real mess. I don't know how they'll afford rebuilding. Their crops took a beating."

Drawn into the Hadleys' plight, Liza clucked her tongue in sympathy. "They are fortunate to have a friend like you to help them."

163

He shrugged. "I can offer Jack a job with the N & D. He can make some good money until winter sets in. I'll mention it to Bram."

Bram. The Gajo with the pipe and the kind eyes she had noticed at the train depot. The same Gajo who had intruded upon their kiss at the Hadleys' that morning and openly frowned his contempt.

"He does not approve of me, does he?" she asked, quietly.

Reese's chewing slowed. He regarded her steadily.

"No," he said.

She had expected nothing less than honesty from him. Even so, the bluntness of his reply hurt. Deeply.

"You are shamed in his eyes because he found you with me. You will be shamed even more when he learns I am staying with you now. In your home." Dismay dulled her appetite further. She set her fork down.

"I'll take care of Bram, Liza. You're my responsibility. Not his. Don't worry your pretty Gypsy head about him."

"How can I not? He is your friend. You respect him."

Reese's brow furrowed. Silently, he finished off the last of the beef, washed it down with coffee, and pushed his empty plate aside. He leaned toward her and rested his elbows on the tabletop.

"Bram Kaldwell took me in when I was just a runny-nosed kid with nowhere else to go. My mother had died a couple of weeks earlier, my father long gone. I refused to be sent to an orphanage, and he found me hiding in a boxcar outside Chicago. Cold and half-starved."

"Oh, Reese," she breathed, aching for the little lost boy he must have been all those years ago.

His features turned pensive. "He got me a job with the Chicago-Northern Railroad. Twelve years old, and I was doing man's work." He grunted, as if amazed he had survived it. "I grew up real fast that year."

"Bram paid me fair," he went on. "I saved what I could and spent the rest of my childhood in rail yards all over the country. Not a life I'd wish on any kid, but I learned the rail industry inside and out. I never wanted to do anything else. Reckon I owe Bram for that."

He nudged her plate closer to her. "Eat. Your supper's going to get cold." Obediently, she picked up her fork again, and he continued. "Railroads were moving west. When I came out here, I fell in love with the land. I was tired of riding the rails all the time. I was ready to settle down and decided Niobrara City would be the perfect place to build my own railroad. Bram agreed."

"You make it sound easy," she said, softly, knowing it wasn't.

A corner of his handsome mouth lifted. "It costs a small fortune to form a railroad, even one as small as the Nebraska-Dakota. I had amassed some savings, but it wasn't nearly enough. Even Bram, with all his wealth, couldn't afford it."

"And?"

"Knowing how much having my own railroad meant to me, Bram used his influence and formed a cartel of investors. He's the N & D's top financier. Reckon I owe him for that, too."

He leaned back in his chair and crossed his arms over his hair-dusted chest. Their eyes met.

"The point of all this is, I'll never have a friend better than Bram. I can't begin to think what I owe him for all he's done for me, but he's not my keeper, Liza. No one is. If I choose to let you stay with me in my house, that's my business. No one else's. Including Bram's. Okay?"

She was not sure. While she better understood his relationship with the older man, nothing changed the fact that Bram Kaldwell viewed her with disdain. To him, she was nothing more than a troublesome Gypsy who would be better off banished from the town than dealt with. She slid her empty plate aside.

And she had not forgotten the beautiful woman named Rebecca Ann.

"I hope my explanation soothes your worries, Liza. Where you're concerned, Bram's opinion doesn't matter to me." He stood and gathered their dishes. "We'll have dessert in front of the fire, okay?"

"If you wish."

He set the dishes in a pan, added soap, then poured the last of the heated water on top. Ripples of muscle rolled across his shoulders and back while he performed the domestic chore, and awareness crept into her tumultuous thoughts. She longed to go to him, wrap her arms around him, lose herself in his warmth.

But the privilege would never be hers.

"What of Rebecca Ann?" she blurted.

A dripping plate hovered in midair. "What about her?"

Liza bit her lip. She cursed herself for asking. "Never mind. It does not matter."

The lie hung between them. Liza cut a giant piece of still-warm cake and left the kitchen.

She did not bother to light a lamp in the main room. The flames drew her, offered comfort. She did her best thinking in front of a snapping fire, and she hunkered on her heels, Gypsy fashion, close to the heat.

The orange-red blaze worked at soothing her lagging spirits, and she tried hard to pretend she was back with the kumpania, a circle of wagons behind her, surrounded by her family in front of the campfire.

But she could not. She was here, in Reese Carrison's

world, in his house, and troubled by the woman in his life.

"Rebecca Ann is Bram's daughter. What else do you want to know?"

His voice came from behind her. Startled, Liza's glance darted up at him. He towered over her, both fists on his narrow hips, feet spread.

He reached for the cake she held; wordlessly, she gave it to him. He set it on a small, doily-covered table, then extended a long arm toward her.

Heart pounding, she straightened and took his hand. He led her toward the blue-tapestried couch and sat, pulling her down next to him.

"I don't want Rebecca Ann between us, Liza," he said. "I'll answer any question you have about her."

Her chin lifted; her pride surged full force. Did he think her a jealous shrew?

"She is your friend. I already know that. What else is there to tell me?" she demanded, her tone more defensive than she intended.

His tawny eyes bored into her. He seemed to strip away the layers of her pride and expose the naked truth beneath. Her chin scooted a fraction higher.

He twisted to face her; his shadowed gaze raked her from shirt collar to hem.

"Warm enough?" he asked, his mouth softening as if he liked what he saw.

"Very." She tugged at the white cotton.

He leaned toward her and took her bare foot in his palm, tucking her other beneath his denim-clad thigh. "You should wear socks, you know. Your feet are cold."

She had not noticed until now. His hands, still warm from the dishwater, massaged her arch and toes and ankle, gliding along her skin with a gentle firmness. Her pride fell away; her protests died unspoken. She could not pull away if she wanted to.

Never had she been so pampered. Imagine. Having her feet rubbed. She almost purred aloud.

Reese's brow furrowed thoughtfully.

"I watched Rebecca Ann grow up," he said. "She was always Bram's little girl, his pride and joy. Even though she never paid me much mind, I admired her. Hell, half the railroad did."

Liza hugged her knees and forced herself to listen.

"Eventually, she went away to school, then married and moved to St. Louis. When Michael died, I attended the funeral with Bram. Before then, it'd been years since I'd seen her. She had blossomed into a beautiful woman. One of St. Louis's social butterflies."

His mouth pursed. "That was last summer. In the meantime, the N & D became a reality. I'd planted roots in Niobrara City. And I realized I needed a wife."

Liza tucked her chin and thought of little Margaret Michelle, growing up without a father. "And Rebecca Ann needed a husband."

Reese nodded and reached for her other foot. "Bram was all for it. Still is. It's the perfect arrangement for everyone."

Arrangement? Did he feel no love for this woman and her child?

Liza frowned. Perhaps it was the way of the Gaje, but she would not have expected it of him. Reese Carrison was a man destined to have a great love. Of that, there was no doubt. She had read it herself, in his Heart Line.

Surely that love would come later. After he and Rebecca Ann were married and living together in this house.

This wonderful, magnificent house.

He had built it for her. Rebecca Ann. Bram Kaldwell's daughter. Liza's gaze stroked the room, wall to wall, ceiling to floor, the faint scent of fresh paint still in the air. Reese needed a woman to put the loving touches on his home, and Rebecca Ann would be the one.

A dull ache weighted Liza's heart. Why should that knowledge bother her? Why should it hurt?

She cursed herself for a fool.

She was getting too used to him. To his ways. To eating with him, instead of after him; of serving him from the front, not behind; of having him lick frosting from her finger and spoil her by rubbing her bare feet when they were only a little cold.

It had been easy. Too easy. How could she have been so weak?

It was the Gajo in her, she thought on a wave of miserable conviction. Mama's sin. The curse she had been born with.

Liza pulled her feet from Reese's grasp and stood. He glanced up at her, one brow raised.

"The hour is late," she said stiffly.

He watched her, clearly wary of her change in mood. "You can have my bed upstairs in the loft."

"No." She drew a breath. "It would not be right for another woman to sleep in this house before your betrothed—"

"Rebecca Ann isn't my betrothed," he said slowly, as if speaking to a child, as if it were imperative he make that fact clear. "I haven't yet asked for her hand."

"I will sleep outside," she said firmly.

He stared at her in disbelief.

"Do not look so shocked, Gajo. I have done it many times."

"That's the most harebrained thing I've ever heard of."

She shrugged. She would not let him sway her this time.

"Come on, Liza," he said, his tone heavy with exasperation. "Take my bed. I don't care what anyone else thinks. It's cold outside."

She headed for the door.

"I'm not kin to a woman sleeping alone in my yard!"

"I have slept in places far worse," she sniffed.

"But it's the *yard*, Liza, for damned sake!"

"I am not afraid of your yard."

He threw his hands up and muttered something about stubborn Gypsies. "Fine. Have it your way." He rose from the couch and jabbed a finger toward her. "But you wait right here until I get back. Hear me?"

Not quite brave enough to ignore the command, she curled her bare toes into the thick rug and waited.

He strode upstairs and returned moments later, his arms laden with folded blankets and a coverlet that dragged behind him, as if hastily pulled from its mattress. He tossed a thick pair of gray wool socks at her.

"Put those on. Refuse, and I'll put them on for you," he said with a growl, glaring at her.

She dared not utter a word of protest and complied, pulling them up to her knees. Her toes wiggled in the cushiony warmth.

He preceded her outside. Chilly air blasted against her fire-warmed cheeks, and she shivered. Some of her resolve left her. She eyed the front lawn with trepidation.

Reese laid a rubber blanket on the grass, then spread the others on top. He stood back, glowering, and waited.

"Thank you," she said and swept past him, lowering herself onto the bedroll and snuggling into the blankets.

He seemed about to say something, but thought better of it.

"I'll see you in the morning," he said roughly. At the front door, he hesitated, throwing a glance over his shoulder. Shaking his head, he went inside. The door latched behind him.

With Reese's departure, the darkness surrounded her, pushing away the Gaje world and comforting her with the familiarity of her own. Lying on the ground, the crisp night air filling her lungs, the tiny stars twinkling down at her, she could pretend Paprika and Putzi were burrowed next to her, that Mama and Nanosh, Tekla and Hanzi were near.

But she could not sleep. Her gaze roamed the yard, admiring its tidiness even in the dark, and succumbing to fanciful musings, she envisioned flowers along the porch, a garden out back.

A garden. Her people never stayed in one place long enough to grow one, but she had gazed longingly at them during their travels, some with tomato plants so heavy with fruit the branches hung to the ground, so many tomatoes that the Gaje never noticed when the Gypsy ate their fill.

Would Rebecca Ann plant flowers and grow vegetables? Would she take pride in Reese's yard? In his house?

Liza could not imagine her with dirt under her fingernails or a scrub brush in her hand. Not the delicate, perfect Rebecca Ann.

She closed her eyes tightly and tried not to think of her. Or of Reese alone in his bed. Without her to keep him warm, as she had the past nights.

She rolled over to her side and tried to quell the longings her thoughts inspired. She had made the right decision to come outside, Liza reassured herself firmly. With Reese, she had abandoned the Gypsy ways. For a little while, he made her forget. Sleeping away from his house would remind her of her people, her world, and where she belonged.

At last, sleep beckoned. Dreams took her, dreams of yellow checkered curtains, of wonderfully modern stoves and iceboxes, and of raisin cake dripping with sweet white icing.

Chapter Eleven

A rooster's cheerful crow ended Liza's slumber, forcing her eyelids open and inviting a languid stretch beneath the toasty-warm blankets. Sighing, she shifted to her back and blinked against the shining sun.

The dew-fresh morning held an invigorating bite that awakened her fully. She put off rising, taking a moment or two to orient herself and recall the events of the previous night, where she slept and why.

A movement near the porch caught her attention. Reese approached, his features hidden beneath the black felt hat pulled low over his forehead. Liza pushed herself to a sitting position and speared a hand through her hair, tousled from lack of a braid.

Unsure if he was still annoyed with her, she watched him. His gait had lost some of its limp, and she knew a flare of relief that his twisted knee had finally begun to heal. A faded pair of Levi's hugged his hard thighs, a tan shirt clung to his wide shoulders, scuffed boots rode his feet. He looked rugged and utterly masculine, and Liza's heart responded with an unsteady beat.

He hunkered beside her, bringing himself down to her level. Beneath the hat's brim, his tiger eyes, unfathomable, intense, rested on her. She boldly met his gaze and waited for his reproval.

But he said nothing. Instead, he handed her a cup, its contents steaming in the cool air. Matching his silence, Liza took it from him and curled both hands around the hot sides.

She waited.

He tore his glance from her and stared out across the horizon. She studied his profile, so strong in the morning light, his chin square and defiant, his jaw faintly stubbled. The cotton shirt, open at the throat, revealed a sprinkling of dark hairs beneath the red bandanna tied loosely at his neck.

"I missed you last night," he said roughly.

Liza's pulse tripped and hammered. The words sounded torn from him, as if he had not wanted to admit them, even to himself. A maiden heat formed between her legs and spread deep within her belly. She drew her knees up tight and resisted the sensation.

Triumph coaxed a tiny smile to her lips. He had missed *her,* not Rebecca Ann. He had been as affected as she by the nights they spent sleeping in front of the fire at the Hadleys' cabin.

"I missed you, too," she said softly.

He grunted, as if unconvinced she suffered worse than he.

Deeply pleased at his scowl, she lifted the cup to her mouth and sipped, expecting coffee and tasting hot, sweet chocolate instead. She had not had the treat in a very long time. Liza's pleasure grew. Reese Carrison was a man full of surprises.

"I have to go into town this morning. I have business to attend to with the N & D," he said, his gaze returning to hers. "I'd like you to go with me."

As quickly as it blossomed, her pleasure died. Niobrara City? With its hostile citizens who had accused her of kidnapping Margaret Michelle? Lowering her lashes, she tightened her fingers around the cup.

"I think not," she murmured.

He squinted into the sun. "People will know you're staying with me by now. It's best to meet gossip head-on."

"I do not want to shame you by having your friends see you with me."

"Under the circumstances, my friends will understand. The others, I don't give a damn about."

A moan of indecision slipped through her lips. She had no desire to see the Gaje's contempt for a Gypsy, and yet to spend the day with him. . . .

Lean fingers snared her chin, forcing her to face him. Tigerlike eyes appealed to her. "Come with me, Liza. You need some clothes and provisions for the kitchen. And I'll send out a few telegrams, try to locate your family."

"Oh, Reese," she breathed, unsure what to do.

A corner of his mouth lifted. He released her chin. "I promised to show you a telegraph, remember?"

A telegraph. How could she refuse a glimpse of this amazing machine that would help him find her people? Excitement welled up within her.

"I will be ready whenever you say," she promised and scrambled from beneath the blankets.

He rose. "I'll see to the chores, then meet you out here when I'm done."

She nodded and headed toward the house.

"Liza?"

She halted and glanced at him expectantly.

His hot gaze ran over her, clear down to the wool socks sagging on her shins.

"That shirt will never be the same again," he said wryly.

A blush touched her cheeks. She laughed softly and ran into the house, hurrying to brush her hair and wash.

After fastening the last of her skirts, Liza smoothed the fabric over her hips. She had chosen the best for a top skirt, the magenta, for it was the newest, the color the brightest. Thank the good saints she had had time to launder them. It would not do to embarrass Reese in front of his people with clothing torn and dirtied from mud.

She reached for the gold-and-crimson striped kerchief, but thought better of it. She would wear her hair uncovered today, bound only by a loose braid. With Reese at her side, she did not care what the Gaje thought of a Gypsy with coppery-red hair.

At last, she was ready. She lingered at the stove, however, stirring cream into a pan of water and chocolate, careful to raise a rich froth on top. A second cup of the sweet drink to take on the ride into Niobrara City would be delightful.

Suddenly, the back door crashed open behind her. She cried out in alarm and whirled about in a frenzy of skirt hems.

The Wild One.

Her heart leaped to her throat. He stood in the doorway, dwarfing the opening with his bulk. A knife in his enormous hand, buffalo skins on his mammoth shoulders, he clomped into the kitchen.

"You Carrison's woman?" he boomed, rage shimmering in his beady eyes.

He was like an enraged grizzly bear. From somewhere deep inside her, a ball of fear exploded.

"Get out," she rasped.

"Not 'til I find him. Where is he?"

He sheathed the knife and lumbered closer, ever closer. He could crush her with one swipe of his powerful fist. She inched backward and thought of the pan of chocolate, hot on the stove.

"Where's Carrison?" he thundered.

With more speed than she would have thought possible, he spread his mammoth arms wide and lunged toward her. Instinctively, she reacted, twisting, her hands finding the pan handle and blindly hurling the simmering contents at him.

He roared in surprised pain and staggered back. Chocolate dripped from his straggly beard onto the buffalo hide. Appearing dazed, he blinked and ran his tongue around his thick lips.

His gaze slammed into hers. His features contorted in renewed rage. With a bellow that shook the rafters, he leaped toward her again.

This time, she had nowhere else to go. His huge hands gripped her shoulders, and she rammed into the wall, jarring her insides with the force and stopping any hope of escape. A scream tore from her throat.

The meaty paws gave her a mighty shake. Her teeth rattled inside her head. She squirmed and kicked with a panic-driven strength she did not know she possessed.

"Damn you to hell, McCrae! Let her go!"

The Wild One froze, his ears pricked to Reese's yell. He grunted and whipped around, dropping Liza without a backward glance. She gulped for air and sagged against the wall.

"Carrison." McCrae snarled the word and moved toward him. "Heard tell you was missin', then I heard you was found agin. Too bad. I was hopin' you'd turn up dead."

"Wouldn't give you the satisfaction, you son of a bitch." A Winchester rifle was braced in both hands. Reese's gaze, sharp, assessing, never left him.

"Yer time's done run out. Jest like Lester when you killed him."

"Lester's death was an accident. I didn't kill him. You know that."

The words circled around Liza's head. McCrae kept moving as if Reese had never spoken.

"And you know I ain't standin' fer yer railroad smokin' up the sky with stink. Yer dirtyin' God's land with miles of track. Yer ruinin' my home and Lester's, and I ain't gonna stand fer it. Not anymore than he did." He halted and swiped a big hand across his beard. He glanced over his shoulder, as if remembering Liza was behind him.

"So what're you waiting for? I'm here. You found me."

Incredibly, Reese uncocked the rifle and sent it sliding across the floor. He straightened. The Wild One watched him closely, clearly unsure what Reese intended. His beefy hand unsheathed the knife at his waist.

"C'mon, McCrae. Let's settle this right now." Reese lifted his arm, beckoning him, taunting him. "Come and get me."

For a moment, the other man did nothing. In the next, a sinister laugh filled the kitchen, stroking Liza's spine with horror.

"I bin waitin' fer this fer a long time, Carrison. Ever since Lester died." The blade sliced the air in a wide arc. He crouched, but did not move closer.

"What's the matter? An innocent woman more to your liking?" Reese prodded him.

The jab worked. McCrae roared and lunged toward him. Reese easily jumped back into the doorway, evading his grasp, and in that instant, Liza realized he was baiting the

177

Wild One, goading him outside, away from her. A sob rose in her throat.

McCrae lunged again, hurling his weight against Reese. They fell against the door and tumbled down the back steps in a tangle of legs and fists and buffalo skins, each man grunting and cursing and rolling over the other.

Heart pounding, Liza bolted toward the rifle and snatched it from the floor. Running outside, she pulled back the hammer and aimed the weapon as best she could at Silas McCrae.

But it was no use. Neither man stayed still long enough to give her a clear shot. Fearful of the knife's blade glinting dangerously in the sunlight, she swung the barrel toward the sky and pulled the trigger. The blast reverberated in her ears.

She had their attention. Both men burst apart. McCrae darted an uneasy glance at Liza, and Reese took advantage of the mistake. His foot lashed out, and he kicked the knife from McCrae's grasp, sending it skidding out of sight.

McCrae made no effort to find it. Breathing heavily, his stance ready to take any blow Reese might send his way, he spat a mocking laugh.

"You put up a mean fight, Carrison. Didn't think a dandified railroad man like you had it in him."

Reese swiped at the blood trickling down his chin. "Get off my land. Leave me and what's mine alone."

"Not 'til I die. That damned railroad of yers is no good."

"Leave the N & D alone."

"Bringin' in poachers and killin' off the animals. A man can't hunt, can't trap, not with some goddamned whistle blarin' all of the time and scarin' away what animals are left. Hell no, Carrison, I ain't leavin' it alone." He bent and scooped up his coonskin hat from the ground.

"Railroads are this country's future, McCrae. We're not

out to take your livelihood. You'll rest easier when you understand that."

"Rest easy? When there's people crawlin' all over the place? Crowdin' me out?"

"It's called 'progress,' McCrae. There's plenty of room in this country for you and the rest of us."

"Me and Lester never wanted your lousy progress. He aimed to stop it. Same as me. And the only way to end it is to destroy your damned railroad. That'll halt it for sure."

Alarm crawled up Liza's spine at the deadly promise in his tone. He yanked the hat onto his tousled head, turned abruptly and lumbered toward his horse. He hefted his bulk into the saddle and jabbed a dirty finger toward Reese.

"Consider yerself warned, railroad man. Y'hear me?" He crackled in satisfaction, as if already plotting a new revenge. "Consider yerself warned."

Long after Silas McCrae left, Reese kept Liza within sight at all times, even going into the barn with her while she tended to Zor and his tender leg. She was glad for it. The fierce fur trapper's attack had scattered her wits and left her shaken to her toes.

He was a man with unclean spirits, possessed by Satan himself. Liza crossed herself in prayer to God every time she thought of him.

Yet, his revelations troubled her. Reese Carrison had killed a man? A Gajo named Lester? Liza could not believe it.

She did her best to put the Wild One from her mind. Assured the stallion would rest comfortably while they were gone, she returned to the kitchen and packed a light lunch in a tin pail. Reese waited for her outside, and she left the house to join him.

He had parked a buggy on the lawn. One boot propped

on a wheel spoke, his forearm resting on a bent knee, he stared into the distance. A cigarette dangled from between two fingers.

The grass rustled beneath her feet as she approached. He straightened. His gaze, like sunbaked whiskey, burned over her, from the earrings swaying in her ears, to the strands of beads about her neck, to the bottoms of her skirt hems and back up again.

He carried the cigarette to his lips for one last drag before flicking the stub away. With no words between them, he reached for her. She went to him, and he took her tight against him. She molded to his embrace, her arms curling around to his broad back.

"Doing okay?" he asked quietly.

She nodded against his hard shoulder. "Better than you, I think."

He made no reply. Instead, the sinewy muscles beneath her palms flexed, as if he relived the scuffle with Silas Mc-Crae yet again in his mind.

"He is wicked," she murmured.

"He's hell-bent on revenge."

She drew back and peered up into his shaded expression.

"Why?" she asked.

His troubled gaze rested on her for a long moment. He pulled her back against him.

"Lester McCrae was Silas's uncle. Raised him from a kid. Far as I know, old Lester was the only family Silas had. They were two of a kind. Cut from the same cloth. They lived off the land and kept to themselves. Hell, years would go by before anyone caught sight of them."

Liza could not imagine two men living so alone, not when she'd been surrounded by dozens of her own family every day of her life.

"They were against civilization. Against people." A corner of Reese's mouth lifted. "Against railroads. We had no idea how *much* they hated us until the night Lester was killed. Only then, did we learn that he and Silas intended to destroy the N & D."

"But your railroad is big and covers many miles. How can only two men do such a thing?" Liza struggled to comprehend the depth of the men's evil.

"Treachery, darlin'. Destruction of railroad property. Any time and any way those two could manage it. They figured it cost money—lots of it—to make repeated repairs to tracks and the train itself." His jaw tautened as he scrolled through the memories. "They were right. They figured the investors would pull out if the N & D proved to be a bad investment. They were right about that, too."

Again, Liza pulled back to study him. Reese had endured so many worries for his precious railroad. Yet he won over them. The N & D had become a reality. His pride and joy.

"How did Silas's uncle die?" she asked softly.

His gaze met hers, steady and unflinching. Without guilt.

"We'd been forced to keep a guard posted while we were building the trestle bridge. We had a fortune tied up in lumber and supplies, and I couldn't take a chance on losing it all on the McCraes' subversion. Late one night, when I was taking a guard shift, I discovered Lester trying to release the brake on one of the cars filled with rails and ties. Since the bridge was only half-built, the car would have started rolling along the track, then plunge into the canyon. I fired a warning shot, hollered at him to stop. In his haste to get away, he slipped under the car. By then, he'd released the brake, and the car had started to move. I managed to stop the car by resetting the brake, but it was too late." Reese hesitated. "The wheels cut him in two. There was nothing I could do. I'd never even come close to the man."

She shuddered. "But Silas blames you."

"Yes."

"You were very brave to fight him," she said soberly and touched a finger to his puffy bottom lip.

He grunted. "Damn near gave me heart failure when I saw him attacking you."

"You must be very careful." An ominous dark feeling came over her. All her years of fortune-telling had never produced such certainty of continued trouble for his railroad.

"I know." A grimness crossed his features. "He's threatened me before. But it scares me he'd go through you to get to me."

"Do not worry so. He did not hurt me."

"This time." Somberly, Reese's arms loosened. "We'd best be going. My men need to be prepared when McCrae retaliates yet again against the N & D." He gestured to the buggy. "Ever ride in one of these before?"

"Never." She eyed the fine-looking rig with its tufted leather seat and elegant fringe along the canopy and shook her head for emphasis. She was glad not to have to think about Silas McCrae, even for a little while.

"Then it's time you do." From beneath the shadowed brim, he regarded her. "There are ways a lady must act, Liza," he said. "It doesn't matter if we're in town surrounded by many people or out here by ourselves."

Unsure what he expected of her, she cocked her head. Did he think she would shame him somehow?

"A man always helps a lady into a buggy. And he helps her down again. When we get to Niobrara City, you're not to walk behind me or some such thing Gypsies are inclined to do. I'll offer you my arm, and you'll walk at my side."

Liza contemplated his words and pursed her lips dubiously. She had never been given such privileges before.

A corner of his mouth tilted, as if he knew what she was thinking. "You're in my world now. We treat womenfolk a tad differently than the *Rom*. A man gives a lady his protection. But most of all, he gives her his respect. I'll do the same with you."

Her heart melted. To be treated like this, revered and honored . . . She lowered her lashes and swallowed down an unexpected welling of emotion.

It was her long-held dream. She had shared her cherished longings to be a lady with no one, yet Reese promised to make the dream come true this very day.

He humbled her. And made her feel proud.

Her chin came up. "I shall try not to embarrass you in front of your people. I will do as you say."

"Takes a lot to embarrass me, Liza. You'll do fine. Just follow my lead." He patted the leather seat. "Ready?"

"Yes."

He extended his hand. Feeling silly accepting his assistance when she was perfectly capable of climbing in herself, Liza laid her palm against his and stepped into the buggy. Settling upon the padded cushion, she tucked her skirts primly about her and put the pail at her feet.

Reese climbed up beside her and took the reins, giving them a firm slap on the sorrel's rump. The rig leaped forward, rolling easily from the yard onto the road leading to Niobrara City.

She marveled at the smooth ride, nothing like the creaking and groaning lurches from Nanosh's old wagon. She leaned over the edge of her seat to run an appreciative glance along the buggy's sleek frame. Enthralled, she reached up and fingered the fringe dancing along the canopy borders.

"There are rigs a lot nicer than this," Reese said, amused.

"I bought this one secondhand and fixed it up."

She sighed happily. "It does not matter if it is not new. To me, it is beautiful. So shiny and elegant."

She sighed again and clasped her hands tightly in her lap. Her back stiff and straight, she did her best to look like a lady. It was not too hard. She already felt like a queen.

Wild grasses, so bountiful on the Nebraska prairie, swayed gently in the breeze. Beneath the buggy's wheels, little clumps of gravel crunched and skittered into the road-side ditch. The sweet smell of clean air blew into Liza's face and tugged at her braid.

"I will buy Mama a kerchief today," she said, remembering her failed attempt with Paprika and Putzi days earlier. The wad of Gaje dollars she had earned from her baskets was still safe in her pocket.

"I'm sure she'd like that."

"I have already picked the color. She is very embarrassed she has no hair, you know. A new kerchief will make her feel pretty."

As soon as the words were out, her breath caught in her throat. Aghast, her eyes darted to Reese.

What had made her blurt the reason for Mama's shame? What would he think?

"No hair? What happened?" he asked. A vein of curiosity laced his tone, but nothing more, not a shred of the disdain or disgust or mockery she expected.

None.

What remained of the walls once erected between their worlds, dividing them, holding them apart, crumbled and fell like age-old ruins. For Liza, there was nothing to stand between them now, not the Gaje, not the Gypsies, but instead a glorious bond of trust and friendship she had not thought to feel with a Gajo before, but which she felt with Reese Carrison.

Deeply. Intensely. Freely.

She told him everything, then. Mama's sin. The strict judgment handed down to her by the kris. Nanosh and his aloof love, her despair of ever finding a husband, her shame from being different from her people.

He listened, asking questions now and again in his low voice, dragging his glance from her only to check the horse's direction, but bringing it back immediately thereafter.

When she finished, Reese braked the buggy to a stop, right in the middle of the road. She glanced at him uncertainly. He turned to her and cupped the back of her head, pulling her toward him. He took her mouth to his, boldly, wordlessly, with not a care for the time of day or lack of privacy or that she was Gypsy and he was a Gajo intended for another.

His lips moved across hers with a deliberate skill, as if he was determined to soothe the past with the devastating power of his kiss. The ploy succeeded, for Liza could think of nothing but the hot pressure of his mouth inflaming her senses. Her resistance flew to the wind; a sighing moan of pleasure escaped her.

Too soon, the kiss ended, yet he lingered, toying with her bottom lip with his teeth, teasing her with the tip of his tongue. She breathed in the scent of him, the taste of him, reluctant to let him go.

He drew away. Desire smoldered in the depths of his eyes, a golden fire he kept tightly banked. She could not meet the intensity of his gaze. He left her too weak, too tormented with longings not quite proper.

"Why did you kiss me like that?" she whispered.

"To prove to you you're worthy of a man," he murmured. "No matter what your people think."

"Oh, Reese." Would she ever make him understand the

ways of the Gypsies, that the Gajo blood flowing in her veins could never be accepted?

"I respect your customs and beliefs. Don't think I don't. But when it comes to you, the Gypsies aren't playing fair." He reached toward her and snared her chin, forcing her to look at him. "We're going to set a few tongues to wagging when we get into town. I want you to know"—the pad of his thumb stroked her jaw, inciting shivers of tingles down her spine—"I'm proud to have you on my arm. Okay?"

Hesitantly, she nodded. A tremulous smile hovered on her lips.

"All right, then. Let's go. I have friends I want you to meet."

He took the reins once again, and the buggy rolled down the road. Liza basked in the warmth of his avowal, made even more glorious by his kiss, still moist upon her mouth. God's saints. Her pulse raced a wild course even now.

But as they drew within the township limits, Liza's confidence wavered. The mid-morning hour yielded few travelers upon Niobrara City's streets. Reese's shiny buggy alone claimed the road and drew the eye of those strolling upon Main Street's wooden boardwalks.

Many stared openly, their curiosity obvious. Women put their bonneted heads together and whispered among themselves; children pointed pudgy fingers; men stopped in mid-task, tilting their hats back to better see across the street, and narrowed their eyes in silent contemplation.

Liza could imagine their minds spinning like a child's top. A wisp of panic curled through her. Reese Carrison, respected, held in high esteem by his people, had just come to town with a Gypsy, accused of stealing a horse and a child and who stayed with him unchaperoned at his magnificent house.

No wonder they stared.

A rueful smile chased away her trepidations. She guessed that, in their place, she would stare, too.

Reese maneuvered the rig to the edge of the street and set the brake. He dismounted, and she waited while he tied the reins at a hitching post, then returned to the buggy for her.

His strong hands spanned her waist, and he helped her to the ground but did not immediately let her go.

"What's in the pail?" he asked.

Scant inches separated them. His hard thighs touched against hers; his hat's brim shaded the sun from her own eyes as much as his. She peered up at him, catching the reckless gleam in his gaze. She sensed his keen awareness of the stares centered upon them and that he deliberately held her close because of them.

Two could play the game, she decided. Leaning against him, she placed a hand upon his solid chest and coyly toyed with a button on his shirt.

"Our lunch." She lifted a shoulder delicately and gave a languid blink of her lashes.

For the second time in precious few minutes, desire flickered and flared beneath his hooded gaze. A man's desire for a woman, powerful and potent. Liza had not thought it possible before, but it had been she, and none other, who had roused it in him.

"We'll come back for it later," he said roughly, releasing her and turning her about, as if he could not trust himself to remain within the bounds of propriety a moment longer. He steered her away from the buggy, but a man's shout halted his step.

"Mr. Carrison! Wait, Mr. Carrison!"

From over the top of her head, he searched the board-walk. Liza turned and caught sight of a Gajo, a broom in his hand, hailing them from the boardwalk outside the Empty Saddle Saloon.

A crisp white apron covered his portly chest. He left the broom leaning against the building and hastened into the dirt street, pausing only to allow a buckboard wagon to rumble past. Behind him, Bram Kaldwell emerged from the saloon, a disapproving frown set upon his face.

"Good morning, George." Reese's hand slid to the small of Liza's back and stayed there.

"Mr. Carrison," the older man puffed, slowing to a stop in front of them. "Ain't you a sight for sore eyes! Don't mind sayin' you gave us all a fright when you showed up missin' a few days back!"

Reese grinned. "Afraid I didn't have much choice. That was one hell of a storm."

"Don't I know it. You all right?"

"Can't complain, considering what we went through."

George nodded in relieved understanding. His puffing slowed, and he slid his glance from Reese to Liza.

She endured his perusal. Keen and thorough, he seemed to inspect every inch of her until she fidgeted and wished for her kerchief.

"Mm-mm, she's a pretty one, Reese," he said. A smile spread across his features and crinkled the corners of his eyes. She sensed his kindness, rare for a Gajo. "Her name's Liza, eh?"

"It is." Reese's mouth crooked. "You heard about her, I gather."

"I did, but not from gossiping folk. Met her brother yesterday."

Liza squeaked. "My brother?"

"Didn't catch his name, little lady, but he was in my saloon asking about you."

Her fingers flew to her mouth. Her eyes widened and darted to Reese.

"Hanzi," she breathed. "Hanzi was here. Oh, my saints." She turned back to the other man. "Are you sure?"

He shrugged. "A nice-looking young'un, 'bout yay tall?" He held a hand out, indicating a height even with Liza's.

She nodded.

"Wears a wool cap? Hair to here?" He tapped the lower edge of his collar.

She nodded again.

"He's the one."

"Yes," she whispered, convinced. The Gajo spoke the truth.

"Where is he now?" Reese asked. His hand slid up from her back and settled upon her shoulder. He gave her a reassuring squeeze.

Regret clouded the kind face. "I don't know. Could be anywhere. He said he was going to keep looking 'til he found her." He grimaced. "Wish I had better news."

"Thanks for telling us." Reese inclined his head. "By the way, I believe proper introductions are in order."

"Of course, of course." George hastily smoothed back the silver strands of hair on his balding pate and stood very straight. He waited expectantly.

"Liza, allow me to introduce George Steenson, proprietor of the Empty Saddle Saloon," Reese said. "George, Liza of the Lowara tribe of Gypsies."

The Gajo practice of meeting one another captivated Liza, momentarily overshadowing her thoughts of Hanzi. Unsure what was expected of her, she reacted on pure instinct.

She extended her hand. George clicked his heels and grasped her fingers, bending low and dropping a light kiss on her knuckles.

Liza's lips parted in surprise.

"Pleasure to make your acquaintance," George said. "I've been mighty anxious to meet you."

"Thank you," she murmured.

"Will I see you again?"

"Most likely," Reese said, answering for her. "She's staying at my place. I'll bring her to town now and then."

George arched a brow and met Reese's challenging gaze. Whatever disapproval the older man might have felt about Liza's living arrangements quickly disappeared, however, as if his deep respect deemed any decision Reese might make as perfectly acceptable.

"I'll look forward to it. Until then, Liza, enjoy your day."

"I will. Thank you."

George hesitated. "You might want to send out a few wires, Mr. Carrison. They could help track down the boy."

"I intend to. If he should stop in the Empty Saddle again asking for Liza, send word to me, won't you?"

"You bet I will."

"Appreciate your help, George."

"Think nothing of it." George waved and hustled across the street back to his saloon. Bram Kaldwell, Liza noticed, was nowhere in sight.

"Mr. Steenson is a nice man," she said.

"You'll find most of Niobrara City just like him," Reese said.

From beneath her lashes, she peered at him doubtfully.

Nonplussed, he took her hand and settled it in the crook of his arm. Together, they strolled down the boardwalk toward the telegraph office.

Chapter Twelve

A bittersweet thing, wiring the telegrams.

The irony of it troubled Reese. He should have been happy to send them, for Liza's sake. Hell, it'd been a good idea. A fitting arrangement for their bargain. Do what he could to find her family in return for her healing his horse.

It was only fair.

But now that the job was done . . .

She would leave him. Inevitably, she would. She missed her family. She belonged with them. Of course, she would go back.

A heaviness weighted the pit of his belly.

Suddenly, the hours and minutes took on new meaning. Already the morning had fled, and the noon hour approached. How much time did they have left? How soon before the telegrams worked their magic and tracked down the elusive Gypsies, inviting their return for Liza?

Time. So little remained.

The visit to the telegraph office presented a new perspective of all he took for granted. Liza viewed his world through a child's eyes, with fascination and wonderment of all those things never before known to her. Up to now, her simple life had no need of electricity or a Morse code, but she'd taken it all in with amazing aplomb.

Estelle's Clothing Parlor had been no different. Liza had been unswayed by the expensive fripperies most women dallied over and had wheedled a bargain over a single kerchief, silk, and of the brightest yellow. She paid for her purchase herself, brushing aside Reese's offer to buy it for her with the teasing explanation her mother would be mortified wearing a gift that was marhime, tainted by a Gajo's money.

Reese understood when once he would've been puzzled. He'd adjusted to her ways, her beliefs. She fit so easily into his life.

Their last destination was Hutton's General Store. Liza hugged her small package to her breast as if the brown paper cuddled a priceless treasure instead of a yellow kerchief. She took his arm and regaled him with an amusing tale about Rollo, Hanzi's puppylike pet bear. Engrossed in the captivating way she told the story, the laughter in her voice, the dancing light in her black eyes, Reese nearly walked right past the mercantile.

He opened the door, and she stepped past him inside. Her glance swept the customers scattered about the organized clutter. Heads turned; conversation ceased. Everyone's gaze centered upon them.

Had Reese not known her so well, he might have missed the subtle lift to her chin, the slight stiffening of her spine. Lest she turn and bolt out the door again, or worse, hurl a curse upon them all, he grasped her elbow firmly and steered her toward the canned goods lined on shelves at the back of the store.

"Get what you need for the kitchen," he said.

"Will you help?" The intensity in her features bespoke a message her pride refused to reveal. "I do not yet know all the foods you like."

"Sure." His eyes met hers. "I'll not abandon you to the wolves, sweet," he said in a low voice. "I'll be right beside you."

She drew away with a haughty sniff. "Do you think I am afraid of your people? I have shopped in Gaje stores many times."

But she relaxed visibly and walked ahead of him with more confidence. Their path took them past three women, prim in their wide-brimmed bonnets, standing near an on-ion barrel. Reese recognized each of them, old biddies with nothing better to do than mill around and gossip about their friends and neighbors.

He tipped his hat and flashed them a broad smile.

"Enjoying the day, ladies?" he asked, aware they were enjoying it immensely just seeing him here with Liza. He doubted they'd had a tastier morsel for ruminating.

"Of course, Mr. Carrison."

"Lovely day, sir."

"Couldn't be better."

Reese kept walking. They broke into frenzied whispers as soon as he was past, and his smile broadened.

Now that Liza had arrived, Niobrara City would never be the same. He took an odd pleasure in the thought and lent his assistance in choosing their groceries. Liza piled cans of beans, tomatoes, and a bag of rice into his arms until he could hold no more. He set them on the counter for tallying; she added molasses, cakes of yeast and a tin of baking powder, giving him a hint of the meals she intended to prepare. Reese eyed the fare with appreciation and de-cided she'd spoil him against his own cooking for sure.

With the store's proprietor busy with two customers ahead of him, Reese settled in to wait his turn. Liza drifted toward the dress goods section. His gaze clung to the delicate sway of her hips and the slight curve of her buttocks beneath the skirt layers. Her bare ankles peeking from beneath the magenta hems, she moved with an unpretentious grace, an artful seduction to his senses he doubted she was aware of. A tight little sigh escaped him.

She halted, her attention snared by a bolt of purple-colored henrietta. She unwound a length, holding it toward the window light to examine the deep hues, then compared the yardage to another bolt in green. Her head cocked in silent consideration, as if she could not decide which she preferred.

Reese went to her and tapped his finger on the latter.

"This one," he said.

She darted him a surprised glance over her shoulder. "Do you think so? But the purple is very pretty. Rich enough for a king."

"True, but the green accents the red-gold glints in your hair." He wiggled the end of her braid to emphasize his point.

"Mr. Carrison is right." From behind them, a woman's shy voice joined in. "The green suits you. You'd look lovely in it."

Reese and Liza turned in unison. Maudeen Hadley, with little Jacob on her hip, peered over at them from a table heaped with fabric remnants. She tucked a cracker into her son's pudgy fist.

"You see? Maudeen agrees with me." Reese smiled. "We'll get the green. How much do you need?"

But his question hung in the air unanswered. Maudeen drew closer, and Liza tensed, her wariness of the other woman evident.

"How are you, Liza?" Maudeen asked softly.

Liza remained silent. Reese imagined her mind churning, weighing Maudeen's attempts to be friendly against her deep-seated contempt for the Gaje in general.

"I am good," she said finally. "And you?"

"Good." Maudeen extended her bandaged hand for view. "The burns are healing, thanks to you. And with Mr. Carrison's help, we made the most important repairs to the cabin. We have a roof and four walls, at least."

"I am glad to hear that."

"We came to town to get lumber and such. Jack and Toby are at the mill now."

"Oh. I see."

They seemed to have forgotten Reese, and he made no move to intrude. He sensed Maudeen's need to assuage her husband's rudeness and make amends for the hurt he'd inflicted on Liza.

Maudeen shifted her son to her other hip. "Would you like some help choosing notions? They have buttons here that would be lovely with the green henrietta."

Liza lowered her lashes and rewrapped the fabric around the bolt. "I had not intended on buying anything so frivolous as this. The cloth is beautiful, but I have no need of it."

"Not so fast." Reese reached forward and tugged the bolt from Liza's hand when she would have returned it to the shelf. "You've nothing to wear but the clothes on your back. I'll buy it for you."

"You will not."

Reese raised a brow. "Is my money marhime?"

She paled. "Of course not."

"Then why do you refuse?"

She chewed on her bottom lip.

Her damned noble pride again. His mouth flattened in

exasperation, and he tossed an appealing glance toward Maudeen. "Maudeen, tell her it's perfectly acceptable for me to do this for her."

Maudeen smiled gently. "It's true, Liza. Mr. Carrison's intentions are quite honorable. He's thinking only of your pleasure. What lady would refuse a gentleman's offer to buy her something pretty to wear?"

"Even if she has to make it herself," he added dryly.

Liza cast a helpless look at Reese.

"I am not accustomed—I have never—" Her lips clamped tight.

"Then it's time you enjoyed a man's attentions. Maudeen, see that she gets all she needs for a new dress, won't you? I'll step outside and have a smoke."

"Of course, Mr. Carrison." Jacob whimpered and squirmed in her arms, and she pulled another cracker from the canvas bag slung over her shoulder. He gummed it contentedly. "What style of dress did you have in mind, Liza? Something to wear in the coming winter?"

Liza ran a palm over the henrietta's lustrous texture.

"Perhaps a skirt with a blouse to match," she said, sending Reese an uncertain glance. "Long sleeves, with the skirt very full."

"Oh, how nice." Maudeen's face danced with feminine eagerness. Within moments, she had spools of thread, laces and braids, and an assortment of buttons laid out on the henrietta.

Head to head, shoulder to shoulder, the two women bent over the fabric. Maudeen, with her plain calico dress and sturdy work shoes, and freckles sprinkled over her fair features, could hardly be more different than Liza with her gay-colored skirts and jangling beads, olive skin, and sharp, black eyes, and yet a friendship had blossomed. Two cultures had merged. A fragile bond between a Gaja and a

196

Gypsy had formed over something as timeless as a shared interest in women's fashions.

Reese grunted in amazement and left them.

Outside Hutton's store, he blinked in the glaring sunlight and tugged his hat brim lower over his forehead. Dipping into a shirt pocket, he retrieved a rolled cigarette and lit it, then leaned against a wooden post and hooked a thumb into his waistband.

Niobrara City bustled with activity. The dirt streets rumbled with horses and wagons and a wide assortment of rigs. The rain-soaked land had begun to slowly dry out, enabling area farmers to return to the fields and bettering the roads for travel. Women and children scurried about making their purchases and chatting among friends in the norm of everyday living.

He looked forward to returning to his own routine. He hadn't stepped inside his office at the N & D for days; he missed his train, his men. As soon as Liza was ready, he'd walk down to the depot and feast his eyes on the great iron beast he called his.

And then he'd deal with Silas McCrae.

From the sea of faces moving about him emerged Bram Kaldwell. Reese watched him closely and hoped Maudeen kept Liza occupied a little while longer.

Bram's gaze touched on him for only a moment before he jerked it away. Outwardly, he looked the same in his expensive tailored suit and spit-shine boots, but an aloofness hung about him. A cool air as tangible as frost on a winter morning.

He halted near Reese and stared out into the street. Finally, he withdrew his pipe from inside his jacket.

"Fine day," Bram said. He squinted up at the clear sky and clamped his teeth on the stem.

"As long as it's not raining, it's fine enough for me."

Reese offered him a match. Bram made no comment to his rueful remark and lit the pipe, sending blue-gray clouds of smoke curling in front of him. They stood together in silence.

Finally, Reese straightened from the post and sought refuge in the one topic that had always bound them together.

"Been into the office yet?" he asked.

"No. Have you?"

"No, but I'm heading that way," he said.

Bram continued puffing. "I just came from the hotel. Went to see Rebecca Ann for a spell."

"Did you?" Reese endured a stab of guilt. He'd forgotten his promise to take her to dinner. "How is she?"

"She's doing well enough, but the baby's sick."

"Margaret Michelle?" Reese frowned. "What ails her?"

"Doc says it's measles. Quarantined 'em both for two weeks."

"Two weeks!" A vision of Rebecca Ann fretting over her daughter, fevered and covered with the rash, the hotel room constantly dark for fear of damaging the child's eyes, loomed. He doubted the rambunctious Margaret Michelle would be an easy patient to care for.

Bram shook his head in grandfatherly concern. "I've already had the measles, so the doc lets me visit. No one else can come to call, though."

Two weeks.

"Never had the disease myself. Did you think to hire a nurse?"

"Rebecca Ann won't hear of it. That child means the world to her. She won't leave her with anyone." Bram speared Reese with a vaguely accusing glance. "Margaret Michelle is all she has in the world. Except me, of course."

"I know, Bram."

Two weeks.

198

He couldn't see Rebecca Ann in all that time. Under doctor's orders, he was forced to avoid a risk to his own health. With a jolt, Reese realized he'd have to put off his marriage proposal until after the quarantine.

He should have been disappointed. After all, his quest for a wife had been delayed. But like the flutter of angel's wings, subtle and undefined, relief brushed over him. He'd been granted a reprieve in a situation beyond his control. He couldn't see Rebecca Ann if he wanted to.

Which he did, of course. And should, given the circumstances.

"How'd you get that swollen lip?" Bram demanded.

Reese had one wild flash of Liza's mouth moving beneath his before he remembered the truth. "Silas McCrae came to call. We've got more trouble with him."

Bram's attention sharpened. "That so?"

"He's demented," Reese said. "He wants revenge on the N & D. We have to be ready for him." Pulling one last drag off his cigarette, he tossed the stub to the ground and crushed it with his boot toe. He exhaled slowly. "I'll not tolerate him coming to my home and attacking me and mine. I'm prepared to do whatever is necessary to stop it from happening again." He met Bram's eye squarely. "Anything."

Soberly, Bram agreed. "I'll meet you at the office. You say you're headed there now?"

"Yes. Soon."

In the next moment, the door to Hutton's General Store opened. Liza appeared on the threshold with Jacob in her arms, one fat little fist clutching the beaded strands about her neck, the other held fast to one of her earrings. With Maudeen's hasty help, she laughingly tried to extricate the hoop before he yanked it off her lobe.

Bram tensed and hissed a harsh curse, his resentment

for Liza a tangible thing, so tangible that even Maudeen did not confuse his reaction. Her sympathetic glance darted to Reese.

The laughter froze in Liza's throat. She appealed to Reese, her expression a mixture of pained dismay and helplessness.

He understood her regret for being part of a friendship going sour, a years-long relationship showing signs of impending death. He felt it as deep in his own gut.

"Bram, we have to talk," he growled.

"Talk? Hell." Bram's lip curled. "She's got your brain so befuddled you've lost all reason." He stepped out into the street, but jerked back, glaring at him, uncaring that Liza heard his every word. "She'll be the ruin of you, Reese. One day, you'll see that."

The razor-edged avowal drew blood. Stunned, Reese watched him go, words of denial flat on his tongue. One by one, his hopes and dreams, his carefully laid plans for the N & D, for Niobrara City, for taking the perfect wife, rolled forth in his mind, reminding him of all he'd worked for, all he'd ever wanted.

Held captive by the ugliness of Bram's prediction, Reese stood riveted and wondered if it could be true.

Great damage had been done.

They ate lunch on the well-tended lawn of St. John's Church when neither of them had an appetite. Conversation failed, yet there were words that had to be spoken. A chasm existed where once there'd been a closeness, a raw awareness of the other, a hungering need that cried out to be filled.

Bram changed all that. He'd hauled to the surface all the hate and misunderstandings Liza had only begun to conquer. He reopened each wound. Every bit of healing Maudeen and George Steenson had tendered with their kindness and acceptance of her, a Gypsy in their midst, had been destroyed.

No wonder she despised the Gaje.

Reese sprawled on his back beneath the shade of a towering maple. He stared through the leafage, oblivious to the cheerful song of unseen birds. Beside him, Liza sat silent, hunkered on the grass, her arms wrapped tightly about her knees.

He put off going to the N & D's office. Bram would be there, still angry and resentful. Another argument would serve no purpose, and Reese wasn't yet ready to make amends.

Bram wanted a husband for Rebecca Ann. Therein laid the trouble. She was widowed and mother to a child needing a firm hand, and he saw Reese, a trusted business partner and longtime friend, as the ideal solution. Rebecca Ann, petite and beautiful, but fragile and alone in St. Louis, needed a man to care for her.

Reese had been only too willing. Ready for a wife, he was sure Rebecca Ann would fit his needs and wants to perfection. In that, he and Bram had been in complete agreement. And up to now, she had been perfectly suited for him.

Or so he thought.

Liza threw his reasoning into a tailspin. Plopping into his world through no choice of her own, she'd been hurt by Bram's frustration and Reese's own selfishness.

His head turned. Her profile carved in the afternoon light, he studied the gentle curve of her chin, the high cheekbones, the proud tilt of her nose. With skin that welcomed the sun with no fear of freckling, hair eager for the wind, and an untamed spirit that flew free from convention, she was like no other woman he'd ever known.

No other.

His intense scrutiny detected the faintest quiver in her lower lip. She may as well have sobbed aloud for the pain it caused him.

He reached for her, his fingers finding her wrist.

"Liza," he said huskily.

She trembled and pulled away from his touch. "I must go."

Tossing the remains of their lunch into the tin pail without her usual neatness, she rose abruptly. Little bells of alarm went off in his head.

He pushed to a sitting position. She sprinted away from him toward the end of the church yard, hems of bright magenta billowing about her ankles, her thick braid swaying across her back. He breathed an oath and rolled to his feet, lamenting her speed and a bum knee yet weak and healing.

He broke into a light jog. She dashed a glance over her shoulder and increased her stride to a near-run, changing direction and circling toward the church rectory.

He veered to the right. He caught up with her and snatched both of her arms in a firm grip. The pail fell from her hand. She yanked and jerked.

"Damn it, Liza. Hold still!" He could not contain his frustration.

She choked on a sob. Behind them, children played on a school playground. A horse and buggy rolled past. Lest they make a public display of themselves, Reese hauled her against the rectory, taking shelter in the shadows offered by a cluster of lilac bushes.

"I cannot stay," she rasped. "Why can you not see that? I have embarrassed you. I have shamed you!"

"Like hell you have."

She squirmed like a trout out of water and pushed

against his chest with a strength he hadn't thought possible. "I will find my family without you. I do not need your fancy telegraph machine. I will find them and be away from your world forever. I vow it!"

His blood ran cold. Desperation seized him. He pressed her deeper into the shadows, using the weight of his body to hold her.

"I won't let you leave," he said in a snarl, fingers gripping her flesh.

"You cannot stop me!"

"I'll go after you." The pledge tumbled from his mouth without a conscious plan, instinct and a simmering fear taking over where logic ceased. "Not all of my people are like Bram. He's only one man, Liza. One! There are many others who will learn to know you as I have, who will welcome you and accept you. Think of George Steenson and Maudeen!"

She held herself taut in his arms and sniffled, her gaze no higher than his chin. "He wants you as a husband for his daughter."

"Yes."

"I am only a Gypsy, a vagrant, not worthy of his—"

"You're a beautiful woman."

"I do not belong with you here in your town. Why can you not understand that? Bram is right. He—"

"*Forget Bram!*" He hurled the command through his teeth with a vehemence that compelled her to flinch. "What of *me*, Liza? Doesn't it matter what *I* want, what *I* think? I've treasured my time with you. I'll hate like hell to lose you when your family finally returns. You've filled a place in my life that needed filling in a way no other woman has done before." Chest heaving, he groped for a way to convince her, to say all the right things, to assuage the pain and anguish tormenting her. "Rebecca Ann pales next to you. You know that? She *pales.*"

Liza grew very still, absorbing his declaration. Her fingers clutched at his shirtfront. She refused to look at him.

"I have shamed you," she insisted, her voice softer, less wounded. "I never meant—I never wanted—"

"Oh, Liza." Frustrated with her stubbornness, he eased his hold on her, bringing one arm around her shoulders and bracing the other on the rough wall of the rectory, his fist clenched above her head. He sighed heavily. "Liza, Liza, Liza."

Droplets of tears clung to her eyelashes, thickening their length, making them shine like polished onyx. He wondered if the hurt would ever go away, if the differences between their worlds would melt and disappear, allowing each other's people to live in harmony.

It seemed an impossible task. He had not the time to ponder the immensity of it; he concerned himself only with her, with himself, and the minutes ticking steadily away.

"I have to go to work, okay?" His head lowered; his cheek pressed into her hair. He breathed in the clean scent of her, wholesome and pure, and damned Silas McCrae for his trouble.

She softened against him. Her hand trailed down his chest; she hooked a finger into one of his belt loops, a tiny gesture that hinted at her vulnerability, an unwillingness to see him go.

Pride kept her from the admission, yet he knew it. The knowledge surged strong within him, and his manhood swelled with a fierce need to prove to her where his words had failed, to take her body to his and drive into her the conviction of truth.

He lingered against the rectory wall, behind the bushes, his blood coursing hot with every breath, every thought.

To forget Rebecca Ann and Bram and McCrae, to forget all of Niobrara City and take her now, hard and deep. . . .

What he would give.

But he denied himself the want. He denied himself the smallest of kisses, the gentlest of touches. He denied himself *her* when he wanted nothing more than to have her.

"I'll take you home," he whispered against her temple.

"There is no need." Her voice was muffled against his shirt. "I can find my way."

"I'll not hear of it." He drew away from her. "It'll be late when I return. Will you be all right while I'm gone?"

She gave no answer but released his belt loop.

Her silence troubled him. A foreboding thought erupted. His heart began a slow, pounding thud.

"Promise me you won't leave," he said, the air between them rumbling with his demand.

She had yet to look him full in the face. He gripped her chin and tilted her head back.

"Promise me, Liza."

Her lashes fluttered, a subtle revelation of the workings in her mind. He cursed and pushed her farther against the rectory, her back at the wall, and wedged his knee between hers.

"Swear to me on a Gypsy bible or whatever your people hold in reverence that you'll be waiting for me when I come back," he said in a hiss. "Swear it!"

She twisted her chin from his grip, full Gypsy pride glaring back at him. "What right do you have to demand this of me?"

"None," he said harshly. "But I demand it anyway."

"Arrogant Gajo!" She turned away from him, yet her tone lacked the haughty sting he expected.

"I've come after you before, remember?" he taunted in

205

her ear. "Once, twice, three times. I'll do it again. You know that, don't you?"

Her head swiveled toward him.

"Yes." Her eyes blazed with a glittering light he scrambled to identify, a brilliance that had nothing to do with the clashing of their wills or the tears she had shed.

"I will be there," she said finally. "Waiting for you to return."

And then he knew the light, its meaning. Its source.

Triumph.

Chapter Thirteen

If nothing else, the incident in the church yard cleared the
air between them. Liza took a great deal of comfort in
Reese's possessiveness. Saints in heaven, she had not expected the strength of it. Perhaps it was not a bad thing to
see him get, well, a little crazy over her?

Her decision to flee had been an impulsive one, a tactic
used by the Gypsies many times to evade an unpleasant
situation. Nanosh was a master at fleeing, yet Liza could
not deny it was more a matter of cowardice than shrewd
judgment, and in her case, definitely that. She hoped never
to see Bram Kaldwell again, not when he despised her so.

Their walk from the church back to the buggy was bereft
of conversation. They had no need of it. While Liza did not
truly expect to see Bram again, she thought Reese walked
a little closer beside her, his clasp on her elbow a little
tighter. But she could not be sure.

They neared the Niobrara City Livery on the way toward
Main Street, and Liza's gaze drifted toward the corral, as it

always did when horses were gathered. The pole fences held a half-dozen assorted breeds, and without conscious thought, her eye skimmed over each one.

The animals were nervous and uneasy. They snorted and pawed the ground, swinging their heads and rolling their big, brown eyes as if grumbling about an unwanted intrusion.

Puzzled, Liza slowed her step and peered closer between the rails. A tiny form in white moved among the horses, and alarm flared within her. It took but a moment to recognize the child's tousled blond ringlets.

"Margaret Michelle!" she gasped.

Reese's glance sharpened in the direction she pointed, then swung toward the Grand River Hotel, a short jaunt from the livery.

"She must've gotten out of her room when no one was looking." He shook his head in exasperation. "The little hellion. Where's Rebecca Ann?"

"Git away from there, young lady!" An important-looking Gajo in a dark-gray suit and black derby hastened toward the corral. Several men followed him, concern carved in their expressions.

"Come on, honey," he said, his tone coaxing but firm. "We got a sick horse in there, and it ain't no place for you to be. You could get hurt."

The urgency in his voice drew Liza and Reese to the fence, the buggy waiting on Main Street forgotten in light of Margaret Michelle's dangerous predicament. She shook her blond head with a pout and stood unmoving in the dirt, her bare feet sullied from mud and manure, her crisp, ruffled nightgown smudged and bearing a tear on the sleeve.

It appeared she had left her sickbed for an adventure at the livery, escaping her mother's watchful eye yet again. In her willful innocence, she seemed curious of the palomino writhing on his side near her, his body twisting and jerking in contorting, spasmodic movements. Low, anguished nickers fell from his throat, and Liza's alarm grew tenfold.

"We'd best get her out of there quick as we can, Mayor," one of the men said. "She could get kicked and never know what hit her."

The man's worry mirrored Liza's. The mayor headed for the corral gate, but Liza took a swifter route by climbing right between the rails. Reese followed close behind.

"Come, little one," she said in a soft voice, extending a beckoning arm toward Margaret Michelle. "You must not get so close to the horse. Shall we find your mama? She is looking for you, I am sure."

The child turned toward Liza. From forehead to chin and down her neck, her porcelain skin was marred from countless spots, evidence of the measles plaguing her. Recognition flared within the heavy-lashed eyes, and she smiled broadly, but made no move to obey.

"Horsey sick. Like me," she said.

"Yes, very sick." Liza kept talking and ventured another step, careful, so very careful not to spook the little girl into toddling closer to the palomino.

An impish expression replaced Margaret Michelle's smile, as if she knew exactly what Liza and the others were trying to do. With her usual contrariness, she scampered closer to the skittish mass of horseflesh.

"Sweetling, come." Liza struggled to keep her voice even when every part of her wanted to scream in fear. "Stay away from the sick horse. You musn't—"

"Horsey sick," she said again and reached a hand toward the palomino, wanting to pet him, her sympathy endearing if not for the danger it presented.

"Please, little one." Only a few more feet, and Liza would reach her in time to pull her to safety.

But the flailing hooves showed no mercy. A glancing blow struck the little girl from the side and sent her sprawling into the dirt. She laid in a crumpled heap, motionless, and Liza cried out in anguish.

Heedless of her disease and the risks it bore, Reese reached her first and scooped her into his arms. He snapped orders to several of the men to empty the corral of the rest of the horses. As they hustled to obey, he carried her limp form to safety outside the corral's fence. He set her down gently, and Liza fell to her knees beside them. Frantic, she checked bones and pulse and for signs of blood.

"Anything broken?" the mayor asked, horrified.

"I do not think so," she said, and brushed the tangled ringlets from Margaret Michelle's cheek.

"Looks like she just got knocked out cold." Reese's grim glance met the mayor's. "But send for the doctor anyway."

"Yes, sir."

Vaguely aware of the growing crowd, Liza's thoughts centered only on the child. She paid little mind to the repulsive Gaje disease covering her from head to toe and rooted, instead, in the depths of her skirt pocket, retrieving her *bujo*, her medicine bag.

"What's she doin'?" someone asked.

"We can't let a Gypsy doctor the young'un. What would her mother think?" another demanded.

Liza ignored them and sprinkled a few grains of black pepper into Margaret Michelle's nostrils.

"Looks like Gypsy hocus-pocus to me," a voice declared. "Oughtn't we stop her?"

Liza flashed the ignorant Gajo a contemptuous glare. "I

am only helping the child wake up. Do you think I will harm her with all of you here to watch?"

"Leave her be." A murderous expression shadowed Reese's features. He rose to his full height and faced them squarely. "If any of you has objections to this woman tending the girl, take them up with me." His tone thundered with the fury he strove to contain. "While most of you have had few dealings with Gypsies in your lives, I'd warrant this one has a gentler, more caring hand than any of us. We'd all do well to trust her."

His scathing glance cut over the crowd. No one spoke.

A hysterical shriek blasted the tense silence, and Liza held her breath, knowing that Rebecca Ann had at last discovered Margaret Michelle's absence. In typical fashion, she came tearing toward them, distraught and frenzied and panicked for her daughter.

Quickly, Liza bent over the little girl and slipped a small piece of *johai* inside the collar of the white nightgown. The Gaje would not appreciate this valuable and powerful Gypsy medicine Liza believed to be ghost vomit, streaked with Gaje blood and scooped from the earth to protect her people from disease. She gladly shared the revered piece with Margaret Michelle. Soon, the child would be well again.

The crowd parted, and Rebecca Ann stumbled through. At the sight of her daughter lying prone on the ground, her face drained of color. Tears sprang to her eyes. Liza feared she would faint.

"Is-is she dead?" she whispered.

Margaret Michelle stirred, and her measle-pocked face twisted. She sneezed once, twice. The thick lashes lifted, and her blue eyes widened in confusion. The crowd murmured in relief and amazement.

211

"Oh, my baby!" Rebecca Ann sank to her knees. "My baby, my baby! What happened to you?"

The little girl howled at the sight of her mother. Rebecca Ann held her tightly, rocking back and forth, her eyes squeezed shut.

They opened again. Her gaze darted to Reese, Liza, then back at Reese again. Distrust warred with uncertainty and fatigue in her face.

"A horse kicked her, Rebecca Ann," Reese said. "She was in the corral as free as you please."

"We could not reach her in time," Liza added softly. "We tried, but she would not come."

Rebecca Ann's chin trembled. "I-I must have dozed off. She'd been napping, and I didn't know she—" She halted and bit her lip.

"Things turned out well enough, as far as we can tell," Reese said. "Her shoulder will be sore. Better have it looked at. I'll carry her back to the hotel for you."

"No." Rebecca Ann shook her head firmly. "I'll carry her myself."

A muscle tightened in his jaw, but he did not press the issue. "I'll send a doctor up then."

Rebecca Ann stood and made her way past the crowd. She halted, ran a glance over the townspeople and Reese, a glance that never touched on Liza.

"Thank you," she said over her daughter's sniffles and left.

It was an acknowledgment that excluded Liza, as if she were as much a part of the dirt as the street they stood on. The rebuff pierced deep. Liza told herself it did not matter.

It did not.

She rose stiffly, slipping the medicine bag back into her pocket. The mayor appeared in front of her, his hand extended to lend her assistance.

"Name's Al Dunning, ma'am. I appreciate what you did for the child. Even if her mother didn't."

Startled, Liza's gaze flew to his. Compassion lurked within his hazel-eyed depths, and she knew his gratitude was genuine.

"It was an unfortunate thing to happen," she demurred. "We must be thankful she was not hurt worse."

"Reckon you're right. That there palomino is gentler'n most. He'd never try to hurt her if he was feelin' better."

In unison, they turned to the corral and the afflicted horse. Mud clung to the sweat, soaking its gold-colored hide. He continued to jerk and twist, as if trying to expel the demons torturing his insides. Liza clucked her tongue in sympathy.

"Have you called for the vet?" Reese asked.

"Yes, sir. First thing, but he's out on another call. No tellin' when he'll get here."

"That horse is in pain, for sure." George Steenson appeared from within the group of townspeople. He moved toward the fence, wiping his hands on a clean white apron.

"Don't I know it." The mayor grimaced.

"He might hurt someone, the way he's rolling and kicking like that." Jack Hadley strode forward, a coil of rope in his hand. Liza glimpsed Maudeen and her two young sons near him. "Best to tie him down so's he won't hurt no one else."

Appalled, Liza sucked in a breath.

"That is the worst you could do!" Everything she had ever learned about horses cried out to deny his intent, no matter how well-intentioned. "You would only injure him further."

A deep red flush crept up from Jack's collar.

"I ain't kin to a Gypsy back-talkin' me," he said with a snarl. "Stay out of this!"

"Jack! Please!" Maudeen pleaded.

He whirled toward her. "She ain't got no right stickin' her nose in our business, Maudeen. She an expert or somethin'?"

"Yes!" Reese flashed him a harsh glance. "She knows more about horses than any of us. She's damned good with them."

"Pardon me, Mr. Carrison, but this town has managed just fine without her before. And we'll manage just fine now," he snapped back.

"Jack Hadley!" Her temper piqued, Maudeen gave his shirtsleeve a firm yank. "How dare you speak to Mr. Carrison that way! After all he's done for us!"

"Reckon it won't hurt to see what the Gypsy lady can do, Jack," the mayor said. "You saw how gentle she was with the child. What've we got to lose?"

Grumbles of agreement rose among the crowd.

Jack's fingers clenched and unclenched over the coiled rope. "All right, then. I've had my say," he said stiffly. "If the rest of you want to leave the horse in a thievin' Gypsy's hands, then I can't stop you. But I ain't havin' no part in it."

He spun on his boot heel and stomped across the street to the Empty Saddle Saloon, the door slamming shut behind him. Maudeen's cheeks pinkened in mortification, but she made no move to follow him. Instead, apology pleaded from her freckled features, and her gaze met Liza's.

Liza lowered her lashes. There was much to say to her new friend, things her husband most likely would not understand or agree with. Would their differences ever be resolved? Could their friendship flourish? It all seemed impossible.

"Will you see to the horse?" Reese asked quietly. His fingers tightened on her waist, and Liza could not deny him. She would not shame him in front of his people by refusing to heal the palomino's ills.

"For you, yes," she said.

His gold-flecked eyes warmed in approval, and he nudged her gently toward the corral.

With scrutiny heavy upon her, she slipped through the fence rails, crooning in the age-old tongue of the Gypsy, as Nanosh had taught her to do. She bent toward the animal, her hand reaching for the sweat-dampened neck.

Without warning the horse whinnied and kicked out, barely missing her. His head reared up and twisted back toward his abdomen. Murmurs of alarm sifted through the crowd. With Reese at the helm, the townspeople sifted into the corral.

"I'm not too sure about this, ma'am," the mayor said uneasily.

"Leave her be, Al. She knows what she's doing." Reese's voice was calm, firm.

"But, Reese—"

"Let her do her work."

Clearly reluctant, the mayor made no further protest. Liza tried again, stepping with a careful tread toward the horse.

"Easy, my pet," she soothed. The horse's ears pricked to the lulling sound; for a moment, he laid very still. "Easy."

Liza knew she must get the horse onto his feet, to walk him to soothe his pain. Her hand stroked his head, slipped along his neck, and then returned to his muzzle. Her fingers gently grasped his halter, and tugged on the leather, trying to get him to raise his head.

He rolled wary eyes toward her, but didn't budge. She continued to croon softly, her voice always even, the gentle sounds inspiring the horse's trust. Still, he refused to get

---

up, and her concern deepened. Was there an injury none of them yet suspected?

She pulled on the halter again and made a soft clucking noise to encourage the palomino to stand. In a sudden eruption he leaped to his feet with a bellowing nicker. Liza hung onto the head piece, his superior strength jerking her upward, her toes clearing the ground by inches before she touched down again.

The crowd rushed to her defense.

"No!" she commanded. "Get back. Give him the room he needs."

Immediately, they obeyed. With feet braced, Liza clung to the halter, talking softly all the while, until the horse showed no further inclination to bolt.

Even so, he stomped the ground, pawing and kicking at the dirt, raising little clouds of fine dust. His head swung back and forth toward his abdomen.

She glanced at the mayor. "A severe case of colic."

"I thought as much," he said.

"Have you ridden him today?" she asked.

"Yes. A brisk ride, out to the river and back."

"He has sucked in some air, which troubles him. Perhaps he chews the wood in his stall, too?"

The mayor grimaced wryly. "Afraid so."

Liza nodded. "Colic."

"She'll get him feeling better in no time," Reese stated with confidence. Liza warmed to the pride he showed for her in front of his people. "Tell us what you need, Liza. We'll get it for you."

Her mind sifted through the best treatments. "First, a blanket, cotton if one can be found, soaked in hot water. We will wrap it around his belly and flanks."

Reese nodded and swept a gaze over the crowd. He

called a tall, lanky youth named Hank to the task. The boy agreed readily and hastened away.

"Do you have any colic medication on hand?" Liza asked the mayor. He shook his head. "We will make a drench of whiskey and water, then, an ounce of each, to give him.

George hustled forward. "Reckon that's my department." He gave her a broad wink. "Be right back, Miss Liza."

"Thank you, George."

Moments later, he returned from the saloon carrying a brown, pint-sized bottle. "Whiskey and water," he said. "An ounce of each. Just like you wanted."

Liza took the bottle. From the corner of her eye, she glimpsed Jack Hadley emerging from the saloon, a glass of beer in his hand. He halted on the boardwalk, not stepping out into the street, not joining them.

But his interest was obvious. He stared, sullen and serious, with the look of a lost pup about him. Perhaps he regretted his outburst; perhaps he felt a fool. Liza did not know.

She put him from her mind. The palomino's drenching was more important than a Gajo full of contempt for her; she could not waste the time thinking about him.

"Someone help me hold the horse," she said, her hands busy with the bottle and her grip on the halter. "We will need a lead line as well."

Four men appeared and stood on either side of the sick animal. Reese took the horse's head and helped to position the beast's nose horizontal to the ground. Murmuring gently, Liza inserted the bottle into the side of the palomino's mouth, and lifted it slightly to trickle a small amount of watered whiskey onto the back of its tongue.

She stroked the golden neck and throat, encouraging him to swallow. She repeated the procedure until he had taken the entire bottle.

"Here you go, ma'am." Hank set a metal tub at her feet. "A cotton blanket soaked in hot water."

"Perfect." Giving him a tentative smile of approval, Liza lifted a corner of the sopping fabric and began wringing the water out.

The young Gajo was hardly older than herself. A sun-faded shirt hung limply on his spare shoulders; denim pants sagged on his hips. He glanced at Reese, then back at Liza, and seemed tongue-tied and in no hurry to leave. He cleared his throat.

"I've been watchin' you, ma'am. You're doin' real good with that horse," he said finally. "You ought to be right proud. Most women 'round these parts wouldn't know the first thing what to do."

"I have lived with horses all my life," she said. "I know them well."

"You shore do." His expression grew reverent. "Need some help?"

"Of course. We must work quickly. He still feels the pain."

Hank took the blanket and set to work with an efficiency that matched hers. With the excess water wrung out of it, he assisted in wrapping the warm length of cotton about the palomino's abdomen, nudging Reese and the other men aside in his importance. Once his initial shyness fled, he kept up a steady chatter, even among the horse's restlessness.

"This will make him feel better," Liza said, eyeing their handiwork. "Now we must walk him." She appealed to the mayor. "If that is all right?"

"By all means, Miss Liza. Do what you must."

"I'll keep you company," Hank said. "Mr. Carrison, I'd best take this from you." He reached a hand toward the lead line someone had found for Reese, so he could more easily hold the horse.

"By all means, Hank."

A subtle irritation hung in Reese's tone, but he said nothing more and relinquished his control over the horse. Liza's brow raised to him in silent question. He gave her no answers, setting both hands on his hips instead and sending Hank an annoyed glare.

The horse did not walk easily. Liza kept her full attention on him, for she had all she could do to keep him from stopping to lie down again. She crooned to him, keeping her arm about his neck while Hank encouraged him from his position near the flanks, rubbing the belly in slow, sure strokes.

She pulled the balking palomino out of the corral gate. With every step, with every passing minute, it seemed some of his discomfort had eased. She kept a tight hold on him and advised Hank to do the same.

The crowd of men and women watched them go. There was no animosity in their faces, but instead a lessening of their uncertainties about her, and she could not help but feel, for the first time, a glimmer of hope for their acceptance.

The horse moved slowly. Maudeen caught her eye and smiled hesitantly, as if she feared her husband had destroyed the fragile birth of their friendship. Their glances held, Liza's full of understanding, free of contempt, and Maudeen visibly relaxed. Swift and genuine, the bond strengthened. The horse would not be sick forever, Liza mused. There would be time to talk when they returned.

"I hear tell you're stayin' at Mr. Carrison's place," Hank said from behind her.

"Yes." Liza pulled her thoughts from Maudeen to the lanky youth. "Only until my family returns."

"That so?"

Liza nodded. As they walked, an iron-clad hoof kicked at a pebble; she watched it skitter across the road.

"Reckon that'll be very long?"

She shrugged. "I do not know. Nor does Reese. We only sent the telegrams this morning." She considered him. "Why do you ask?"

A slender shoulder lifted. "Talk is that Mr. Carrison plans on weddin' Bram Kaldwell's daughter."

Her hackles rose. "Reese has done nothing dishonorable. He has not even asked for her hand yet, but when he does, she should be very proud to have him for her husband."

"Aw, now, Miss Liza, don't go gettin' all fired up. I didn't mean nothin' by it." He seemed eager to make amends. "It's just that—" His mouth tightened.

"Speak your tongue, Hank," she demanded.

"It's just that, if Mr. Carrison don't have no claim on you, then maybe I'd—maybe I could—if you don't mind—"

Puzzled over his stammering, she stared at him. "If I do not mind what?"

"Miss Liza, I'd be right happy to call on you sometime. Leastways, 'til your family came back."

Her step faltered. She could hardly believe her ears.

So bold, the Gaje. Impulsive. With little thought to the consequences. In their own words, this blushing boy wanted to court her. Saints in heaven. Their parents had never even met to arrange it.

"Now I reckon we don't know each other yet, but if you'd like, I'll talk to Mr. Carrison and all. It's just that, well, you most impressed me with how you treated this horse, and it's always been a dream of mine to own a fine horse ranch someday. I was hopin' you could teach me some of what you know. Not that I would take advantage of you or anything, because you're a right beautiful woman with that purty hair and all that there gold jewelry and stuff, and well, I'd be right proud to be with you."

His long explanation left him breathless. And left Liza stunned.

The palomino threw his head in another fit of colic. Liza was glad for it. She needed the distraction to collect herself.

"Shall I speak to Mr. Carrison?" Hank persisted.

An image of Reese loomed in her mind, vivid and true. An image of raw masculinity and power and strength, of honor and respect, of muscled arms that held her with gentleness, of a mouth that kissed with taut passion. For the life of her, she could not see Hank the same way.

She could not.

"Miss Liza?"

Her head spun. She was tortured by a lifetime of unfulfilled dreams and the yearnings in her heart, by the hopelessness of all the things beyond her control.

Maybe now was the time to confront them.

"That will not be necessary," she said finally. "I will speak of it to him myself."

Liza decided a second drenching was needed. Afterward, the mayor insisted upon detailed instructions on the care of his horse and the preparation of his stall. The palomino had stopped sweating and improved greatly, enough to be taken home, and the mayor was most appreciative.

"You're sure I can't pay you something, Miss Liza?" he asked. "What you've done is worth every dime of a vet's fee."

His insistence pleased her. She basked in the novelty of having a Gajo, especially one of his prominence, feel gratitude toward a Gypsy.

"Of course not. I would not think of it." Being gracious

came easily; she gladly buried her contempt and disdain for a man as kind as he. "I am happy he is feeling better."

"So am I. Well, I assure you, I won't forget what you've done. If there's anything I can do for you in return, you have only to ask."

"I will remember that," she replied, though she could not imagine herself asking anything of a Gajo, even one who was a mayor.

"It's getting late, Liza. Are you ready to head home?" Reese asked.

Knowing his impatience to return to his railroad, she made hasty good-byes to Al Dunning, George Steenson, Hank, and even a few Gaje whose names she did not know. They returned her waves with smiles of friendship on their faces, each promising to look forward to seeing her again.

Reese took her elbow to escort her back to the buggy.

"They're besotted. Every one of them," he said.

"Do you think so?"

"You've charmed the whole bunch."

She thought of Hank and his enamored attentions. Her mouth pursed. "Is that so bad?"

A rueful laugh tumbled from him. "Let me put it this way." He paused beside the shiny rig and set his hands on his hips. "Someday, your husband will have all he can do to keep the men away. Half the county will want you."

She snorted. "Your brain plays tricks on you. Your tongue speaks of lunacy."

"Ah, my sweet, but you're wrong."

Wryly, he extended his hand to help her into the buggy. Liza lifted a foot to climb in.

"Mr. Carrison!" A horse thundered down Main Street at full speed, its rider waving his hat wildly. "Mr. Carrison!"

An ominous fear clutched Liza's heart. The Gajo's frantic yell could only mean something terrible had happened. She

stepped back from the buggy, her heart thrumming errat-
ically.

Reese's gaze sharpened on the Gajo, a spry man she
guessed to be in his forties. He wore a red bandanna around
his neck, a sign that he worked for the N & D. "Whoa,
Clements. Take it easy. What is it?"

Clements drew his mount up in a spray of dirt and
gravel. "We've got trouble," he panted. "Quarter mile of
track burned out. Completely gone."

"Damn it!" Reese spat the oath. "Silas McCrae."

"Yes, sir. I reckoned it'd be him."

"What of the trestle bridge?" he demanded. "Any damage?"

"None, sir, that I can tell."

"Thank God for that, anyway." Reese let out a breath,
his expression hard. "Have you seen McCrae?"

"No, sir." Clements heaved in air. "But I thought I spotted his horse hidden in some brush. When I saw the fire,
I went to check it out. On my way back, his horse was
gone."

Guilt stabbed Liza. She knew how anxious Reese had
been to meet with his men, to devise a plan against the
crazy fur trapper. She knew how much his railroad meant
to him. She knew how much he wanted to prevent *this*.

And yet he had been kept from it because of her, sending
telegrams, buying green henrietta and having lunch on the
church lawn. Trivial things. Things that could have waited
until after he protected his railroad.

"Oh, Reese," she breathed and touched a hand to his
arm. "I am sorry."

He seemed not to hear. A grim line slashed his mouth.
He began unhitching the sorrel from the buggy.

"Gather as many men as you can," he ordered Clements.
"I want them armed and ready to ride. Have them meet at

the depot, and send word to Bram. And I want guards posted on the bridge. We can't let McCrae get to that next."

"Yes, sir. Anything else?"

"No. Get moving."

"Yes, sir!" In an instant, he obeyed, kicking his mount's ribs as he tore off, yelling for volunteers at the top of his lungs.

"Liza." Reese's fingers worked deftly at the harness. "I'll run you home. We'll take the sorrel—he'll be faster without the buggy."

"I will not think of it!" she said, aghast.

His fierce gaze told her he would not tolerate an argument. "I want you safe. Away from this."

All about her, townspeople responded to the urgency in Clement's calls, spilling from businesses and crowding the boardwalks. A horse-drawn water wagon clattered around the corner. Rifles and revolvers appeared from nowhere. Liza's alarm increased tenfold.

"I will find my own way home, Reese. Do not worry for me."

"Excuse me, Mr. Carrison." Jack Hadley stood uncertainly behind him, Maudeen and the boys at his side. His glance touched on Liza, then skittered away. The look was without accusation, but rather, surprisingly, held a hint of remorse. In a fleeting thought, Liza wondered if Maudeen had rendered him with some stern wifely chastisement to affect the change in his mood.

"Mind if I ride with you?" Jack asked in a stiff tone.

Reese did not immediately answer, as if he, too, pondered the difference in him. He gave a terse nod. "I'll be glad to have you."

Jack seemed relieved. "Maudeen can take . . . Miss Liza home, if you like. I'll leave 'em our rig and borrow a horse."

Liza sensed Reese's reluctance to let two women drive

themselves home with children in tow, given the volatility of McCrae.

"I'll be happy to take her, Mr. Carrison," Maudeen spoke up. "We won't dally. I promise."

"I will go home with Maudeen," Liza said firmly.

After a long moment, Reese consented. "Thanks, Maudeen. I owe you."

She rolled her eyes. "No, you don't!"

"I'll see you at the depot, then." Jack waved at Reese and embraced Maudeen and his sons. He sprinted toward a group of men already headed that way.

"Our wagon is parked on the next street, Liza," Maudeen said in her quiet voice. She took Toby's hand.

Reese delved beneath the buggy's seat and retrieved their brown-wrapped purchases, stowed there for safekeeping, and handed them to Liza. He delved again and produced a gleaming rifle.

"When you get into the house, Liza, I want you to lock the doors," he said, dropping the lever to check the chamber. "I'm guessing McCrae won't bother you when it's me he wants, but please be careful anyway."

Liza nodded and swallowed hard, her eyes riveted to the gun. The full impact of the danger he was in struck with ugly force. The use of weaponry had never been condoned by her people. They shunned violence and confrontation, and yet the Gaje did not hesitate to fight viciously for what was theirs.

Seeing Reese with a gun terrified her. He would do anything to save his railroad and its massive trestle bridge.

"You must not get hurt," she said, her voice quavery. "I am afraid of what could happen." She bit her lip, knowing Maudeen waited discreetly, knowing she should join her, and knowing, too, they stood in full view of all his people.

"I'm well-armed and well-manned. McCrae'll be at a disadvantage with us." He dropped a handful of shells into his pocket.

"Will you stop the fire?"

"I'll do everything in my power. I just hope it hasn't turned into a full-blown prairie fire by now." He took the reins and led the sorrel from the buggy. He paused in the street. "I'll see you later. Tonight. After dark, most likely."

Her chin lifted. Beneath his hat brim, his tiger eyes met hers, challenging, demanding her to deny she would be there when he returned.

"I will wait for you," she said firmly.

A flash of emotion flickered through his gaze.

"You damn well better," he said roughly.

She had delayed him long enough. He turned, ready to mount the sorrel without benefit of a saddle, eager to join his men.

"Reese." Her fingers closed over his forearm, halting him.

He turned back. She did not care that Maudeen watched, that the entire town could see him here with her, saying good-bye to a Gypsy when everyone knew he was intended for Rebecca Ann.

She did not care.

She flung her arms about his neck. Tight and fierce.

"God be with you," she whispered into his shoulder.

He crushed her to him in one brief clasp. His mouth touched her hair, so fleeting she might have imagined it. She cursed the tears that threatened to fall.

He released her. She spun about and ran to Maudeen. She would not look back.

In the next moment, the sorrel's hooves pounded the dirt road. Too soon, the sound faded. Liza sniffled and shifted the packages in her arms, freeing her hand to hold Toby's. Maudeen repositioned Jacob on her hip.

"Is Mr. Carrison's railroad gonna burn down, Liza?" Toby asked, peering up at her with the innocence of an angel.

"No, sweetling." She took a long breath, regaining her composure. "He is very smart. He will save his train. You will see."

"Good. I'm gonna ride on it someday. Just like my pa."

"Of course you will."

Maudeen and Liza exchanged somber glances. Without saying anything, they walked to the wagon and perched Toby between them. Liza held Jacob, giving him her beads to chew on, and he slobbered over them with delight.

Within moments, they left the tense town behind and headed for home. Maudeen kept Liza's troubled thoughts at bay with talk of her garden and the storm's damage to her green beans. Liza politely considered her invitation to come over and help with the mammoth chore of canning the produce growing in abundance.

Eventually, the wagon slowed.

"Our cabin is that way," Maudeen said, pointing in the opposite direction than which she turned the rig. "You must come over again soon, Liza. I promise you won't recognize the place."

Maudeen's proud mention of her cabin brought memories crashing back to Liza, filling her head of the time she'd spent there after the tornado.

"Yes," she murmured. "Reese has told me much has been done already."

How different it would look now, she thought to herself as Maudeen prattled on about the new shed and chicken coop and the barn-raising they planned in the near future.

Yet its destruction would remain ever vivid in Liza's mind, no matter what it looked like now. She would always remember eating dinner on the floor, sleeping on a table-cloth, and quilts hanging on a line, shutting out the rain.

How could she forget? For it was there that she had fallen in love with Reese Carrison.

Chapter Fourteen

When Reese came home, he searched the expanse of the front lawn, expecting to find Liza wrapped in blankets on the grass and sleeping peacefully beneath the obsidian sky. He searched along the porch, too, and then the sides and back of the house. He found no sign of her.

She was gone.

The clock in the kitchen read nearly two in the morning. He stood in the tidy room, not moving, the only sound greeting him the steady drip, drip, drip of ice melting in the icebox, a solemn cadence to the pounding of his heart.

She had promised to wait for him.

He swallowed down gall from the lie. He'd believed her, like a fool.

He hadn't expected the lamp glowing in the kitchen, though, a beacon of welcome for his return. Or the bowl of thick vegetable soup, now cold, covered with a clean towel on the stove. To keep him occupied after he discovered she'd left? His lip curled.

He smelled the smoke on his body, the sweat and grit from riding hard and from overworked muscles, weary of fighting the fire. It'd been a night of frustration and failure, a night without a sighting of Silas McCrae, a night of gut-wrenching damage to the N & D track.

But he bore it all to come home to Liza. It'd been the one thing that kept him going hour after hour after god-damned hour.

How he hated the house's silence. He'd lived with it before, but now, suffocating and harsh, it closed in on him, choking his every breath.

He sucked in air, filled his lungs, cleared his mind of the self-pity. She could be anywhere. He'd vowed, more than once, to go after her, but in the reality of the moment, his despair cried out for a reason why he should track her down. She had made her decision. She didn't want to stay.

She didn't want him.

Ignoring the bowl of soup, he doused the lamp and left the kitchen. Embers glowed in the main room's stone fireplace and cast a muted orange glow in the darkness. Out of habit, his eye swept the room and found nothing out of place. Empty. So damned empty.

He moved toward the stairwell leading up to the loft. In the quiet, a faint sound reached his ears.

A tremor raced through him. He turned slowly.

She lay on the couch facing the fireplace, hidden from view from behind. She slept deep, her breathing soft and regular, and blissfully oblivious to the hell she'd put him through.

A grin touched his mouth, hesitated, then spread wide. In his relief, he nearly laughed out loud.

He went to her. One arm was stretched out in front of her, relaxed in sleep, her fingers slightly bent. On the floor, next to the couch, cutout pieces of green henrietta were folded in a neat stack.

He hunkered down beside her. She was barefoot and nestled against the cushions, a shapely leg peeking from beneath the profusion of her skirts. Freed from its braid, her hair pillowed her head in a red-gold mass that trailed over her shoulder and hung over the couch's edge.

For a long moment, he watched her sleep and pondered the power she wielded over him. It amazed him, this power, for he didn't know how to resist, or, just as perplexing, didn't know if he should.

He slipped his arms beneath her and lifted her from the couch. Her mouth puckered, but she hardly stirred more than that, merely snuggled into him with a gentle sigh. In spite of his weariness, his muscles treasured her weight, and he carried her to the stairs, up to his bedroom in the loft.

There would be no front lawn for her tonight. Not this Gypsy witch who'd charmed him with an unfamiliar hex. She was in his world now, in his house, and he gifted her with his own bed.

Already, the covers were turned down, in readiness for his return. As carefully as he could, he laid her upon the cool sheets and held his breath lest she awaken and protest.

She did not and rolled to her side. He pulled the quilts over her, and she burrowed deeper, seeking their warmth.

In the darkness, he delayed leaving. His gaze strayed to the other side of the bed, unruffled, unused; to the second pillow, empty and unneeded. She looked small in the massive bed. Surprisingly small. He was consumed by a yearning to make love to her so strong his temples pounded from the force of it.

There were few more foolish than he. But he would not sleep with her tonight. Though his body sought release in hers, release from lust and tension and worries about Silas McCrae, he would not touch her. He would not give in.

He was bound by intent to another. A vague unease riffled through him at the knowledge, and his mouth grew taut.

Liza had stayed. For now, that was all that mattered.

A hint of an early autumn nipped the air, filling Liza's lungs with its crisp bite. She perched on the top rail of the corral fence, her gaze captured by Reese as he rode the stallion at a brisk walk.

The breeze toyed with her hair, sending strands flitting across her cheek. She never wore a kerchief these days, and a braid only on occasion. Reese preferred her hair cascading down her back, swept aside by combs and ribbons, and she obliged him, often using the intricate carved tortoiseshell he had given her, the fashion used by the women in his society.

She lifted a hand and tucked the strands behind her ear. Reese coaxed his horse from the walk into a high-stepping trot. Watching him, she smiled in pleasure. In contentment.

She had grown comfortable living with him. More than she had ever imagined. His home was hers now, or so it seemed in her heart, and she had formed a great attachment to all that was his.

It did not seem that she'd waited more than two weeks to hear from her people, for every day was filled to overflowing. She spent time with Zor whenever she could, happy that he had grown steadily stronger. And when she was not in the corral with him, she gladly cooked, and cleaned, and cut Reese's grass while he worked long days at his railroad. With Maudeen's help, she had learned to plant a vegetable garden—a garden!—and to weed it and water it and nurture it with loving care.

A woman did these things for the man in her life. Be it the Gaje blood flowing in her veins, or, right or wrong, the love in her heart, she did them all willingly, living each day to the fullest, and trying not to think of the time when her people would come, and it would all end.

They had not heard a single word in all this time. Liza was not surprised. The Gypsies could be elusive when they wanted to be, hiding in woodlands and canyons and out-of-the-way places to trick the disapproving Gaje. Nanosh was very shrewd. He would not be found until he was ready. And with Hanzi's help, they would search for her in their own way, sending secret messages among their people and leaving behind the vurma for the many friends and relatives traveling in Gypsy tribes scattered all over the prairie.

She did not think about it so much anymore. The telegrams would find her people when nothing else could. She must be patient.

Her mouth pursed. Yet Reese's world was not without its worries. She feared the Wild One's return almost as much as Reese did. She listened with trepidation as he told of his men's efforts to secure the N & D against his attacks, of rebuilding the burned-out track, of the endless hours of keeping watch. But, in more than two weeks, Silas McCrae had not let his grizzled face be seen. Liza could not help but hope perhaps he had realized the folly of his ways and given up.

Saints in heaven, that it could so easy.

Reese's exultant yell scattered her wayward thoughts. Smiling at his enthusiasm, she leaned forward on the rail and stuffed her turquoise skirts between her knees.

The stallion's midnight-black flanks gleamed in the sunlight. Reese rode him in an easy canter around the corral. The horse responded to his commands with a lithe grace, all signs of lameness gone, every movement free and spirited. Reese's beaming approval made the countless hours Liza had spent treating the animal worthwhile.

After they finished, she clapped her hands in proud delight.

"He is beautiful, is he not?" she asked as Reese reined the stallion in at the fence.

"I've never seen him better, that's for sure. You've done a fine job with him, Liza."

"And to think you wanted to shoot him dead." She shook her head in mock disapproval and clucked her tongue. She could not resist teasing him.

"Keep reminding me of that, woman, and you'll find yourself sharing the barn with him."

Her eyes widened in feigned dismay. "You mean you would toss me from your magnificent bed?"

"I would. Being's I can't join you myself, why not?"

Her heart fluttered at his unexpected admission. "It was not my choice to take the bed. I woke up one morning, and there I was."

A side of his mouth lifted; he leaned on the saddle horn. "And yet you don't complain and sleep there every night now," he said softly. "I think you prefer it to the lawn."

She shrugged and thought of her tiny cot in Nanosh's wagon. "Your bed is more comfortable, yes. I have learned to like it. Very much."

He grunted. "You'll like it even more when you have a man to warm you."

Heat swirled through her belly. It was true. She could not fall asleep without thinking of him cramped on the couch downstairs, or the strange emptiness she felt being separated from him, nor could she deny the constant ache to twine her legs with his and fill her arms with the breadth of his body.

"I do not think of such things," she lied.

His unwavering gaze suggested he knew better. "Funny. I think of them all the time."

The stallion swung his head, as if miffed at being ignored. He sidled closer and nudged his black nose against Liza, nearly knocking her from her perch. She scrambled to regain her balance.

"Do you think you are so wonderful that you can push me around, you silly horse?" she scolded, planting a kiss near his ear. "Here, then. Have this, but mind your manners next time."

He burrowed against her palm and chomped at a small turnip. Reese dismounted and flipped a stirrup over the saddle's seat to loosen the cinch.

"Has Hank come to call lately?" he asked nonchalantly.

She peered around the stallion's face. "Yesterday again."

Reese glowered at her. "He's a pest. Thinks he knows everything in the world about horses."

She hid her smile. "He is anxious to learn. He comes to see me and asks many questions."

Reese rolled his eyes and hauled the heavy saddle off, swinging it onto the top rail next to Liza. "Yeah, I'll bet."

"He has been a gentleman. His intentions are most honorable."

"He's a man with a man's desires."

"He is only a boy." Mentally, she compared Hank's rangy frame with Reese's hard-muscled bulk, his youthful features to Reese's chiseled planes. "A boy," she insisted.

"He'd best not lay a hand on you, if he knows what's good for him. I'll not stand for it."

"He has not." Reese's jealousy was most endearing. No other male in Liza's life had been afflicted with that sweet malady. She found it quite pleasant to be at the center of not one man's attentions, but two. "I do not think he likes my cooking, though."

"Really?"

"Too spicy."

After removing the bridle, Reese pulled off the saddle blanket and waved it at the stallion, spooking him into a run toward the other side of the corral. He draped it over the fence, then stood in front of her and hooked both thumbs into his hip pockets.

Liza looked down at him expectantly.

"Not only is he a pest, but he doesn't appreciate a good cook when he sees one," Reese said roughly. "Maybe that's for the best. Leastways, he won't come to call when he's hungry."

The air tinkled with her laughter, and she reached for him, her hands grasping his broad shoulders. He took her waist and swung her from the fence, gently settling her to the ground.

"You are the only Gajo that matters to me," she said softly. "I cook for no one else but you."

"An easy promise to make, sweet lady, until another man claims you."

"I speak the truth."

"So do I."

She cocked her head and wondered at his change in mood. "You will believe me when you see that I have planned a special supper for us. Roasted pork with apple-sauce. Maudeen gave me her recipe and showed me how—"

A shadow crossed his features. His glance fell away, and he released her.

"I won't be eating here tonight," he said.

She blinked.

"I have an appointment with Rebecca Ann for dinner at the Grand River Hotel." He frowned into the sky. "I pick her up at seven."

His quiet explanation rocked her. He did not have to tell her why.

"I see." She pasted a brittle smile to her face. "It does not matter, Gajo. I will eat my share of dinner and save yours for lunch tomorrow."

Liza stood in the middle of the kitchen, surrounded by the delectable aromas of seasoned meat and fresh-baked bread, and could find no appetite for them. Her stomach churned. Her heart ached. Her head pounded with resentment.

Tonight, Reese would ask Rebecca Ann to marry him. What a fool she had been, to fall in love with him when all along she knew he could never be hers. Of course he would choose a woman of his own world, one beautiful and sophisticated. Why would he want a simple Gypsy?

Her lip curled. Rebecca Ann. Pah! She could not heal a horse or pluck a chicken or climb trees to pick apples for sauce. She was too fragile, too perfect. She would only melt in the sun.

Liza snatched a knife and a fresh carrot and began scraping with a vengeance, her pique flying free with the peelings. Did Rebecca Ann worry when Reese worked too hard? Did she fret over his railroad and Silas McCrae? Hardly! She would not know to do such things.

Liza's hands slowed. She bit her lip.

What could she do? She did not know how to keep him. She had not learned the tricks a woman used to win a man. Reese would be ready to leave soon. Any minute. How could she make him stay?

She must try before it was too late.

The knife and carrot fell to the table with a clatter. She

spun about, flaring her skirts in a blur of turquoise, and left the kitchen.

The door to his bedroom stood open. At least, in that regard, he had not shut her out, had not clung to privacy. She walked in without hesitation.

He stood at the mirror buttoning his shirt, the tails hanging outside his black pants. Their gazes met in the glass. Liza could not think of a thing to say.

She turned and plopped on the bed, sitting cross-legged on the coverlet, and watched him finish dressing. His scent reached her, bay rum and soap, all in preparation for his proposal to Rebecca Ann.

She drew in a breath and let it out again. "The child, Margaret Michelle. She is feeling better?"

He stretched his chin to manage his tie. "Bram tells me she is. I haven't seen her myself."

"Oh." She plucked at the coverlet. Then, "You must be looking forward to having dinner at the hotel."

"Not really."

"I am sure it is a lovely place to go."

"Nice enough. I'll take you sometime."

She snorted at the impossibility of it. "Do not make a promise you will not keep, Reese."

His brow raised at the snap in her tone. "If I say I'll take you, then you can be sure I will."

"After you are married, or before?"

Her wounded heart could not stop the words, and as soon as they were out, she regretted them. With slow, measured movements, he faced her and leaned back against the dresser, gripping the edges until his knuckles showed white. "So that's what this is all about."

She could not look at him. "I am sorry. I did not mean to say that."

A heavy breath left him, one fraught with frustration.

"It's time for me to take a wife, Liza. I'm not getting any younger. I want a family. Children."

"Of course."

"I've given this a lot of thought. She's the best—she'll be good—" His teeth clamped tight. Hot and fierce, his gaze raked her, as if demanding her to deny it, to give him reason not to see it through.

But she could say nothing. From the moment Liza had met him, Rebecca Ann had been his, an important part of his life. How could she deny him what he wanted most?

The air strained with their silence. Abruptly, Reese pushed away from the dresser and snatched at the suit coat lying on a corner of the bed.

"I'll be late tonight. Don't wait up." He ground out the words.

Shoving his arms into the sleeves, he left.

She flinched at the front door's slam. A sudden panic gripped her that all of her time with him would be lost, all her happiness gone, the tender feelings nurtured in her heart these past weeks forgotten, trampled beneath another woman's feet.

She could not allow it. Saints in heaven, she could not!

Bolting from the bed, she lifted her skirts and dashed down the stairs. She feared she might not catch him in time, that he might already have left, that he would forget if she did not make him remember. The front door swung open with the same loud bang with which it had closed.

"Reese!"

He halted from his climb into the buggy and turned toward her.

She had little to give him. She was only a poor Gypsy, but she had herself, did she not?

Liza flew to him, then, in a blur of skirts and beads and bare feet. His arms opened, an instinctive action, and he

239

took her weight against him, falling back a step to regain his balance. She gave him no time to speak, but wrapped her arms tightly about his neck, pressing her mouth to his with all the love and fervor she possessed.

Like a spark to flint, passion ignited between them. He crushed her to his chest, lifting her, her toes clearing the ground by inches. Her lips opened, his tongue thrust inward, invading the moistness with ardent demand, until she was consumed with the taste, the feel, the want of him.

He groaned deep in his throat and set her down again. He could not seem to hold her close enough, or tight enough, or long enough. His hands roamed her spine, roughly, passionately, never still, sliding down to her buttocks. His palms opened, and he cupped the rounded flesh, kneading them against him. His male arousal pressed against her feminine softness through the layers of skirts, and a new kind of fire raged inside her.

His brazen possession burned her senses. She had not expected his response; she could not have guessed the strength of it. A sound trembled in her throat.

"Say the word, Liza," he rasped against her mouth, as if he could not bring himself to break away even for a moment. "Say it, and I'll stay. I'll call everything off."

Her bosom heaving, she twisted from his kisses.

"I cannot," she whispered, her pulse thundering inside her. "I cannot."

She pushed from his embrace, knowing her lips were ravaged and swollen, that he was as shaken as she, and just as tormented.

But he must decide without her. He must learn for himself when there was no passion between them, when his head was clear, his mind rational.

Only then, would he know the truth in his heart.

* * *

Reese leaned back in his chair and swirled the whiskey in his glass. He stared broodingly at the amber liquid, spinning and whirling like a golden tornado, reminding him of *her*, the golden temptress with golden skin who made him lust with the fury of golden fire.

He lifted the glass, tossing back the whiskey in one gulp, and relished the heat in his throat. It matched nicely with the heat in his loins that refused to go away.

He scowled and tried not to think of her.

Next to him, Rebecca Ann dabbed at the milk her daughter spilled over the hotel's starched tablecloth. Margaret Michelle couldn't sit still through the meal, which further grated Reese's patience. Conversation was near impossible; the child had neither the discipline nor inclination to obey her elders. And Bram just sat there, puffing on his pipe with a grandfather's indulgence, smiling at his granddaughter's antics. Reese glowered at him.

He hadn't intended on the dinner being a family affair. He had wanted to spend the time with only Rebecca Ann in a quiet meal to discuss their future. Up to now, the subject had never even come up, and as the evening wore on, Reese wondered if it would.

Margaret Michelle poked a finger into a dish of peach tapioca pudding. Ignoring the spoon nearby, she pulled out a dripping slice of fruit and stuffed it into her mouth. A plate of diced roast beef and potatoes sat untouched, save for the gravy smeared on the front of her blue crinoline dress.

Watching her, Reese frowned. "It might be a good idea if she ate her meat and vegetables first, Rebecca Ann. Having dessert now will spoil her for the rest of the meal."

Rebecca Ann merely smiled and pulled a smashed pea from one of her daughter's perfect blond ringlets. "She has always had a sweet tooth, just like her daddy. Why, I re-

241

member when Michael and I were married, he took all the leftover cake with us on our wedding trip."

"Ate it all, too, as I recall," Bram said, chuckling around the pipe stem.

"Yes, he did." A faraway look stole into her china-doll eyes. "And he was as trim and fit as ever. Right up until the day he died. Do you remember, Papa?"

"I sure do, honey. He was a mighty handsome man. For as long as I knew him."

A quavering sigh left her. She blinked rapidly and sniffled, Bram murmured something compassionate, and Reese nearly rolled his eyes heavenward.

They'd abandoned him to the outside of their private circle of memories, and he chafed at it. With a grim certainty, he realized he'd forever compete with a dead man's ghost, like it or not, and he'd damn well better get used to the idea.

He reached for the bottle of whiskey.

"Mama! Out! Out!" Margaret Michelle howled.

In her determination to be done with her dinner and out of her seat, the child toppled a glass of ice water and pushed at the table, yanking the starched cloth and sending the lighted candle in the centerpiece swaying. All three adults leaped to their feet. Reese lunged for the taper, Bram right-ended the water glass, and Rebecca Ann grabbed for her daughter.

"Rebecca Ann," Reese said in a low voice, his patience at an end. "I don't claim to be an expert on child-rearing, but she needs a firmer hand. She's getting a mite too much to handle."

Clearly aghast at his opinion, Rebecca Ann's gaze darted to Bram, then back at Reese.

"She's tired," she said defensively. "She's not yet totally recovered from the measles, you know."

The disease had long since run its course. Margaret Michelle had returned to her usual contrary form, but he said nothing more and gestured to the nearest waiter to bring them a damp cloth.

"I think it's best we go to our room now," Rebecca Ann said, washing the little girl's wiggling fingers as best she could. "I'm taking an early stage back to St. Louis tomorrow."

"You're what?" Bram and Reese asked in unison.

"Being cooped up in this hotel has driven me near to madness," she pouted, oblivious to the unexpected detour she'd caused in Reese's plan. Her gaze drifted to her daughter who wandered among the other diners. "Margaret Michelle needs to be back in her own house and playing with her own toys. Niobrara City is so small, why, there's nothing to do here, and with that train whistle blaring all the time—I'm sorry, Reese, I know it's your train, but in St. Louis, we don't have trains so close to our home."

Bram cast him a pointed glance. "I'll take Margaret Michelle for a walk. Wear her out some before bed. That'll give you two time to yourselves."

"But—" Rebecca Ann said, her perfect brows furrowed.

Obligated to see this through now that Bram had gone through the trouble of arranging it, Reese cleared his throat. "I'd like a few minutes with you, Rebecca Ann, if you don't mind."

"Of course not." But her eyes followed her daughter and father out into the lobby.

He took her elbow and led her from the dining room to a tiny rose garden at the back of the hotel. Niobrara City had little to boast of by way of romance; it was the best he could do under the circumstances.

"Reese, is there something special you wanted to talk to me about?" She peered up at him, a vision of perfection in the gathering dusk. He detected no coyness in her, or even a true desire to be outside. Beneath the hem of her plum-colored dress, her toe tapped impatiently.

He pushed his hands into his pants pockets. Countless times he'd planned this conversation, practiced it and re-lived it. Now all the right words evaded him.

"Have you given any thought to living anywhere besides St. Louis?" he asked finally, taking a coward's road.

She appeared perplexed. "Oh, no. Why should I? St. Louis is my home."

"Niobrara City will grow in time. The people here are good, God-fearing citizens who work hard for a living."

"Reese, are you saying I should live in Niobrara City?" She seemed appalled at the thought. "You've got to be jok-ing."

His hackles rose. "You'll not find a nicer town anywhere. The N & D offers prosperity and respect, not only to Ni-obrara City, but to the state of Nebraska, as well."

She studied him, as if trying to understand his way of thinking. "You're so much like my father," she mused. "Per-haps it's the railroad you built together. I don't know." She shivered and crossed her arms over her small bosom. "I shall never leave St. Louis, Reese. My house is there. I re-member vividly the day Michael and I decided to buy it. We shopped for weeks for just the right neighborhood." She shook her head. "Before he died, Michael chose the school he wished our daughter to attend when she's old enough. Of course, I'll honor his wishes."

A man of Reese's years should not have been so blind, so stupid. From the beginning, he had closed his eyes to the truth, so obvious now, so implacable. All along, he had been a first-class idiot.

"Of course," Reese said quietly. Inch by inch, a heavy

burden slipped from his shoulders, Rebecca Ann's decision freeing him from his own.

"Was there anything else, Reese? I'm cold."

"No, nothing." A small smile formed on his mouth, his well-laid plan gone awry. Or had it? "I'll take you inside."

They met Bram waiting in the lobby. Margaret Michelle was busy turning somersaults in the middle of the floor, but went willingly enough to her mother. They made proper good-byes, and pensive, Reese watched Rebecca Ann head toward the stairs.

She hadn't reached the top before Bram spun toward him.

"You didn't ask her to marry you, did you?" he demanded.

"No."

"Are you going to?"

"No."

"Why the hell not?"

Reese narrowed his eyes at the insistence in his tone. "She doesn't want to be married to anyone but her husband, that's why."

"What're you talking about? He's dead."

"I know it. So do you. But to her, he's still alive. Leastways, in her head."

A deep red crept over Bram's cheeks. Rarely did Reese see him this angry. "You're making a big mistake. Rebecca Ann is perfect for you and the N & D. You said so yourself. But you're letting her slip through your fingers because of that troublemaking Gypsy you've been shacking up with all these weeks."

"Leave Liza out of this."

"Deny it, then."

"Damn you, Bram."

"Damn *you!*" Bram fairly shook with rage. "That's the end

245

of it between us, Reese. I'm pulling out of the cartel. Finance the N & D on your own. You're not using Kaldwell money to keep your lousy train running on its track!"

"Bram, listen to me!" Reese grabbed his friend's arm, but Bram jerked free with a snarl and stormed from the hotel.

He might as well have landed his fist into the pit of Reese's belly for the wind it took out of him. He couldn't move, couldn't speak to beg reconsideration. For one irrational moment, Reese thought of Rebecca Ann, of marrying her after all, of finding a way to make it work. His glance shot to the stairs, but she was long gone to the shelter of her room. A sick feeling of defeat washed over him.

In the dining area, the clatter of dishes penetrated the lobby. A waiter busied himself clearing their table, dumping dishes and glasses into a large metal pan for washing. Only the whiskey remained.

Reese strode over and snatched the near-full bottle.

"I'm not through with this yet," he muttered and tossed a bill onto the soiled tablecloth. "Here's payment for the meal. Keep the change."

And he strode out of the hotel.

By the time he braked the buggy to a stop on his front lawn, he'd given the whiskey a good share of business. He stepped from the rig carefully, testing his legs, and once down, dragged in a long breath of air. The cold helped clear his head.

The house loomed dark in front of him, but a shadowy, white-clad figure huddled on the stairs drew his eye.

Liza.

"I told you not to wait up." His voice was harsher than he'd intended, his mind already envisioning the picture she made whenever she wore his shirt for a sleeping gown. His step faltered, whether from liquor or from wanting, he couldn't be sure.

"I could not sleep," she said softly.

He grunted and managed his way toward her. He kept a firm grip on the bottle neck with one hand; with the other, he pulled his tie loose and let the ends dangle down, then fumbled with the top button of his shirt and managed that, too. Crossing his arms over his chest, he tucked the whiskey into the crook of his arm and leaned against the stair rail.

"You've ruined me for other women, y'know that?"

Her faint gasp reached him; she eyed him warily through the darkness.

"You might be interested to know Rebecca Ann won't be my wife. Not now or ever," he drawled. "It'd never work, anyway. We don't agree on child-rearing, and I'm not a part of her past. She clings to it and won't let go."

"Oh." She sat very still, her knees hugged to her chest. "I am sorry."

"Don't be. I'm not." He doubted she understood his ramblings. It didn't matter. "I do blame you for the mess I'm in, though."

She stiffened. "Me?"

He scowled darkly, a fine testament to his mood. "Kiss me like you did and expect me to forget it. To act like nothing ever happened between us, then ask another woman to marry me. Hell." No other man deserved this punishment, this torture. Why should he? "You haunt me wherever I go, y'know that? Whenever I sleep, you're there. I think of you every minute of every day. Not Rebecca Ann, Liza, but you. Always you. From the moment I saw you take my damned horse."

Her jaw lagged open prettily. She stared at him.

"There'll never be a woman like you in my life again."

She was the reason his world was falling apart. He'd lost an entire railroad over her, years of work and dreams gone. His life would never be the same.

But if his world were shattered, he wanted her at his side to pick up the pieces again.

"Will you marry me?" he asked quietly.

Her breath caught, the only sound in the night save for the beating of his heart.

"You have had too much of the whiskey," she said, her voice a tremoring whisper. "It has befuddled your mind."

"My head has never been more clear."

"But your people, Reese. Your town." Her fingers touched her mouth. "Bram."

"I don't care about them. You are all that matters to me."

She made no reply. After an eternity, she stood and walked to the door. One hand took the knob. She faced him.

"This is what you want?" she asked. "Truly?"

"Yes," he whispered. "Truly."

She didn't move for a long time. God, so long.

"Then it is what I want, too. Yes, Gajo. I will marry you."

Chapter Fifteen

They were married on Saturday afternoon. Liza wore the green henrietta, the crisp folds and shimmering luster transforming her from a shabby Gypsy to a beautiful Gajo bride. She treasured her new clothes, worn by no one before her and fitting to perfection, for she had not shamed Reese by wearing them. He had clearly been proud to have her at his side, but God's saints, the looks he gave her seemed to strip every thread from her body.

Afterward, there had been a wedding supper on Reese's lawn. All of Niobrara City came, with only Bram Kaldwell conspicuously absent. Maudeen outdid herself in planning the celebration. Everyone helped, new friends whose names Liza struggled to remember. Gaje who accepted her as Reese's wife out of respect for his prominence and influence in their town.

Now, the celebration was over. The games of roundball, horseshoes, and wrestling matches had ended. Tables dismantled, gifts opened, food put away. Everyone had left, tired but smiling, leaving nothing behind but a trampled lawn and a heartful of memories.

Liza stared out the bedroom window and relived each one. It had been a wonderful day. A day carved from a lifetime of dreams. But a dark cloud shadowed her joy.

She missed Mama. And Paprika. And Nanosh. Her brothers, cousins, the entire kumpania. She wanted them here to rejoice in her new husband and to take part in her wedding day, for it had been an occasion to rival the finest of ceremonies practiced by her people.

Except Mama would be horrified.

Liza had no need of divining or palming to know that. No tea leaves or sticks and stones were necessary. From the deepest recesses of her soul emerged the awful worry that she had made a terrible mistake marrying a Gajo, and Mama would be devastated.

The sun had long since faded into the night. A full moon took its place, a bright globe in the blackness. Its brilliance escaped her, as did a worried sigh of dismay that maybe her mother was right. She should not have married Reese Carrison.

He waited for her downstairs, giving her the time she needed to prepare herself, a wife for her husband on their wedding night, but here she stood, fully dressed and pensive. He would come to her soon, and she would not be ready.

Her pulse pounded a dull throb inside her head. To lie with him in his magnificent bed and consummate their marriage . . . She would be ostracized from her people, forever marhime, the final shame for marrying a Gajo.

The agony of being torn between two worlds wrought a moan of dismay from her throat. She had not felt it for a very long time, this anguish. The intense love she had for Reese had made everything seem right. But how could she give up the Gypsy world in which she had been raised, the world in which her family lived? How could she give herself to Reese when there was not enough of herself to give?

The door opened with a raspy squeak of its hinges. Knowing he came to her at last, she drew a deep breath, dredged up the courage to face him and slowly turned from the window.

His smoldering gaze touched on her but for a moment before swinging toward the bed, not yet turned down in readiness for their coupling, then back again, gliding over the green henrietta draping her from shoulder to ankle. She lifted her chin.

"Second thoughts, Mrs. Carrison?" he asked coolly.

"Yes."

A dark brow raised; he moved farther into the room. He had rolled his shirtsleeves up to his elbows, exposing his muscular forearms and a dusting of crisp hairs over his tanned skin. His masculinity reached out to her, and she swallowed down the stirrings of desire. So much a man, her husband. How could she not want him to make love to her?

"I won't hurt you if I can help it," he said, his voice low. "You know that, Liza."

She sensed his puzzlement in her reluctance to go to him when their kisses of late had been frenzied with passion, their touches tightly restrained from too much intimacy, saving themselves for now, for this moment.

"I am not afraid." Her glance fell from his, and she swept past him. She could not think straight when he looked at her like this, his longing a hot flame in his eyes.

He grasped her arm, a gentle but unyielding grip. "Then what is it?"

Their gazes clashed.

"Tell me," he said, strands of urgency in the words.

She pulled from his hold and pivoted, finding herself in front of his dresser and staring at their reflections in the mirror. He stood behind her, the top of her head at his chin. The breadth of his shoulders absorbed her slender form, and she could not help but know their bodies were a perfect match.

But in the soft glow of the kerosene lamp, she saw the wreath of wildflowers nestled in her hair, upswept in a coiffure with coppery-gold tendrils curling down her nape and over her forehead. No beads hung from her neck, no hoop earrings from her lobes. Preparing for her wedding, she had foolishly thought herself elegant and beautiful and very much a part of the Gaje world. Now, she could only feel shame.

"God's saints. Look at me." Her fingers plucked at the hairpins in disgust and dropped them to the dresser top. "I do not look Gypsy. Your people have changed me. *You* have changed me."

One half of her hair drooped. Reese caught the flower wreath before it tumbled to the floor. "You changed yourself, Liza. No one did it for you."

"I am Gypsy!"

"And you are Gaje. You're both."

Little bursts of panic swelled within her at the truth. How could she fit in with two very different worlds?

She yanked out the last pin. Her hair spilled over her back and shoulders. She frantically searched her mind for her striped kerchief, but for the life of her, she could not remember where she had put it.

She turned her face from the glass and coiled her arms about her. Suddenly, she felt terribly alone and a need to cling to the old ways.

"It is tradition for a bride's family to weep when they unbraid her hair after she is wed," she said hoarsely. "Then her new mother-in-law helps her tie her kerchief in the special knot used only by the married women."

Reese dipped his hand into the silken tresses, fingering the strands, stroking their texture.

"There's no one here to weep for you," he said. "And there's no braid. No mother-in-law. No kerchief."

She shook her head. "No. None of those things."

"Only me for the rest of your life, Liza. Your husband. Isn't that enough?"

She bit her lip and resisted the lure of his closeness, the warmth emanating from his body. "I do not know."

He stilled and let the locks of hair drop. "Your family won't be happy to learn we've married." In terse movements, he unbuttoned his shirt and removed it, hurling it to a far corner of the room. "What will they do?"

Miserable, she shrugged. "The Gypsies do not recognize a Gaje wedding. To them, it is only a ceremony that has no significance."

She flinched at his vehement curse. He snatched her left hand, lifting it for her to see, showing her the heavy gold band circling her finger.

"This is proof that you're mine." His voice was low and intense. " 'Til death do us part.' "

"The Gypsies have no need of these symbols."

"The Gaje do. We take them seriously. *I* take them seriously. And God forbid if anyone tries to take you away. I'll kill them first."

Her lower lip quivered.

He swore again.

Roughly, he took her against him, holding her stiff body tight to his chest, and pressed his jaw to her temple.

"What do I have to do to make us right by your people?" he demanded, a pleading desperation to his low voice. "I'll do anything. Anything."

She closed her eyes and sniffled. "You must ask permission of Mama and Nanosh."

"What else?"

Humiliation seared her. "There is a bride-price."

"I'll pay it. Whatever it costs to have you."

Swallowing, she drew a hopeless breath. "There must be complete agreement on both sides. Only then—but it can never be—I do not think—"

"It will be, my sweet." His lips touched her eyelids; his scent filled her. "I'll do everything in my power. I swear to God."

His chin swept the length of her cheek as he searched for her mouth. There was more to tell him, something so terrible that she could not now speak of it, not when she needed him like this, to hold her so possessively that all her worst fears and worries disappeared.

She melted into him, then, surrendering herself to his protection. Her head lifted, eager to meet his seeking lips. Their mouths locked in joint mating, tongues thrusting, twining, their breaths building to heavy pants of passion.

A tremor went through Reese. His hand came between them, to the buttons at her throat, her breasts, her waist, and the green henrietta fell open. With an impatient tug, he pulled the blouse from her shoulders; another, and her skirt drifted to her feet.

He cupped her face tenderly and broke their kiss, his eyes a physical caress over her features. "You're mine, Liza. Mine, forever."

"Yes," she whispered, for she wanted to be his with her whole being, no matter the consequences, no matter the future.

He bent and slipped an iron-thewed arm behind her knees, carrying her the short distance to the bed. He set her down gently, removed her stockings and shoes, and

pulled her chemise over her head. She wore no corset—
she could not abide them, though the women in his world
thought them necessary—and stood naked before him.

Cool air touched her skin, puckering her nipples, and
she released a shaky breath. His fierce gaze, hot with longing, evoked a rush of new and exciting sensations. She
trembled beneath the weight of them.

"I knew you'd look like this," he said huskily. "A million
nights I've dreamed of it."

He drew her snugly against him, crushing her breasts
against his heated chest, skin to bare skin, and Liza's breath
caught at the pleasure. His hungry mouth stifled her sighs.
Her arms wound to his back, her palms flattening against
the rock-hard muscles, holding him tight.

He rained fevered kisses down the column of her throat
and across her shoulder, lowering to the swell of her breast.
His tongue stroked and flirted with the dark crest, laving
it into a pebbled hardness. He suckled like a babe with a
man's need to be sated by a woman, and her knees nearly
gave way.

"Oh, Reese." Her fingers speared into the thickness of
his hair, and she held his head to her even as she wished
him to stop. "Saints in heaven."

A ragged laugh rumbled from him, as if he knew he
pleased her and delighted in it. He straightened and nuzzled her neck. "Ah, precious wife. There's more, and you'll
like it even better."

Bold in her quest to find the truth in his promise, her
fingers worked the buttons on his pants. "Do not dally,
then. This is more than either of us can stand, I think."

The black fabric parted, revealing his heated shaft throbbing in readiness for their joining. Reese guided her hand
to him, closing his fingers over hers. She lowered her lashes

and savored his velvety heat. A ripple of reaction rocked his body, and he sucked in a jagged breath.

He stepped away and removed the rest of his clothes, dropping them on top of her chemise. Muscle and sinew corded his taut, lean body, its manly symmetry boldly proclaimed in his nakedness. Liza's pulse quickened at her first glimpse of his raw maleness, the blood heating in her veins as she drank in the sight.

Splendid and perfect, her husband. Had she not known he would be so?

He reached around her to sweep the coverlet aside, then moved, bringing her down with him to the mattress, the sheets cool on her back, his body deliciously warm on her front.

He claimed her mouth in unquestioned demand, the fire of his desire igniting an answering blaze within her. Never would she tire of him kissing her like this, his lips hard and soft, his passion rough and gentle, his want deep. So very deep.

His lips slid sensuously to her jaw. He murmured her name again and again, his whispers ragged and fervent. The tip of his tongue stroked the inner curve of her ear, and she shivered from the tingles he wrought. His teeth nipped at her lobe, and her head turned upon the pillow, seeking him, wanting him to kiss her again.

Their mouths clung, and her caresses grew frantic over his body. His palms cupped her breasts, each thumb tantalizing a sensitive peak with feathery-soft strokes, inciting panting moans of pleasure from her. His hand slid over her belly, over the curve of her hip. Her breathing quickened with anticipation of his intent, exciting and wicked and wonderful. His hand slid lower, then lower still, and she ached from the mastery of his touch, from the exquisite sensations building inside her.

"Reese. Please."

She could stand no more of this scintillating torture. She writhed from the need of him, this fiery-hot want consuming her. Her thighs loosened, ready to take him. He rose above her, all male muscle and hardness and aching want, and probed her glistening feminine softness with his manhood. Her flesh resisted, and she gasped with the first sting of pain.

"I'll go easy, Liza," Reese breathed, his chest heaving, arms shaking as he held himself back for her. "It won't hurt long. Only seconds."

She trusted him, as she had long since learned to do, and accepted his tentative thrusts. His hips moved over hers, gentle but insistent. Then, a sharp burn shot through her, and she sucked inward. He plunged deep, erasing the hurt, filling her until she feared she could not hold all of him.

His mouth found hers, hungry and consoling, his tongue sweeping aside the memory of his entry and stoking, instead, a strange, budding sensation. He moved again, deep, so deep, her tightness taking him, stroking him, inviting her hips to lift and sway with his. Belly to belly. Thigh to thigh. Man to woman. Liza cleaved with him and rode the peaks, until wave after wave of physical ecstacy washed over her.

Groaning, shuddering, Reese poured his seed into her, staking his claim on her as his wife, solely his for any who dared to deny it. Liza reveled in his possession, for in return he would be hers now and forever, and when his body drifted onto hers, spent and fulfilled, contentment swathed her soul. She held him in her embrace, his body pleasingly heavy on hers, for long after their breathing had eased, their bodies cooled, their passions complete.

*   *   *

"We have all night, Liza. And the rest of our lives." Warmly amused, Reese ran a knuckle across her chin.

"It is not my fault I have learned to like one more thing you taught me," she murmured, tracing a lazy line down the middle of his chest to his navel with her fingertip.

Deliciously cozy snuggled next to him among the pillows and sheets, Liza propped her head up on one hand and tucked a foot between his hair-roughened shins. For the life of her, she could not sleep, even after the excitement of their fervored coupling.

"You don't know the half of it, what we can do to pleasure each other," he said softly. "I'll be happy to teach you those ways, too."

"When?"

"Soon." His low chuckle tumbled through the sheets. "A man needs a little time when a woman wears him out like you did me. To catch his breath, so to speak."

"Oh." She frowned.

"You're insatiable, y'know that?"

"I do not know what *insatiable* means," she said and snuggled closer, laying her head on his shoulder.

Reese grunted, settling her against him. "Every husband should be so lucky."

"Then it does not matter if I understand the meaning or not." She sighed contentedly and drew her open palm against his lean, flat belly. She could not touch him enough. Not in her lifetime.

Against her will, traces of her past melded with the present, and her mouth pursed. As her husband, she wanted Reese to know of her people, their ways and customs, always so different from his.

"It is very important to the Gypsy to have a virgin for his bride," she mused. "Is it so with the Gaje?"

"A man takes a lot of pride in knowing he's the first to

bed his wife, that she's saved herself for him." His arm tightened about her. "But I guess in a few cases a man has to take what he can get. In some parts of the country, women are mighty scarce."

"Oh." Her lashes lowered; a light blush touched her cheeks. "A Gypsy bride must display proof to the entire kumpania that she was pure for her husband on their wedding night, a blood-stained sheet perhaps, or else she brings much shame to him and his family." She hesitated. "Will you expect that of me as well, to show your people I was pure for you?"

"Hell, no." Though he voiced no criticism of the practice, it was not difficult to see he thought little of it. "That's a private matter between you and me. No one else."

"Thank the saints." Liza had always been embarrassed with the custom. She could not visualize such a thing with Maudeen or Mayor Al Dunning or Hank in attendance. Her cheeks blazed anew just thinking of it.

Reese shifted, and he lifted her chin with a crooked finger. His tigerlike eyes darkened with concern. "If your people place this much importance on a virgin among their own, what will they do when they learn a Gypsy virgin has wed a Gajo?"

Her blood faltered in her veins. She could not bear to tell him. She pushed at him, wanting to leave the bed, to avoid answering, but he held her fast.

"Liza, I need to know. For your sake."

She swallowed; still, she hesitated.

With a sweep of his mighty arm, he lifted her atop him, their bodies oblivious to the other's nakedness. His hands gripped her waist.

"I'm not kin to secrets between us," he said, a hint of warning in his tone. "I'll not ask overmuch of you as my

259

wife except honesty and truth. Always. I'll give the same to you."

He was her husband. Strong and powerful and shrewd, and how she loved him. If she could not share with him all that was in her heart, especially her worst worries, what kind of wife would she be?

Even so, she could hardly say the words aloud. With a worried sigh, she lowered her head and nestled beneath his chin, her hair splayed outward in a silken mass over his shoulder. She took comfort from the steady beat of his heart and slid her arms around him, holding him close.

"I did a very serious thing in marrying you," she said finally. "It will be a matter for the kris to decide."

Under the sheets, his hands stroked her spine, slow and soothing. "Why would they deny you the man you choose to marry?"

"You are Gajo. No other reason."

"And these are the same men who ordered your mother's head shaved?"

"Yes. They are very respected and wise. Their word is to be honored and obeyed."

He fell silent, his hands continuing their stroking magic. "I understand the power they wield," he said. "Similar to judges and juries. But our marriage is legal and binding, Liza. The kris is forced by the law of this land to recognize it. What's the worst they could do to you?"

She shuddered in revulsion. She found her courage and faced the truth. "I could be banished from the kumpania. An outcast. I would never be able to see my family again."

His arms flexed, pulling her up to look at him. He appeared stunned. "You're serious."

"I could never jest about something so terrible."

"No wonder you had second thoughts afterward," he muttered.

She nodded soberly. "The shame to my family will be very great. I fear I will pay dearly for my decision. For a Gypsy, there is no greater punishment than to be declared marhime."

"Oh, Liza." Cupping the back of her head, he brought her back down against him, wrapping his strong arms around her. For long minutes, he said nothing, and she imagined his logical mind working, sifting through all she had told him.

As she lay on him, her cheek pressed to his warm skin, a strange form of relief veiled a portion of her worries. She did not feel so alone now, nor so fearful and apprehensive. She had opened her heart and emptied it into his own, giving him everything of her world, holding nothing back. Perhaps some of the mystery would be eliminated, making reality less daunting and more easily confronted.

"Listen to me." Reese pulled her up again. He tucked her hair behind her ears, the movement tender and pensive. "You read my palm once. Remember?"

"I will never forget."

"You told me I'd have a great love someday, that the woman I married would make me happy, and our love would last forever."

"Yes," she whispered.

"We both assumed you spoke of Rebecca Ann. We were both wrong." He took her hand, twining their fingers, and dropped a soft kiss to the inside of her wrist. "You were speaking of yourself. I know that now because I love you so much it scares me."

Emotion welled inside her. Her head dipped, her mouth hovering over his. "I love you, too, Reese. More than anything. Anything."

"We'll get through this." His fingers speared into her

hair. His breath melded with hers. "I don't know how, but we will. Together."

"My wonderful, precious husband."

She kissed him long and slow, a drugging kiss that told him again of her love for him, of her gratitude and belief in everything he told her.

A slow fire built within her, flame by flame. She strained toward him. She wanted more, demanded it. The sheets slid downward, bunching at her hips, but she did not bother with modesty. Why should she, when he now knew her body as well as herself?

Against the softness of her abdomen, his burgeoning manhood throbbed in response, fanning the fire inside her. She knew the pleasures that lay ahead, and suddenly impatient, her blood raced hot.

"Love me again, Reese," she breathed. "Love me now."

She raised over him, her hair a red-gold curtain around them. Her knees parted, straddling his hips, and she took control, giving where once she took, bringing him home and discovering a new kind of ecstacy.

His breathing grew ragged. Gasp for gasp, the bed rocking with their rhythmic thrusts, they rode together into the sky and touched the stars until they shattered into a thousand pieces and came drifting down, glorious and glittering and delightfully sated.

A persistent dinging pulled Liza from the blissful depths of slumber. She frowned, resisting the sound, and snuggled closer against the solid warmth of Reese's body.

An annoyance, those Gaje alarm clocks.

She did not want to get up. She wanted to stay tangled in her husband's arms and legs forever, never leaving their wonderful big bed. But already the sun's brilliant rays beamed into the room, hinting of a dawn long since past.

A heavy groan rumbled from Reese, and he rolled to his side of the mattress, reaching over to stop the ringing. His arms came back around her.

"I have to go into town," he mumbled against her hair.

"No. Stay with me another day." Though she had not yet opened her eyes, her lips found his chest easily in a brief, pleading kiss.

"I have to meet with the cartel."

"Stay with me." Her tongue swirled lazy circles around his nipple.

"I have to work for a living." Amusement laced his tone. He nuzzled her cheek with his whiskery jaw until, fully awake, she giggled and pushed him away. "We've hardly left this bed for three days, my lusty wife, except to eat and bathe and see to the chores. And you want another?"

"I do. I am insatiable." Having deciphered the true meaning of the word at some point throughout their loving, she lifted her bare shoulder in an uncaring shrug. "You said so yourself."

"That I did. And it's my great fortune you are." He planted a loud kiss on her mouth. "However, I have to get up."

He tossed the covers aside and heaved himself out of bed, but Liza delayed, her mouth pursed in a pout.

She had been shameless with him these past days. The hour had not mattered. Early or late, she wanted him. It seemed so long ago she despaired of being desired as a wife, as a woman, yet Reese proved her wrong. Every touch, every spoken word, every fervent kiss affirmed he treasured her as his.

Her gaze riveted to his lean, naked body as he moved about the room washing and shaving and choosing his clothes. Little muscles rolled in his taut buttocks, bigger ones in his thighs. She relived the feel of his flat belly beneath her palms, the hard flex of his biceps. God's saints, even the dark thatch in his armpits excited her.

A liquid heat pooled between her legs, and she squirmed, resisting the need to pull him back into bed for another around of coupling, knowing this time he must refuse and understanding why. She reluctantly slipped from beneath the sheets and doused her longings by making quick work of her own washing and dressing, then departing for the kitchen.

By the time she fried eggs with ham and potatoes, he joined her, dressed in the same crisp black suit he had married her in, and ready for his important meeting with railroad investors. Losing Bram Kaldwell's backing had been a great worry for him, she knew, to say nothing of the blow to their friendship, and she prayed silently that all would go well so that he would not forfeit both Bram and the N & D.

All too soon, he was ready to leave, and at his urging, she walked with him to the corral. While he saddled the stallion, her spirits plummeted, for the day stretched out before her, unusually long and lonely.

She clasped her hands behind her back and twirled the toe of her shoe in the soft dirt.

"I will miss you today," she murmured.

He glanced up from the clinch. "I'll miss you, too."

Though she knew he spoke the truth, most likely he would be very busy with his men and his railroad and would not miss her as much as he thought he would. She, on the other hand, had no one to talk to or be with. Even Hank would not come to call, now that she was married.

"Maybe I will go to Maudeen's for a visit," she mused.

"Good idea. She loves having you."

"Or maybe I will pick gooseberries for a pie."

"That's good, too."

With her kumpania, she was never lonely with so much family around. Even little Tekla and Putzi provided company, along with all the other Gypsy children. Oh, to have a child of her own . . .

On impulse, she flung her arms wide and spun about, flaring her bright red skirts and jangling her bead necklaces. "I wish I had a dozen babies to take care of when you are at work. Babies in the house, in the yard, in my arms. Babies everywhere!"

"Ah, Mrs. Carrison." Reese stepped behind her, his hands winding around to splay across her abdomen. "Nothing would please me more than to fill your belly with my seed and watch it grow round with our child."

She leaned into him, covering his hands with hers. "And we will have beautiful children, will we not? Children with dark hair and golden-brown eyes—"

"—and burnished copper hair and black eyes, and the girls will wear earrings and bracelets—"

"—and they will all love trains and horses and—"

He twirled her around to face him, his hard kiss smothering the words, igniting a not-long-banked passion in them both. Through her skirts, his swollen maleness cried out his want, a want Liza ached to fill.

He dragged his mouth from hers. His breathing jagged, he tilted his head back and squinted into the sun, as if gauging its position in the sky. He grunted his decision.

"Ten minutes, wife," he said. "That's all I'll give you."

And he scooped her into his arms and carried her back into the house.

Chapter Sixteen

Reese strode across the depot and burst into his office. The door swung shut with an inadvertent slam, the glass panes, emblazoned with the words *Nebraska-Dakota Railroad*, rattling with his arrival.

Harriet Browning jumped, nearly toppling her inkwell onto the ledger pages spread out before her. The gray-haired grandmother of ten came in a few mornings a week to assist in the mountain of paperwork required to run a railroad, but rarely arrived before Reese.

"I'm late," he said needlessly, plucking his hat from his head and tossing it on the coatrack near her desk.

"So I see."

"Are they here yet?" He indicated the closed door leading to the tiny workplace he called his.

"Yes, sir. Have been for a while now."

He brushed the dust from his cuffs, tugged his sleeves lower about his wrists, checked his tie to make sure it hung straight. After raking a hand through his hair, he drew in a deep breath and grasped the knob.

Harriet's pen hovered once more over the inkwell. Her lips twitched. "Setting the alarm clock one half hour earlier allows plenty of time for marital companionship. Leastways it did for Arthur and me."

Reese's mouth quirked wryly. "Thanks, Harriet. I'll remember that."

He opened the door and faced the quartet of pinstripe-suited, cigar-smoking men who waited for him.

For two hours, he plied the benefits of the Nebraska-Dakota Railroad to the northern part of the state and Niobrara City itself; provided figures of costs and income from shipping crops and livestock to Omaha and points east, stressed the profits made, small but steady and with a potential to grow higher over time. In a quiet voice, he told the cartel all these things while his heartbeat tight with fear in his chest that they would not see them as significant, that they would deny him the precious financial backing he needed to keep his train running on its track.

Afterward, he dined with them at the Grand River Hotel, sparing no expense and wishing Bram was with him. Far more experienced at wooing and wheedling, Bram had a natural ability to charm and sway in both business and social circles, while Reese relied on gut instinct to find his way. But then, he reminded himself grimly, had Bram been here, the cartel would not.

As they lingered over after-dinner brandies and leisurely smokes, he invited the men on a horseback guided tour of the railroad, its track and stations, and of course, the trestle bridge. To his great relief, they accepted, and everyone saddled up.

The weather worked to his advantage. It was a clear day, with the sun high enough in the sky to warm their backs without drawing a sweat, the air crisp and clean in their lungs. They conversed constantly, questions and answers flying forth between them with ease.

They paused at the ridge overlooking Skull Canyon. Below, the bridge towered over a narrow stream glistening on the canyon floor. Reese spoke of the bridge with pride, pointing out the hundreds of wooden planks that crisscrossed across the massive opening, shoring up the rails that would guide the train from one side to the other.

The cartel was duly impressed.

"A fine piece of workmanship, Reese."

"Stupendous!"

"But what of Silas McCrae?" Jim Worthington, his portly belly straining his vest buttons, pointed to the heavy timbers. "He burned out a quarter mile of track, didn't he? There's a hell of a lot of lumber in that bridge, Reese. What will keep McCrae from destroying it as well?"

Up to now, the day's discussions and tour had worked in Reese's favor. Obviously, the cartel's concern over Silas McCrae would not.

"We'll post a guard if we have to." Reese pointed toward a stretch of sparse woodlands nearby. "I've thought of clearing this area of land and building a post—"

He halted, his attention caught by a snippet of blue fabric waving from a cottonwood branch high over their heads.

He frowned but continued. "If we ride over here"—he urged the stallion forward twenty yards, and the men followed—"you can see that a man can easily watch—"

He halted again, another piece of the fabric catching his eye. His concentration faltered, and he shot a glance to the ground.

Deep grooves in the soft dirt wove the entire length of

the ridge, the tracks pummeled by countless well-shod hooves.

"A guardpost, you say?" Worthington prompted.

A strange arrangement of stones with a single stick pointing forward to the north, a symbol Reese had never seen before but one he recognized.

The men of the cartel faded out of his awareness, their questions dying to a buzz in his head. Filled with a slow, heavy dread, Reese mouthed a fervent curse.

Liza hummed an old Gypsy tune while she picked gooseberries, choosing only the ripest and best, and filling the tin bucket to near overflowing. The shrubs lined a trickling stream located a pleasant walk from Reese's house, and they grew wild for the taking. She had grown partial to Gaje pastry and could already taste a flaky pie on her tongue, juicy and sweet and baked to perfection.

With a tinkle of her bracelet, she dropped the last berry on the pile and straightened, easing the ache from the small of her back. Her mind busy with thoughts of washing and stemming the fruit for the next step in preparing the pie, she hardly noticed the shadow rising over her.

It loomed larger. The grass behind her rustled, prickling the fine hairs on the back of her neck. A horse blew softly nearby, and an instantaneous image of Silas McCrae flashed in her mind. She whirled.

"Hanzi!"

The sight of him jolted her when she had fully expected to see the raging fur trapper in his buffalo hides and dirty beard. A cry of joy bubbled in her throat.

But there was no elation, no answering smile, on her brother's young features. Stone-faced, he stared back at her.

"What is this thing you have done, Liza?"

His chilling demand sent cold reality whirling through her brain.

The time had come.

The sound of jangling harnesses seeped through her dread. One by one, high-wheeled wagons, too many to count, certainly more than the entire Lowara tribe, rumbled to a stop. The horizon was filled with them, her people, all of whom had finally come back for her.

Nanosh leaped from the last rig. A door creaked open, and Mama stepped out. Behind her emerged Paprika with Tekla in her arms, and Putzi, his little legs scampering to keep up.

Like an angry boar, Nanosh stormed toward her. Before Liza could greet him, he drew close. His beefy hand came up, striking her across the cheek with a force that sent her sprawling into the weeds.

She cried out in surprise and pain. Her hair, held back only by the tortoiseshell combs Reese preferred, flung over her eyes and face, and she clawed at the strands, lest he hit her again.

"She-dog! For nineteen winters, I raised you as mine, and you repay me only with dishonor!" he said in a snarl.

"No!" she gasped, pressing her palm to her fiery cheek. Her mind reeled from the blow, from his accusations.

Mama rushed forward. "I prayed to the great spirits it was not true, that my daughter would not be so stupid. In God's love, Liza, tell me you did not do this!"

"She wears his ring," Hanzi said dully.

"Yes." Nanosh's features darkened with contempt. "The Gajo speaks the truth, then."

He lunged for her, as if to land another punishing slap. Liza scrambled to her feet and, through sheer agility, managed to dodge him. Bosom heaving, she watched him with

270

a wary eye, watched all of them as they centered her with their dark, accusing gazes.

"For many days and many nights we searched to find you," Mama said, her weathered face full of anguish. "We leave behind the vurma, but you do not find it. We leave messages among our people, but no one has seen you. You disappear—*poof!*—into thin air. Even Hanzi cannot find you when he goes back to the Gaje town where we saw you last."

"And then we hear of the big wedding." Hanzi's lip curled. "A Gypsy and a Gajo. Everyone talks. The Rom are amazed. They cannot imagine anything more shameful."

"All the tribes mock us." Tears streamed down Mama's cheeks. "Have I not taught you well, daughter? Have I shamed you so much that you must shame me back?"

"No, Mama!" Liza said hoarsely. She never dreamed a pain as terrible as that which speared her now, a pain as deep and burning as any sharp-bladed knife might wield.

"We travel along the railroad tracks to find our way quickly back to Niobrara City," Nanosh sneered. "A Gajo who works with the big train tells us how to find Reese Carrison. He says you will be with him." He pursed his lips and hurled a stream of spittle at her skirt hems. "Why do we come back? Why? You do not deserve to be Gypsy!"

Liza sucked a breath inward. There was no worse curse than that.

"Look at you, Liza!" Mama sobbed. Her features twisted with torment, she sank to her knees and spread her hands wide. "Your hair—no braid, no kerchief. Nothing! Free to the wind for all to see—have you no honor?"

"Mama, please!"

Liza had never seen her so distraught. A high-pitched wail filled the air, dredged from the deepest bowels of her mother's soul. Her faded kerchief clinging to her hairless scalp, she curled into a tight ball of hysteria, her brown fists pounding the weeds and grass.

"Oh, Mama. Do not do this! I cannot bear it!" Arms outstretched, Liza bent toward her, needing to comfort her for the pain she had wrought and hold her grief-wracked body against her own.

"Do not touch her!" Nanosh's bark stopped her cold.

"She is my mother!" Liza cried.

"She gave you life, but you do not deserve to be called daughter," he spat.

Liza jerked back as if he had struck her again. Her chin trembled. "How can you say such a thing?"

"I say it because it is the truth."

"Enough, Nanosh!" Another man's authoritative bark halted Nanosh's fury. "You do not give her a chance to defend herself."

Liza's gaze darted toward a short, slightly built man, a man whom she had not seen in many years, but one she recognized with much dread.

Uncle Pepe. Mama's brother. Leader of the ominous kris.

Her knees wobbled beneath her. His presence explained the extra wagons, the many Gypsies staring through windows and doors. In that instant, she realized the kumpanias had banded together to find *her* and that justice would be served.

Her stomach heaved with horror.

"Calm yourself, Pesha," Uncle Pepe commanded.

Immediately, Mama's wails ended, softening to little hiccups. Her body unfurled to lay limp and prone in the weeds, as if she did not have the strength to rise.

Uncle Pepe's black-eyed glance fastened on Liza.

"We are in the Gaje world now." His slender arm swept before him, indicating the cultivated fields of corn and wheat adjoining Reese's land, the ribbon of road leading

272

into Niobrara City, the tiny shapes of barns and houses in the distance.

"Yes," she whispered.

"This is not the place for us to settle the grave matter of your marriage," he said. His glittering perusal held her captive with the immensity of his power among her people. A pencil-thin mustache lined his upper lip. His gold tooth shined in the sun. "Come with us, and we will find another."

He turned, obviously expecting her to follow. Hanzi went to Mama's side and curled his arm about her shoulder, urging her back to their wagon in a quiet voice. Nanosh joined him, and they lifted her, sniffling and exhausted, to her feet. Not giving Liza a backward glance, they made their way back to the kumpania.

Only her siblings remained, silent and haunted by all they had seen. Even little Tekla, perched on Paprika's hip, did not squirm or howl with her usual two-year-old enthusiasm.

"What will you do?" Paprika asked softly, her eyes wide and sorrowful.

Liza could not speak past the huge lump in her throat. Tears threatened, and she angled her face from the children, that they would not see her torment, the agony that threatened to tear her apart.

She blinked furiously and focused a longing gaze on Reese's house—*her* house. Gay-colored asters and brilliant clematis waved cheerfully in the breeze. The well-trimmed lawn, the white clapboard siding, the spacious porch lining the entire front of the structure. Her garden, with its well-tended rows and thriving vegetables. In a flash, she relived all the memories sheltered within the walls of her new home.

Her home.

She envisioned the kitchen and the cast-iron stove where she had learned to cook Reese's meals. She thought of his magnificent bed, of the pie she intended to bake for him that afternoon.

Putzi tugged on her skirts, his angelic face in need of a washing, his tousled locks begging for a comb.

"Are you coming, Liza? Are you?" he demanded. His pudgy fist grasped the red fabric in a tight grip, as if he refused to take no for an answer, as if this time, he would not leave her behind.

In the weeks she had been away, his front teeth had grown back in, and he lost the endearing lisp. He seemed taller, more grown-up. A little man. Her heart ached with love.

She drew in a long breath and wavered beneath the awful weight sagging on her shoulders.

She had a price to pay. She owed Mama for the hurt. She must account for the decision she made at the cost of Reese's love and the happiness he had given her. Her people expected little else. It was the Gypsy way.

A part of her died accepting it.

She smoothed Putzi's hair and reached for Tekla, settling her on her own hip, relieving Paprika of the responsibility. With all the strength she possessed, every ounce and shred, she turned toward the endless line of wagons and the stern, disapproving faces staring back at her.

Putzi's hand slipped inside hers. He peered up at her hopefully, the unanswered question shining in his eyes.

For his sake, Liza managed a tiny smile. "Yes, little one. I am coming."

Several fires blazed in the camp and sent hazy tendrils of smoke twisting into the black night. Listless and uneasy, wild-haired mongrel dogs roamed and paced, low growls in their throats. Barefoot children hovered close to their mothers. Subdued voices rose and fell, gripped by the somber mood of the kumpanias.

Eighteen battered wagons curved around the encampment in a protective half-circle, shielding the Gypsies from inquisitive Gaje and opening onto the banks of the Niobrara River. Tethered by long ropes, a large herd of horses grazed at the edge of camp. Somewhere in the trees, an owl hooted in song.

A tautness hung in the air. Nerves stretched tight from the waiting . . .

Liza huddled on a fallen log and wrapped her arms about her knees. She endured the wait with thoughts of Reese, filling her head with memories of him. Did he work late, not yet knowing she rejoined her people? Or did he search frantically, tortured with worry and guilt, any place she might be? The kitchen, the barn, Maudeen's? Had he found the pail of gooseberries she left behind?

Would he understand?

He would not tolerate her decision. That, Liza knew with grave certainty. She knew, too, he would come in search of her, and he would find her. More than once, he had vowed it.

But would it be too late?

Near her, sprawled on the ground, Hanzi tossed chunks of red meat to Rollo, chained to the back of Nanosh's wagon. The tame brown bear gobbled every morsel and sniffed out more.

Hanzi's gaze lifted, meeting Liza's. Compassion flickered in the dark depths, and she sensed his longing to spare her the kris. It seemed his disapproval had filtered into grim acceptance of what she had done, and she derived great comfort that he still loved her, despite her dishonor.

Mama's hurt would not go away so easily. Surrounded

by several other women, she squatted in a small clearing by their wagon and wept softly. Liza knew she must grieve in front of the entire kumpania, to show them she did not approve of what Liza had done, yet the display stung deeply. Did Mama not know Liza never meant to cause her such pain? Surely, she did. But her hate for the Gaje would close her eyes to reason.

Paprika tiptoed out from inside Nanosh's wagon, pausing on the wide board that served as a porch to close the door with a gentle click. The task had fallen to her to see that Tekla and Putzi slept peacefully beneath their eiderdowns, and Liza was glad they would be spared the grim proceedings ahead. She could only imagine the terrible punishment the kris would hand down to her.

Paprika skittered down the wagon step and sat next to her on the old log.

"Is it true you married the handsome Gajo? The one we saw at the train depot?" she demanded without fanfare. Keeping her voice low, she wiggled close, for this had been the first opportunity they had to speak alone.

"Yes, Paprika. I have married him."

Her dark brows furrowed. "But he already had a wife. And a daughter, too."

Liza blinked. Then, she remembered Margaret Michelle on that fateful afternoon, her infatuation with the small yucca basket, and Rebecca Ann who had said all the hurtful things about her people.

How long ago it seemed! A lifetime. And yet only a short while.

"No, Paprika. We were both mistaken that day." A faint smile touched her mouth. "Reese has never been married. I am the only wife he has ever had."

Paprika pressed a hand to her small bosom and heaved a solemn sigh of relief. "I did not think it would be proper to have more than one wife, even for the Gaje, but I did not know for sure."

"The Gaje are not as terrible as the Gypsies think," Liza said quietly. "I have learned this for myself."

"Perhaps not." Paprika regarded her seriously. "Do you love him?"

Emotion clogged Liza's throat.

"Very much," she whispered.

"Then you are very lucky."

Dear Paprika. So adultlike. How could she know the terrible price that must be paid for the decision to wed Reese? Did she not understand the awful shame and disgrace that had been heaped upon Mama and Nanosh?

"I do not feel so lucky," Liza murmured and swept a nervous glance toward the men stirring across the flickering campfire.

"You are." Paprika hooked her arm through Liza's and whispered confidentially. "Mama tells me Spiro has offered to marry me. I cannot think of a worse husband. He smells."

"Spiro comes from a respectable family." Liza tried to be tactful.

"So? I do not love him. I want to choose my own husband. Like you."

"It is not easy, Paprika. But you are only twelve. You have several years to get to know him."

Her glance strayed again to the members of the kris, smoking quietly and sharing bottles of whiskey. A few rose from the ground and found makeshift seats from whatever oddities they could find on hand—an overturned pot, a tree stump, an unwieldy bale of hay. Finally, Uncle Pepe himself rose and produced an abandoned chair, one leg shorter than the other three. Nanosh hurried forward with a chunk of wood to bolster the troublesome lean, and after a brief testing, Uncle Pepe nodded his approval.

Liza's stomach flip-flopped. "Saints in heaven, Paprika. It is time."

"Yes. Have trust, Liza." Her black eyes pools of sympathy, Paprika's arms tightened around her in a quick hug before she scurried away to join Mama and the other Gypsy women.

Liza stood, her legs far less steadier than Uncle Pepe's rickety chair.

Behind her, Mama rasped her name and hurried forward with a jangle of necklaces and bracelets. Her brown cheeks were stained with tears. An amulet hung from her neck, smelling of red and black pepper, salt and vinegar spices, and she clasped Liza tightly with her strong arms.

"God give you luck, my child," she whispered. She removed the amulet and draped it over Liza's head; the little drawstring bag dangled between her breasts. "I would lay down my life to keep you from this," she said, her voice quavery. "I was not much younger than you when I had to stand before the kris. They have great power. They hold your honor in their hands."

"I am not afraid," Liza said, as much for Mama's sake as her own.

"I am afraid for you." As if she realized they tarried too long at the expense of the court's patience, she kissed each of Liza's cheeks. Choking back a sob, she ran back to the women and squatted, hiding her face in her palms.

"Liza. Daughter of Pesha, my sister. Come forward," Uncle Pepe commanded.

She drew a breath; her heart pounded and raced.

But she obeyed, standing before them, a semicircle of men who earned their place on the kris with their wisdom and experience over the years. She knew them all: Yojo, a master metalsmith; Stevan, a musician; Dominic, a skilled horseman; Tinya, an artisan; and of course, Uncle Pepe.

Ordinary men with extraordinary power. They dressed no differently than the rest of the Rom, wore no jewelry or special robes. They acted without arrogance. But they carried a dignity about them that held them apart, a solemnity that inspired respect and total allegiance.

Uncle Pepe leaned forward and fastened a stern gaze on her.

"Do you promise to answer the questions we put before you with truth, Liza?" he demanded.

She bowed her head. "May my mother die a horrible death if I mock you with lies."

He nodded. "*Bater*. May it be so."

Likewise, the court responded with rumbles of agreement.

It seemed forever before Uncle Pepe spoke again, so long that Liza clasped her hands tightly before her, keeping her head lowered. Starkly alone, she stood, living the nightmare, the reality of the kris, with scores of black-eyed gazes centered on her, none of whom would trade places with her for all the gold in the world.

Nausea rolled in her belly. That she could prevent this from happening . . .

"You have shamed the Gypsies by marrying a Gajo," Uncle Pepe said finally, startling Liza with the sound of his voice. "You have brought great disgrace to your family. There are few worse things you could have done."

Her chin lifted. She swallowed hard.

"What do you have to say to this?" he asked gravely.

She garnered her courage and willed herself not to shake like a leaf in the wind.

"There is a saying among us," she began. "Which is greater, the oak or the dandelion?"

"Yes," he murmured and stroked a fingertip along his thin mustache.

"The answer is ponderous and wise. Whichever one achieves fulfillment." She drew a breath. "By the accident of my birth, I have been a dandelion among my people. A weed to be stepped on or cast aside. Because the blood of my natural father flows in my veins, I am not a true Gypsy. I do not belong among the sturdy oaks—the Rom."

The entire camp was silent; even the children listened.

"When I married Reese Carrison, I knew the cost. I knew the shame," she said. "But I married him, anyway."

"Why?" Yojo asked.

"Because I had fallen in love with him. Even now, as I stand before you with great respect, the sight of him never leaves my eyes. The smell, the taste of him never leaves my senses. The strength of our love never leaves my heart."

In the golden glow of the firelight, members of the kris stared, their expressions thoughtful.

"I am nothing but a dandelion, Uncle Pepe, but I have achieved fulfillment with my husband. I have learned his ways. His people accept me. I have more honor with the Gaje than I do the Gypsy."

"You feel this to be true, with your soul and your mind?" he said, frowning.

"I do."

"Have you had such a terrible life with our people? Have we not fed you and protected you? Have you not been included in the celebrations and happiness shared by the kumpanias?"

"Yes, all those things." She drew courage from the keen interest shown by the entire court. "I do not seek pity for myself, but in truth, consider my mother, my brothers and sisters." Her mouth pursed. She chose her words with care. "Twenty winters ago, Mama made a mistake. Adultery, as you know. But she was very young, and since then, Nanosh, her husband, has forgiven her."

She ventured a glance toward him, hunkered near a tree. A cigarette burned, forgotten, between his fingers. No movement came from him, as if he, too, listened with sharp interest.

"For many years, we have lived by the harsh judgment handed down to her by the kris," she said. "It is a part of our lives. But how long must we endure the shame from the past?"

Tinya rested an elbow on his knee and propped his chin in his hand. He considered her for one long, agonizing moment. "Tell us of the shame, Liza."

She detected a hint of challenge in his tone, as if she dared to defy their wisdom all those years ago. She met that challenge.

"Already Paprika speaks of a husband of her own." Liza thought of Spiro and managed not to grimace. "But those who want her for a wife are few, and not, perhaps, her first choice. And there is Hanzi."

With the eyes of all the Gypsies upon him, he met Liza's gaze, proud and erect.

"See him?" Her heart swelled with love. "So strong and honorable, yet because he has not yet taken a wife, he cannot be called Rom. He hesitates to take his rightful place in the community. He does not want to shame his wife and children, as he has been shamed, and Nanosh, his father, before him."

Finally, she gestured toward her mother, sweating with anguish, her bosom heaving with deep, heavy breaths.

"Of all of us, Mama has suffered the most," Liza said softly. She faced the kris once more. "Do you realize I have never seen her with hair? Nanosh told me once she had beautiful hair that shined in the sun, with curls that grew wild and thick beneath her kerchief."

"Yes," Uncle Pepe murmured. In the flickering flames, a hint of moisture shimmered in his eyes. "I remember, too."

In the sea of bodies that surrounded the campfires, several women sniffed. Mama wept openly. Even Nanosh hid his face in his hands, his shoulders shaking in silent torment.

Liza struggled with the emotion lodged in her own throat. "I am only a dandelion among the oaks. Yes, I have married a Gajo. Cast me aside like an unwanted weed, if you must. But spare the children the shame, I beg of you. Hanzi and Paprika, Tekla and Putzi, they are innocents. Do not punish them for what I have done."

Dominic cleared his throat. Stevan studied the toes of his battered boots. Pensive, Uncle Pepe rubbed his jaw and opened his mouth to speak.

A rustle in the brush halted the words on his tongue. The mongrel dogs bolted to their feet, growling viciously, running as a pack into the shadows. The men rose in unison, their alarm obvious, their gazes riveted to the unseen intruder.

The mood of the court had been shattered. Heart hammering, Liza peered into the darkness and clutched a hand to her breast.

A horse emerged. A stallion. Black and gleaming and magnificent.

Zor.

She gasped.

Reese swept an impassive glance over her people, then touched on her for a cool, brief moment. He gripped a long-barreled rifle in his hand, clearly ready to use force should her people refuse him entrance. The stallion stepped easily, casually, around the campfires and drew to a stop in front of the entire kris.

They eyed one another suspiciously.

Reese's mouth quirked.

"Sorry to interrupt," he said, "but I've come for my wife."

Chapter Seventeen

Their hostility was a volatile thing.

It buzzed around Reese like bees on clover, and he braced for its sting. He didn't immediately dismount from the stallion but kept his eyes open and senses primed. How far would they go in their refusal to relinquish Liza?

He detected no weapons around them. Not a pistol or rifle or knife could be seen. Their attack would be in the strength of their contempt rather than physical violence, and in that regard, he decided he'd be safe enough.

He returned the Winchester to its scabbard. A few of the younger men inched closer, their admiring gazes riveted to his horse. Reese let them look and dismounted.

His glance sought out Liza. He soaked in the sight of her, for the scare she'd given him, for the agony and worry he'd endured. He wanted to throttle her and hold her, all at the same time.

She kept her eyes downcast, her face angled away from

him, her body stiff and straight. Humiliation emanated from her.

Cast me aside like an unwanted weed, if you must.

Her words haunted him. He was too late. He hadn't reached her in time. She stood before the ominous kris, heart-wrenchingly alone, forced to account for their marriage without him.

Spare the children the shame, I beg of you.

He knew she hadn't wanted him to see her raw and exposed, pleading in front of everyone, her own shame suffocating, her dishonor crippling.

Do not punish them for what I have done.

. . . for what I have done.

The words rippled in his brain. God, that she had to go through this, that he couldn't keep her from it, that he was helpless and inept and, worse, a total outsider.

The Gypsies swarmed closer, keeping him from her, preventing any hope of private conversation. The women wore flowing, layered skirts and loose, low-cut blouses. Gold necklaces and bracelets abounded, and heavy earrings dangled from elongated lobes. The men faced him with sharp, piercing eyes, unshaven cheeks, and fierce mustaches. As a group, their posture was proud, defiant, and noble.

Liza's people. They carried the power to pamper her with love or destroy her with rejection.

"So you are Reese Carrison." Bearing a dignity that belied their primitive surroundings, a short, wiry man rose from his rickety chair. In the muted firelight, his gold tooth glinted.

Reese regarded him, recognizing the influence this man held over the Gypsies, over Liza, as they waited for his guidance to receive a Gajo in their camp.

"Yes," he said, cautious.

"I am Pepe." A tight smile stretched his thin lips. He gestured to the somber-faced group huddled around him. "We were just discussing you."

"I know." Reese leveled him with a steely gaze. "What did you decide?"

"It is a very serious thing you have done."

"Yes." He refused to be intimidated by this man's authority. "Do you deny Liza happiness when she's known only scorn all her life?"

Pepe stiffened as if Reese had slapped him across the face. "It is not for you to question."

"She's my wife," he said roughly. "You can damn well be sure I'll question anything that pertains to her welfare."

"It is a Gypsy matter. You are only a Gajo. You can never understand."

"Oh, I understand. Better than you think." Reese strove to keep his voice calm when he wanted to yell his frustration over their stubbornness. "Liza is a beautiful woman. She's talented and loving, with a heart hungry for a home of her own, a husband and children. She'd make any of the men here a perfect wife. But no one wants her. She's not good enough because she's half-Gaje."

Pepe glared at him.

"Well, she's mine now," Reese said softly. "And I want her more than anything."

"She is marhime," Pepe said, as if that explained everything.

"Yes, marhime. Because she's different, through no fault of her own. And she's marhime because she's married to me. She'll always be marhime to the Gypsy. Why deny her acceptance in my world when she has no chance with any of you?"

No one spoke. Reese's pulse hummed in his ears. Everything hinged on this moment, on the kris's reaction to his desperate pleas.

And to him.

"The Gajo speaks the logic of his people," Yojo said.

"It seems a hopeless case." Stevan shook his graying head sadly.

"No," Reese said in a hiss. "Not hopeless."

"What is it you want from us?" Pepe demanded.

"A compromise."

"Why?" Tinya spread his hands wide. "What will it prove?"

"It's a beginning," Reese reasoned. "A way to make my marriage work."

"How?" Dominic asked.

"Let me talk to her parents. Have they no say in this?"

Again, his question appeared to throw them off guard, as if, in their collective wisdom, they hadn't considered that avenue.

Pepe nodded seriously. He snapped his fingers, his glance sweeping the Gypsies surrounding them. "Nanosh! Pesha! Come meet your new son-in-law!"

The men and women murmured among themselves. Reese searched the shadowed faces for Liza and found her peeking over the top of the kerchiefed head of the woman in front of her. She made no move to join him. Another Gypsy ritual, he surmised, expecting him to pave the way for the marriage without her.

A barrel-chested man with thick sideburns made his way through the crowd and halted in front of him.

"I am Nanosh," he said. He appeared fatigued, emotionally drained. Dark circles ringed his eyes; his lids were slightly swollen.

"Reese Carrison." Reese extended his hand and hoped

Nanosh wouldn't insult him by refusing it, but the older man took the clasp in a tight grip.

"You married Liza," Nanosh said quietly. "In spite of everything."

"Yes." Their handshake ended. "I'll take good care of her. You have my word on that. She's bewitched my people and made many new friends. They love her almost as much as I do."

From around Nanosh's shoulder, Liza's mother glared at Reese. She was shorter than Liza, slender yet shapely for having borne five children. A faded kerchief was pulled low over her forehead, accentuating the stark shape of her scalp. Their gazes met, and she scowled, her black eyes darting away to stare determinedly at the ground.

"Pesha," Nanosh warned.

He slipped a burly arm behind her, firmly nudging her forward. She resisted; he muttered something in Romani and pushed her a little harder until she stood directly in front of Reese.

Still, she refused to look at him. Reese's mouth softened. He found her muleheadedness . . . endearing.

"I've always thought Liza incredibly beautiful," he said softly. "Now I know why. She takes after you."

Pesha sucked in a breath. With a flutter of her long lashes, her gaze lifted to him in surprise, then fell again. A faint blush touched her cheeks.

"The Gaje are very good at lying through their smiles," she snapped.

"I don't lie. Ever." He wondered how long it had been since someone paid her a compliment. Unable to help himself, he leaned over and kissed her cheek.

She flinched and trembled, squeezing her eyes shut.

"I know how hard this is for you, losing Liza to a Gajo,"

he said. "But as God is my witness, I swear to you, I'll make her happy."

Her black eyes, silent and distrustful, opened once more and flitted over him, but no scathing rebuttal left her lips.

A tiny victory, Reese thought. Satisfied, he turned to Nanosh.

"I'm prepared to pay an honorable bride-price," he said. "Whatever is fair."

Nanosh looked skeptical.

"In addition, I offer you winter quarters here, along the river, where there's shelter from the wind and plenty of water and grazing for the horses."

His voice carried over his captive audience. Dark brows rose in unison.

"If you choose to stay, there will be no trouble from my people. You'll be free to come and go among us without harrassment." He squared his shoulders. "So long as the agreement is mutual."

"How can you make these grand promises?" Yojo asked.

The women stirred as Liza moved forward. Her head held high, she maneuvered her way through the maze of bodies.

"He is greatly respected by his people. They will do whatever he asks of them," she said. She came to a stop near Reese, close enough for him to feel her heat, but not touching him. "He is their leader. They adore him."

She glanced at him proudly, then, her eyes deep, fathomless pools, and his loins churned with longing.

"Your offer is most generous, Gajo," Nanosh murmured.

"We will call upon the magic powers of the dead," Pepe said in finality. "Their wisdom will guide us in our decision. Do you agree, Pesha?"

"Yes," she said in a small voice, staring at Reese.

"That is enough for tonight. It is late. We have traveled many miles today, and we must rest."

With that, Pepe dismissed the kris.

All around him, the Gypsies began to disperse. Disappointment knifed through Reese. He cocked his head toward Liza.

"When we will know?" he asked in a low voice.

She shrugged. "It is hard to say. Perhaps tomorrow. Perhaps the next day."

"Not 'til then? Why can't they decide tonight?"

"In a grave matter such as this, the kris must take great care. They may choose to call forward witnesses to my integrity. Who knows?"

Reese groaned and chafed at the delay.

Liza moved against him, a subtle, intimate touch of her breasts against his arm, a wife's touch against her husband

"I am glad you are here," she whispered and lowered her lashes.

He soaked in her close presence. A potent gladness of his own soared through him.

"You deserve a sound thrashing for leaving. I was terrified I'd never find you again," he whispered back.

"Do not scold me, my love." She peered up at him, her expression beseeching and apologetic. "It was something I had to do. Besides, I knew you would find me again. You told me so yourself. Many times."

He grunted at the logic in her words, at the truth of them, for they rendered him without power to chastise her further.

"Yes," he said, wanting to hold her tight against his body but frustrated by the watchful band of men and women who kept him from it.

"Come." She tugged at his hand. "Paprika is anxious to meet you."

His fingers twined with hers. She led him around a campfire to a wagon situated on tall wheels. Painted a deep red with gold scrolls around the windows and door, it gleamed from thick layers of varnish. A young girl stood nearby, her gaze fixed on them, her features expectant.

Before Liza could speak, Paprika smiled, showing her strong, white teeth. "He is even more handsome than I remember, Liza."

No coyness or shy looks with this one, Reese thought, and grinned.

"Paprika." Liza clucked her tongue. "Do not be so bold. Thank the saints Mama did not hear you."

Nonplussed, Paprika dipped into a deep curtsy, spreading her full skirts wide. "No matter what the kris decides, he is a man with honor, Liza. I want a husband just like him."

Reese inclined his head. "My new sister-in-law has the charms of a grown woman. I think Nanosh will have his hands full. I'm most pleased to meet you, Paprika."

"She does not know her place." A youth in his late teens appeared and glowered with brotherly annoyance. He removed his wool cap. "I am Hanzi."

"I guessed as much," Reese said, nodding. "I hear you came looking for us in Niobrara City. I'm sorry we missed you."

"It would have saved us much worry had you been there." Hanzi regarded him steadily. "My sister deserves the best. She has not had an easy life."

"Oh, Hanzi," Liza breathed, her embarrassment obvious.

"She'll be cherished forever," Reese vowed. "Please know that."

The words had no sooner left his mouth when a raucous roar filled the air. From out of the shadows, a shaggy-furred bear lumbered toward them on all fours, his mouth open, teeth showing.

Reese's jaw lagged. Before he could react, the bear raised up on powerful hindlegs and lunged toward Liza, throwing his burly arms around her, swallowing her in a mammoth hug.

She squealed. Reese broke out in a cold sweat and leaped to save her, but in a few heart-stopping seconds, she pushed free, amazingly safe, her giggles mingling with the animal's low-throated grunts.

Only then did Reese see the chain around the bear's neck. Only then did he hear the Gypsies' laughter.

"Do not be afraid for me, my husband," Liza said, her eyes twinkling. "He is only Rollo, wanting to tell me hello. He has missed me, I think."

She gave the bear an affectionate scratch beneath his chin. Reese swore in delayed reaction.

Hanzi barked an order, and the animal immediately crouched back into the shadows, disappearing from sight behind the wagon.

"Sweet mother." Reese let out a deep breath, lifting his hat to rake an unsteady hand through his hair. "He just took ten years off me."

"Oh, I am sorry. I did not see him coming or else I would have introduced you first," Liza soothed. "Would you like to meet him?"

"No, thanks." He shook his head firmly and replaced the hat. He tossed a cautious glance toward the wagon.

Liza laughed again. Raising up on tiptoe, she dropped a light kiss onto his lips.

Beyond the realms of the Gypsy camp, a sudden explosion blasted through the night, sending repercussions of sound thundering down Reese's spine. Beneath his boot soles, the ground trembled. From its hook on Nanosh's wagon, a lantern swayed slightly.

The Gypsies murmured among themselves in alarm. Reese shot a glance into the blackness. His brain deciphered his bearings, a possible location of the blast. Icy fingers of dread clawed at his stomach.

"Saints in heaven. Reese." Horror laced Liza's features. "The trestle bridge."

Her words confirmed what he feared most, that Silas McCrae had finally made good his threat to destroy the N & D.

To destroy him.

"The son of a bitch," he breathed and started toward the stallion.

"You must not go," Liza gasped. Her hand on his arm stayed him. "He will kill you."

"He's got to be stopped," he said tersely.

"Then I am coming, too."

"Like hell." Over her head, he gestured to Hanzi. "See that she stays. Don't let her out of your sight."

"I will do as you say," Hanzi said solemnly and planted himself next to her, one brown hand banding her wrist.

"I want to go." She pulled at her brother's grip and glared at Reese. A tempest brewed in her ebony eyes.

"No. I'll be back for you later."

"Reese—"

Her voice trailed off behind him as he sprinted toward the stallion. He vaulted into the saddle, and the concerned Gypsies parted to give him his way.

He left the camp at a full gallop, leaving behind the scattered campfires and plunging into the moonlit night. The horse's iron hooves hammered the road in a hard run. He needed no lantern. He well knew the lay of the land, every hill and valley, each crack and crevice. He could find Skull Canyon blindfolded.

After what seemed an eternity of a ride, he reined the stallion in at the canyon's ridge.

Nothing could have prepared him for the destruction of the mighty bridge that had taken weeks to build and drained the strength of two dozen men, that only hours ago stood mighty and awe-inspiring and garnered the cartel's admiration. Thick timbers cut from trees scarce to the prairie lay mangled and splintered on the canyon floor, useless for little more than kindling to feed a hungry fire. One end had collapsed like a heap of toothpicks, leaving the other bent and weakened. In the breeze, loosened planks groaned and creaked.

Reese stared.

Nausea rolled inside him.

The stallion nickered low and swung his head. Reese's searching glance skimmed along the demolished bridge and the shallow stream beneath, but no movement drew his eye, no sound reached his ear.

Yet something—or someone—was there. He'd long ago learned to trust his horse's instincts, high-strung and fine-tuned to anything amiss. And he'd bet his last dime that McCrae had stuck around to gloat over his handiwork.

Reese coaxed the stallion down the steep canyon wall. The horse picked his way around iron bolts and shards of wood strewn from the blast. At the base of the bridge, Reese dismounted and withdrew the Winchester from its scabbard. He left the stallion to nose a drink from the stream.

Eerie silence gripped the canyon. Reese bettered his hold on the rifle and scoured the darkness around him.

"Lookin' for me, Carrison?"

He whirled.

"Up here."

A maniacal laugh skittered down Reese's spine. His head jerked toward the sound.

Directly above him, Silas McCrae stood at the highest point of what little remained of the ravaged bridge. Muted gleams of moonlight silhouetted him against the sky. He made an ominous sight with his feet spread and the buffalo coat heavy and thick upon his shoulders.

A wild man, as wild as the creatures he sought to protect. Hate unfurled inside Reese like the sails of a ship, so deep he could feel no fear.

"I could kill you for this," he said with a snarl.

"Reckon I got the advantage, railroad man. See?" From the voluminous folds of his coat, he produced a stick of dynamite in each fist, their dangling fuses a harrowing reminder of their potential to destroy. "From your own railroad yard. A little visit to one of your sheds, and no one even noticed."

"Be careful, McCrae, damn you."

He cackled like a crazed coyote. "Dynamite to build the railroad. Dynamite to blow it up."

Reese's blood ran cold at the singsong in his tone. "Think about what you're doing."

"I'm done thinkin'. I ain't puttin' up no more with that blasted train blowin' smoke and screechin' its horn. And I ain't gonna stand for it haulin' in buffalo poachers, neither."

"Not my train, McCrae. Others maybe, but not mine." Reese grimaced. "I've seen it, too. Entire herds of buffalo wiped out while the train runs past. But the N & D is here to help Niobrara City, to make it grow, not kill the buffalo."

"Shootin' from the windows, like they was shooting at toy ducks." He seemed to relive a nightmare from the past. Reese wondered if the old man had heard a single word he'd said. "Laughin' and havin' a good time while they picked off the herd one by one, then leavin' the carcasses to the wolves—"

"The farmers and ranchers need my train for their crops and stock—"

"—and the hides to rot in the sun." McCrae's voice thundered downward from the unstable bridge. "This is my country, Carrison. And it was Lester's, too, until you killed him! We was here before any of you! Now all kinds of people are crowdin' me and the animals out!"

"No, no." Reese shook his head furiously. "The land can't remain untouched forever. I'll share the land if you share my railroad."

"I'll die first!"

In despair, Reese realized Silas McCrae was a case of dementia long past reason, and nothing he could say or do would calm him.

"Get down from there, or I'm coming up and dragging you down," he grated.

Again, the maniacal laugh shivered along his spine.

"I'm not done yet, Carrison. I ain't leavin' no part of this bridge standin'." In devious glee, he waved the dynamite in the air.

Reese moved toward him. "You can blow up every bridge and rail along the N & D line if you want."

"That's just what I'm plannin' to do." McCrae shook a meaty fist to punctuate the promise. He wobbled on a loosened timber and regained his balance with a hasty flail of his arms.

"I'll build another," Reese said. "Bigger. Stronger. You'll never win."

McCrae spat in disgust. In the blink of an eye, he produced a match and lit it. The orange-red flame sputtered and sparked, then flared into brilliance.

"Stay back, Carrison, or I'll blow you up right along with your precious bridge," he warned.

True to his word, he touched the match flame to the fuses. Reese swallowed hard, never thinking, never really thinking, that McCrae would see his threat through.

His instincts urged him to run, yet McCrae had to be stopped. Could he get to him in time? Indecision warred within him. Save himself or McCrae?

How could he do either?

The fuses grew shorter, gobbled up by the match flame.

"McCrae, you're a damn fool!" he yelled.

A splintering crash drowned out his words. Beneath the fur trapper's weight, a timber gave way, hurling him toward the edge of the bridge. McCrae bellowed a surprised curse and fought for solid footing. The sticks of dynamite fell from his fingers and arced into oblivion somewhere behind him.

He danced a macabre jig to stand upright, but failed. As helpless as a rag doll, he hurtled over the side with a scream that shredded at Reese's core, the buffalo coat floating out behind him like suddenly sprouted wings.

In a blinding light, the dynamite exploded. The force yanked at Reese like a clawing ghost, jerking him from his feet and flinging him to the ground. A spray of gravel and debris pelted his body. Pain coated him. A low groan squeezed from his throat, and he fell unconscious.

Liza tucked her toes beneath her skirt hems and sat tautly on the step of Nanosh's wagon. Her fingers clutched at the amulet hanging about her neck, and for the hundredth time, she poked her gaze toward the road outside of their camp.

Reese should not have gone alone. Certain trouble awaited him in Skull Canyon, and she would not rest easy until he returned. Apprehension knotted her insides.

Most of the Gypsies had retired to their wagons for the night. They did not concern themselves with skirmishes in the Gaje world, but Liza could not be so carefree. She loved her husband too much. She had learned to love his railroad as well, and all that concerned it, even its bridges.

Several men lingered around a campfire, quietly smoking and finishing the contents of a whiskey bottle. Nanosh sat with them, his features somber and preoccupied as he stared into the fire. Near him, Hanzi whittled at a chunk of wood. He would not sleep until Reese returned, Liza knew, for he was honorbound to make good his promise to stay with her and keep her safe.

Behind her, the wagon door opened with a faint squeak. "Liza?"

She turned at Putzi's timid voice. He peered around the door as if afraid she would send him scuttling back to his bed.

"Come sit with me, little one," she said softly, opening her arms to him.

Still warm from his eiderdown, he came to her eagerly. Liza made room for him on her lap, snuggling him against her and absorbing his warmth. Her chin rested on the top of his tousled head.

"Liza, why are you out here when it is so late?"

"I am waiting, little one."

"For your husband?"

"Yes."

"Where did he go?"

"Away. For a little while."

"Why?"

A sad smile touched her mouth. The innocence of a child. She hoped to keep him from the harsh realities of the adult world, for soon enough he would learn them.

"He is working very hard for his train, sweetling."

"Will I get to ride on the big engine someday? Do you think he would let me?"

Unexpected tears burned Liza's eyes. She could not tell him of Silas McCrae's evil intent to destroy the N & D, of the terrible explosion and what it must have done to the trestle bridge. He would not understand her fear that the old fur trapper may have already demolished the magnificent Number 929 engine and the cars it pulled.

"Perhaps someday," she said quietly. "When it is safe. And then Reese will be very proud to give you a ride in his train."

A lazy, mournful whine drifted over the camp, so faint in the distance that Liza's troubled mind gave it little thought. But Putzi sat up, his angelic features bright with hope. "Not 'til then, Liza? But the train is coming now. Do you hear the whistle?"

Her stomach lurched.

In the flash of a second, she recognized the whistle that had always fascinated him, and in the next, another explosion rocked the earth, this one as terrible and frightening as the first.

Talons of terror gripped her. She stabbed a glance past the tops of the wagons to learn the direction the train traveled. The whistle sounded again, closer this time, and she knew the 929 traveled at a healthy clip, as strong as ever as it drew nearer to the Gypsy camp.

And the trestle bridge.

Her heart stopped. The train would not know of the explosions. It would not know of the trouble that lay ahead. And this, *this*, was the terrible evil that Silas McCrae had planned.

She bundled Putzi off her lap and thrust him toward the wagon door.

"Paprika, come quick!" she cried. "Take Putzi to bed. I must go."

The door flew open, and her younger sister's face appeared. "Go where? What is happening?"

"I will explain later."

Liza bounded down the wagon step with Putzi's protesting wail filling the air behind her. From the campfire, the Gypsy men bolted to their feet and called out to her, but she ignored them. She had not a moment to waste.

She ran to the horses. A bay mare lifted her head, nickering softly, and without fanfare, Liza unhobbled her. She halted at the firm grasp on her shoulder.

"I have promised your husband, Liza," Hanzi said.

"I must help him. I cannot stay here and do nothing!"

"The Gaje have their troubles, yes, but you are not to leave the camp, as Reese said," he warned. "No matter what the reason."

Frantic, she clutched his shirtfront in her fists. "I fear for my husband, Hanzi. His train comes. And the bridge is down. Do you hear me? The bridge is down. *And his train will not know!*"

"Let her go." Nanosh's deep voice came between them. "This she must do for her husband."

Liza's breath left her in a grateful rush. If Nanosh had never showed her compassion before, he did so now, when she needed it most. She spun about and snatched a bridle, slipping it on the mare.

"I will come with you," Hanzi declared.

"No, I can go myself. But you must ride into town and get Bram Kaldwell. Ask anyone you see and they will tell you where to find him. He will know what to do."

He responded to the urgency in her tone and disappeared into the shadows of the remuda for his own horse. Nanosh found a sturdy branch and wrapped one end with a rag soaked in kerosene. He dipped the torch into the campfire, and flames erupted.

"You will need light to find your way in the dark," he said. "God's luck be with you, my daughter."

Liza leaped onto the mare's back. Without a word she took the torch in one hand, the reins in the other.

In the next moment, she was gone.

Reese came to, disoriented and burning with pain. As if through a foggy tunnel, his brain registered the call of a whistle, faint but insistent. In bits and pieces, it all came back to him.

He groaned. His eyes opened, and he struggled to focus on the dark shape surfacing near him. The shape drew closer, nuzzled him on his shoulder, and nickered softly.

His horse. Relief stole over him that at least the stallion had survived the blast when he had very likely lost everything else he had ever worked for.

He grimaced and shoved aside the self-pity, forcing himself to sit up. Blood trickled from his forehead down his temple. Pain lanced his knee. Every bone in his body hurt.

His gaze shot to the bridge. Nothing was left.

Sickened, he searched for McCrae, half-expecting him to materialize out of thin air, taunting and cackling with fistfuls of dynamite. But the night was hauntingly quiet, save for the persistent howl of the whistle.

The whistle.

No. God, no.

Reese's mind screamed the words. A darkened form lay in the stream bed. Reese sucked in a breath and tried to stand, but his leg buckled beneath him, the knee useless, too far gone for even Liza's loving heat treatments.

He crawled like a half-wit, dragging the leg behind him in the dirt, cutting his palms on splintered steel and jagged rock tossed by the explosions. By the time he reached the stream, he was breathing heavily, his battered body begging for respite.

The whistle called again. Closer. Louder.

No. No. No.

He clamored into the shallow water and yanked at McCrae's crumpled body.

"I should let you die right here," he ground out through clenched teeth. He clutched the sodden buffalo coat and tried to roll him over. "I'd love to see my train fall into this canyon and crush every inch of you. Only God knows why I don't let it. C'mon, you son of a bitch. Wake up!"

He managed to flip him over. Water splashed onto them both. McCrae coughed and moaned.

The dynamite's explosion had torn off half of the fur trapper's face. Blood and muscle dripped onto the scraggly beard. Reese swallowed down bile.

"Leave me be, Carrison," McCrae rasped, his one remaining eye crazed with the threat of death. "I got what I wanted. I got . . . your railroad."

"Yeah, maybe, but you're going to live and pay the price." Reese clutched the wet coat and gave him a vicious shake. "Come on, damn you! The train'll come barreling down here any second. We have to get out of here."

"Leave . . . me."

"I'm not going to give you the pleasure." He yanked again and barely maneuvered him out of the water. How would he ever get him out of the canyon? Reese's lungs heaved. "Silas, please."

But McCrae didn't answer. His head rolled back. A strangled gasp escaped from his throat, and he breathed his last.

The mighty locomotive made a commanding sight.

A mammoth beast, it thundered down the track toward

Liza with unfathomable power sheathed within its iron belly. Clouds of steam hurtled from the funneled smokestack. The whistle blew again and again, a nagging cry soaring over the prairie.

Liza's chest heaved with a rush of adrenaline. The whistle was meant for her, a frantic warning to abandon the rails for safety, for her life and that of her horse. But she remained on the tracks and desperately swung the torch from side to side, pleading a message of her own.

Skittish and uneasy, the bay mare pranced over the cross ties. Liza controlled her with a taut grip of the reins. The ground rumbled with the train's ferocity, its claim to the land and tracks. Yet again, the whistle blew.

On a panicked sob, Liza glanced over her shoulder. A gaping emptiness reigned where once the trestle bridge stood. Somehow, somewhere, Reese was there among the rubble. Liza longed to go to him, to search him out, but first the train must be stopped. She could not allow it the same untimely death as the bridge.

Down the ribbon of track, the engine's headlight swelled larger. Liza's gaze fixed on the beam, her heart pounding, her lips mouthing a fervent prayer that Clements would see the waving torch and stop in time. The V-shape of the cowcatcher parted the night, loomed ever closer and glinted brighter with every roll of the iron wheels.

And then, behind the glare of the headlight, Clements appeared, his body leaning out the cab's window, his arm furiously motioning her away. Liza defied him, keeping her stance on the tracks when every fiber of her being screamed to jump aside. She waved the torch with renewed fervor.

Abruptly, Clements disappeared inside the cab. The 929's throttle worked its magic. With a loud *chiiiff-ff*, the locomotive began to slow.

Liza gasped in relief. She loosened the reins, and the

303

mare leaped from the crossties in a frenzied run along the tracks of the train. As she neared the tip of the cowcatcher, Liza jerked the horse into a sharp turn, reversing her direction so that she traveled the same as the 929.

Again, Clements leaned from the window. The rush of air whipped at his hat. His eyes widened. "Mrs. Carrison! Is that you?"

"Stop!" she cried. "You must stop! The trestle bridge—"

Clements didn't wait to hear the rest. He lunged for the brake handle and pulled. With an ear-splitting whine and hiss, the engine wheels squealed to a slow, agonizing stop. Harley, his fireman, scrambled to set the manual brake to keep the train from going another inch.

"Lord Almighty, what is it, Mrs. Carrison?" Clements demanded out the window.

She allowed the mare only a moment of rest.

"Silas McCrae," she said, her pulse racing, her hair a wind-tossed mane down her back and shoulders. "You must not go any farther. The trestle—my husband—"

But the mare broke into a hard gallop before she could finish. Horse and rider charged toward the bridge, their outline shrinking into a pinpoint dot of torchlight, until it, too, disappeared altogether.

Clements and Harley stared after her for a long moment; in the next, they hustled into action.

"What d'ya reckon that was all about?" Harley asked, opening the cab door.

"Reckon we got trouble. Like she said, somethin' about the trestle bridge and Silas McCrae and Mr. Carrison. I don't like the sound of it." Clements climbed down the ladder in great haste and set off for the trestle bridge, leaving Harley to hurry after him.

* * *

The buffalo hide slipped from Reese's fingers.

A man had never died in his hands before. The starkness of death numbed him, left him bereft of emotion. Silas McCrae had been a sore spot, a real pain in the ass, but Reese had never wished him dead.

It all seemed so pointless.

He drew a shaky breath and sank to the ground. Defeated by the harshness of reality, bone-chilling exhaustion set in. His eyes drifted closed, and he wished for McCrae's oblivion, that all-encompassing solitude that would take him from the cruelties of life.

Only then did it hit him. The night was quiet. No whistle. No hissing chuff of the train engine. No impending crash.

His eyes flew open. He whirled, his glance flying to the top of the canyon.

There, on the ridge, bathed in the glow of a single torchlight, stood Liza, her skirts full and swaying in the breeze. She stood motionless, as if she stared into the deepest recesses of Skull Canyon, searching for him and afraid of what she might find.

Someone ran to her side. Clements, swathed in torchlight, and then Harley, all of them together, their gazes scouring the canyon. For him. For the bridge.

Emotion clogged in his throat. Only Liza had known. She had saved their lives. She had saved the Nebraska-Dakota Railroad.

Epilogue

Paprika knew a secret. Liza had not yet figured out what it could be, only that it would be revealed very soon, and that whatever magic it held drove Paprika to near madness.

Her sister could hardly sit still. Liza knew it went far beyond her first ride in a Gajo buggy, even one as shiny and grand as Reese's. And she knew, too, that the team of horses could not pull the rig fast enough to suit Paprika.

But Liza could wait. Reese had not left the house since the surgeon ministered his knee, and in the days following, he had grown steadily stronger as the cuts and bruises he suffered from the dynamite explosion gradually faded. Beneath the bandages, the knee would heal. But his worries for the N & D Railroad would not go away so easily. Liza hoped today's outing held those worries at bay, at least for a little while.

"Young lady, I'd warrant you had a hornet up your skirt the way you keep scootin' around on that seat," Reese said, his tone mildly exasperated. "This buggy is hardly big enough for the three of us. You're going to wiggle me and Liza right out of our own seat if you don't settle down some."

"You will understand soon enough," Paprika said, the promise shining in her black eyes. "It is a good thing I did not bring Putzi with me today. He would have told you long ago."

"It must be a very special thing you are taking us to see," Liza commented softly, the buggy's ride rocking her body against Reese's.

"It is."

"Has Nanosh painted his wagon a new color?"

"No." Paprika smiled and smugly clasped her hands in her lap.

"Then Hanzi has taught Rollo a new trick. A fancy somersault perhaps?"

She giggled. "No, no. You will never guess, Liza. Do not even try."

Liza sighed dramatically. "I give up."

"She enjoys torturing us with the suspense." Fondness shone in Reese's features. He and Paprika had grown fast friends from the moment of their introduction. They adored each other.

Liza's heart warmed. "She is a terrible tease. It is probably nothing."

Clearly offended, Paprika clucked her tongue. "Stop here, Reese. There is something I must look for."

They had reached a fork in the road, with a right turn taking them into Niobrara City, a left heading them out into open prairie. Reese did as she bade. Paprika hopped from the rig and ran ahead.

Grateful for the quiet moment, Liza peered up at Reese, handsome and robust in his gray cotton shirt, open at the throat, his faded Levi's snug against his muscle-hard thighs. Her breast swelled with a surge of love.

"Does your knee bother you?" she murmured, leaning against him and curling her arm around his.

"I am not an invalid, sweet wife. The knee is fine." He bent low and touched his mouth to hers, taking his time to savor the kiss.

"I do not think you an invalid." She nuzzled his jaw with the tip of her nose. "God's saints, the surgeon had hardly put away his needle before you took me to bed and exhausted me with our coupling."

His low chuckle surrounded her. "I'll never hurt too much to make love to you."

"You are insatiable."

"Aren't you glad that I am?"

Paprika cleared her throat loudly and reclaimed her place on the bench seat. With a mingling of reluctant sighs, Reese and Liza drew apart.

"Sit back, you two. They say we can come now," Paprika said, reaching for the reins draped across Reese's leg. "I will drive the rest of the way. But first, you must put on these." She reached into the large pocket in her skirt and withdrew a pair of kerchiefs. "Quickly now."

Liza frowned. "Paprika, this is foolishness."

"No, I think the Gaje call them blindfolds." Her impish expression danced with excitement.

Liza exchanged an uncertain glance with Reese.

He grinned. "Best do as she says. I doubt she'll budge this rig an inch until we do."

He reached for one of the kerchiefs and pulled it over Liza's eyes, knotting it behind her braid. Then he repeated the procedure on himself with the other. Unable to see anything, Liza felt his hands on her, pulling her against him as he slouched back in the seat. She snuggled for the duration of the ride.

From the best of her abilities, she determined Paprika headed toward the prairie, but could guess their destination little more than that. Before long, the buggy stopped again.

In the unfathomable distance, horses snorted. Shouts and mismatched bits of conversation hung in the air. Next to her, Reese tensed, as perplexed by their whereabouts as she.

Paprika left the seat and jumped to the ground.

"I will help you down," she said. "Do not take off the kerchiefs until I tell you."

Reese dismounted amid Liza's wifely admonishments to take care with his injured knee. She followed, her foot finding the way to solid earth. At Paprika's word, the kerchiefs fell away.

Reese and Liza stared.

A brand-new trestle bridge graced Skull Canyon. The scent of fresh-cut lumber was everywhere. The new tresses criss-crossed the canyon like the latticework on a mammoth pie, as strong and lasting as the first, and just as impressive.

Tucked amid the crossbeams, men worked, clinging like squirrels on a tree while they measured and hammered. On top of the bridge, too, men scurried about, laying rails and ties. On the far end of the canyon's ridge, the 929 engine waited in silent dignity for its turn to test the planks.

Paprika laughed and clapped her hands. "Did I not tell you I had a fine secret?"

Liza pressed shaking fingers to her mouth.

Reese continued to stare, his stunned gaze roaming over every truss, every bolt, every inch of his new bridge.

As if on wings, word of their arrival rippled throughout

the canyon. Men stopped their work, straightened and waved. Smiles burst on their faces. Applause erupted.

"Oh, Reese," Liza managed through the lump in her throat. "Look. My people. And yours. Together."

It was true. Hanzi and Jack Hadley, their shirtsleeves rolled to their elbows, stood side by side, their faces beaming. Nanosh and George Steenson labored on the rails. Hank and Uncle Pepe manned the horses, hauling dirt and debris. Liza's uncles and cousins mingled among Reese's friends, indeed, all of Niobrara City's citizenry. Even Maudeen was there, laying food out on tables arranged in a clearing with other women from town. Mama helped, along with her sisters and aunts from the kumpanias.

Liza could not believe her eyes.

Two worlds meshed as one, dark-skinned mixed with fairer, all joined for a common goal. Without animosity, without suspicion. Only friendship. And the surprising desire to replace a bridge in the Gaje world.

"I never thought I'd see it." Emotion shimmered in Reese's eyes. He took Liza tight in his arms, both of them too moved to speak, overwhelmed by the enormity of it all.

Bram approached with a roll of blueprints in his hand. Reese turned to him, and they stood, silently assessing the other's reaction. Liza knew they had not spoken together since their argument.

"How are you, my friend?" Reese asked finally, his voice low, a trifle unsteady.

"Good." Somber, Bram nodded. "And you?" He indicated Reese's knee. "Heard tell McCrae nearly took you with him."

"I'm all right."

Bram nodded again and shuffled from one foot to the

other. He gestured toward the bridge with the blueprints. "I took the liberty. I hope you don't mind."

Reese blinked. "You headed all this up?"

"It's the least I could do for the N & D. Got to where I missed it. Railroading's in my blood, Reese. You know that. I couldn't stay away."

"I never wanted you to, Bram. You're a part of the railroad as much as I am."

The older man glanced away, as if he considered himself unworthy of Reese's forgiveness. "I spoke to the cartel. They want in. The future's bright for the N & D. This is going to be one hell of a little railroad someday." A wan smile appeared on his mouth. "Going to give the Union Pacific a real run for its money."

"I doubt that." But Reese grinned with pride anyway.

Bram hesitated. "I couldn't have done it without the Gypsies. They can put in a hard day's work when they set their mind to it." His gaze touched on Liza, then darted away. "Much as I hate to admit it, they didn't do it for me. Or you, either, Reese. They did it for your wife. We have her to thank for your bridge."

He seemed reluctant to leave. Liza sensed he had not yet said all that was in his heart.

He sighed heavily and shook his head. He squinted toward the bridge. "Rebecca Ann never belonged here, you know. She couldn't care less about the N & D. I was wrong to want her married to you. It would've ruined you both." Regret furrowed his brow. "You married the right woman. A beautiful one, too. I wish you the best."

Reese extended his hand. "Thanks, Bram."

Bram moved to complete the handshake, but emotion got the better of them, and they fell into a brief, manly embrace.

Liza rejoiced in the reunion. Bram turned to her, appearing almost shy, and she raised up on tiptoe and pressed a warm kiss to his cheek. "You are welcome in our home anytime. Please come to see us."

"I'd be right proud to do that. You can count on it."

His lips pursed, and a tuneless ditty whistled forth. Bram left them to return to his work on the trestle bridge. Reese's fingers twined with Liza's. Finding his cane, he led her slowly along the canyon ridge, and had his knee not prevented it, he would have been deep among the men, working as hard as any of them.

They had nearly reached that part of the canyon ridge where the 929 waited. From the shade cast out by the mighty engine, Uncle Pepe called out to them. At his command, Nanosh and the other members of the kris set down their tools and joined him. Reese groaned.

"I've been expecting this," he murmured.

A ball of apprehension formed in Liza's stomach. "Me, too. I had hoped the kris would forget. I was foolish to even think it."

Uncle Pepe gestured to Mama, who hastened forth with cups of strong coffee. Her new silk kerchief, as bright as the sunflowers, hugged her head.

"Stay, Pesha," he said. "This is a matter that concerns you, too."

Mama kept her eyes downcast and obeyed, taking a place beside Liza.

Uncle Pepe's grimace was apologetic. "A momentous day, is it not? The trestle bridge is nearly finished, and we have worked hard for a Gajo. Who would have guessed, eh?"

Amusement rumbled through the men. Only Liza and Reese did not smile.

"But the matter of your marriage is still unresolved. Now, we must finish the case. We must give Liza and her Gajo husband our decision." Ponderous, he swilled the coffee in his cup. Liza thought she would die from the wait.

"I think we must not be too hard on Liza. See how she fidgets? She is afraid we will banish her from the tribe." Dominic, always the fun-loving one, could not be trusted to tell the truth. Liza stared and hoped this time he did not tease.

"No, she has suffered long enough," Pepe said quietly. "Far too long. It is time we welcome her as one of us, as if she is full-blooded Gypsy."

"But she leaves us to live in the Gaje world," Yojo commented.

"She is happy there. Why not? She deserves to be happy. We will not bring her any more shame."

Mama's head lifted, disbelief creased in her weathered face. Liza was afraid to hope.

"The Rom have talked. All of us have seen the respect Reese Carrison receives from his people. We are amazed that an entire town will come out for him and build his bridge. They worry for him when the dynamite explodes. They worry for his bridge. They are eager to make him another."

Pepe's black-eyed gaze fastened on them. "When Nanosh came to us with his idea to help the Gaje, it was difficult to agree. But now that we have"—Pepe shrugged, a sheepish smile revealing his gold tooth—"it is not so bad, eh? The Gypsies can be friends with the Gaje, at least for a little while."

"Does this mean my wife is free to travel between both worlds?" Reese demanded. "No longer marhime?"

Pepe faced him squarely. "Yes."

Liza nearly crumpled with relief. A whimper escaped from Mama. Liza grasped her hand in her own.

"There will always be those among us who will remember the disgrace and shame, but the marriage between you is done. We will honor it. Be proud to be husband and wife."

"I owe you, Pepe," Reese said. "How can I thank you for what you've done for us?"

"You have promised us winter quarters along the river. Does your offer still stand?"

"Of course. And I'll see that you have all the meat you need until spring."

Murmurs of delight went through the men.

"Fair enough?" Reese asked.

"Fair enough." Clearly pleased, Pepe exchanged nods of approval with the court.

"And what of Mama?" Having Reese at her side gave Liza the courage to speak so boldly. "Has she not suffered long enough as well?"

"How she loves her mother." Pepe finished off the last dregs of coffee and tossed aside his cup. Sadness dulled the remnants of his smile. "I remember the day the kris punished you, Pesha. I was very young, too young to protest that every woman loves her hair. I could do nothing for you then." He rose and took Mama in his arms. "By this time next year, you will have curls again, my sister. You will be beautiful once more for Nanosh."

A roar of applause went up among the Gypsies who had abandoned their work on the bridge to listen to the kris's decision. An impromptu celebration ensued, drowning out Mama's exultant cries and drawing the curiosity of Reese's people.

In the midst of the clapping and dancing, Liza became separated from Reese. She slipped to the edge of the throng to search him out and found him with Nanosh, their heads bent together in earnest conversation.

She luxuriated in watching him. In the privacy of their

bedroom, they would celebrate in their own way, but for now, she would bask in the victory they had won together.

"He haggles a bride-price, hmmm?" Mama asked, pulling Liza with her to a quiet spot next to the train. Tears of joy stained her cheeks. Liza smiled and kissed them away.

"Perhaps," she said. "But Reese will not haggle too much. He will give Nanosh whatever he wants."

"For a Gajo, he is generous."

In light of all that had happened, Liza detected a trace of reluctance in Mama's admission. It would not be so easy for her to toss away years of resentment.

"It pleases me to hear you speak kindly of him," she said softly. "Do you think you will accept him as your son someday?"

Mama shrugged. "Maybe it will not be too hard. Who knows?" She reached out and stroked Liza's face tenderly. "But I will try, sweetling. For you, I will try." She managed a tremulous smile. "I see the way he looks at you. It will not be long before he leaves my grandbaby in your belly."

"A grandbaby, yes." Liza's gaze met hers. "More Gaje than Gypsy."

Mama released a long, long sigh. She squinted into the sky. "Yes, well, it is in the stars, I suppose. A Gaje grandbaby. With red-gold hair, eh?"

Liza smiled at the thought. "Maybe."

They embraced. Mama stepped away to rejoin the celebration, but turned back.

"Will you braid my hair, Liza? When it is long enough?"

"Of course. And it will shine in the sun, just like it used to."

Mama laughed, a sound of pure delight. As if a young girl again, she swung her skirts and sashayed back into the crowd.

WYOMING WILDFLOWER
PAM CROOKS

Armed with an arsenal of book knowledge on ranching, Sonie retruns to the Rocking M Ranch determined to prove that despite her sex she can be the sonn her fahter had always anted. Lance harmon has beat her to the punch, though. She rides in on her high horse, determined to unseat him. but lsance knows sonnie toppled him years ago, for he has always been head over heels in love with the rancher's youngest dauhgter. And yet, he plans to chase her away. Trouble on the range demands it. soonie doesn't shy away when danger comes rustling through, though proving to Lance that the one thoing that means motre to him than the only home he's ever knowm, is the only woman he's ever loved, his . . . Wyoming wildflower.

__4843-4 $4.99 US/$5.99 CAN

Lori Morgan
Autumn Star

Morgan Caine rescues Lacey Ashton from a couple of pawing ruffians, feeds her dinner, and gives her a place to sleep. He is arrogant, bossy, and the most captivating man she has ever met. He claimed she will never survive the wilds of the Washington territory. But Lacey sets out to prove she not only belongs in the untamed land, she belongs in Morgan's arms.

Morgan is completely disarmed by Laceys's innocence and optimism. Like an autumn breeze, she caresses his body, refreshes his soul, invigorates his heart. At last, the hardened lawman longs to trader vengeance for a future filled with happiness—to reach for the stars and claim the woman of his dreams.

___4892-2 $4.99 US/$5.99 CAN

A Case Of Nerves
Angie Kay

Standing on the moors of Scotland, Alec Lachlan could have stepped right off of the battlefield of 1746 Culloden. Decked out in full Scottish regalia, Alec looks like every woman's dream, but is one woman's fantasy. Kate MacGillvray doesn't expect to be swept off her feet by the strangely familiar green-eyed Scot. But she is a sucker for a man in a kilt; after all, her heroes have always been Highlanders. Wrapped in Alec's strong arms, Kate knows she has met him before—centuries before. And she isn't about to argue if Fate decides to give them a second chance at a love that Bonnie Prince Charlie and a civil war interrupted over two centuries earlier.

___52312-4 $5.50 US/$6.50 CAN